CW00540805

FACING
THE MUSIC

BRIAN SMITH

To Anne + Denis

*How the building
industry works in Melbourne*

Best wishes

Brian

Published in Australia by Sid Harta Publishers Pty Ltd,
ABN: 46 119 415 842
23 Stirling Crescent, Glen Waverley, Victoria 3150 Australia
Telephone: +61 3 9560 9920, Facsimile: +61 3 9545 1742
E-mail: author@sidharta.com.au

First published in Australia October 2013
This edition published 2013
Copyright © Brian Smith 2013
Cover design, typesetting: Chameleon Print Design

The right of Brian Smith to be identified as the Author of the Work has been
asserted in accordance with the Copyright, Designs and Patents Act 1988.

This book is a work of fiction. Any similarities to that of people living or dead are
purely coincidental.

All rights reserved. No part of this publication may be reproduced, stored in a
retrieval system, or transmitted, in any form or by any means without the prior
written permission of the publisher, nor be otherwise circulated in any form of
binding or cover other than that in which it is published and without a similar
condition being imposed on the subsequent purchaser.

Smith, Brian
Facing the Music
ISBN: 1-922086-12-6
EAN13: 978-1-922086-12-9
pp298

For Bish

'All happy families are alike but an unhappy family
is unhappy after its own fashion.'

Tolstoy
Anna Karenina

1

Mike Georgiou believed he could tell the state of a building site by listening to its sound. Not a single sound, but a collective voice that might include the pulsating growl of a concrete pump, the strident tone of a compressor, the staccato hammering of the carpenters, the slow and muffled thump of a sledgehammer, the whine from a chorus of hand tools, the sharp scream of a concrete saw or the rattle of roofing sheets. By listening he could tell what was being done and how well. On a good day the energy and cohesion in the sound approached a form of music. He found it hard to explain and didn't risk trying with any of the crew on site. And when he had mentioned it to Lissa the other day, she laughed at him.

'Ever since they gave you the CityView project, you've become obsessed by it,' she said. 'Now it's playing music to you. Who do you think you are – a band leader?'

She had never shared his love of music. It hadn't mattered in the past. But perhaps she was right, he thought as he stood up from his desk. This was by far the most important project he had been assigned to manage – important for the company and important for him. The building was more complex and the work force larger than he had led before. He could not be as hands-on as he had been on previous jobs and needed to work through others, be more desk-bound and take a more strategic view of the project. It was challenging, it was absorbing and up until a few weeks ago he was confident he would make a success of it. Now he was not so sure.

He put on his hard hat and stepped outside the prefab that

served as his site office. He was pleased to hear a strong rhythm in the sound of construction. Too often in recent weeks he had been confronted by the listless tempo of the site working at a sluggish rate or, far worse, the silence that shrouded a complete shutdown. The troubles had started when the concrete supplier claimed the order had been cancelled and failed to deliver. Until then the project had been progressing well and Mike had begun to think of completing the job ahead of schedule. Soon after there was the unexplained failure of the gearbox on one of the tower cranes and vandalism on some of the completed floors. Adding to his problems, the union delegate, Ted Horton, had found a new militancy and begun calling out the men whenever he saw the slightest reason. It seldom took long to deal with the issues he raised, but the damage to the schedule was difficult to repair.

Mike screwed up his eyes against the glare reflected from the structure rising from the dusty ground in front of him. The next concrete truck had arrived and stood waiting its turn. Several of the men, returning from a break, entered the Alimak elevator before it rattled up the side of the building. The all-encompassing mesh on the lower levels prevented him from seeing any of the work going on in there but higher up, beside the central lift core that bore the banner FINDLAY CONSTRUCTION – CITYVIEW, he could see the hard hats of the crew spreading the concrete pour that formed the next floor plate. Highest of all, the northern tower crane made stately progress, raising one of the complex prefabricated inserts into place. These were one of Jeff Richards' innovations. Mike hadn't worked with this architect before and had been dubious about the way he wanted to change some of their construction methods, but Mike's boss, Ben Findlay, had insisted.

'I've known Jeff for years – we were at Grammar together,' he said. 'He's a top guy, always looking for new approaches and not stuck in his ways like some around here.'

The computer images suggested the finished building would look great, but it was soon apparent Jeff knew very little and cared even less about construction. To keep the project on schedule, Mike was forced to find ways to work with and around the architect. It didn't help that Ben Findlay was short of direct experience on construction sites as well.

Looking to the west, Mike could not see what the other crane was doing. A threatening build up of storm clouds across the horizon was the only notable sight in that direction. He hoped the front would hold off until the end of work for the day.

A pallet of iron pipes, due to be used to extend the safety fencing on the upper levels, rose above the intervening line of containers on its way to the loading platform jutting from the building high above. Immediately he could see a problem: the pallet was slipping from its canvas sling and was tilting to one end, putting all the weight on to one arm. Suddenly aware of the problem, the crane operator halted the lift so hastily that the lopsided load spun in a circle. It struck the side of the building and the arm bearing most of the load parted. The pipes spilled from their cradle and tumbled down in a widening metallic shower that quickly disappeared from Mike's view.

He sprinted across the site and rounded the end container. The air was clogged with dust. The falling pipes had each caused its own eruption that now mingled in the light breeze and rose slowly to form a single choking cloud. One pipe had bounced off the bonnet of the truck that had brought it and pierced the windscreen where it poked from the shattered glass. The driver, still clambering from the cabin, shook his head in disbelief.

'Look what you've done to me fuckin' truck,' he ranted, shock numbing his awareness of how narrowly he had avoided being impaled by the pipe.

Others were not so lucky. One of the men, Joe Frederico, who would have attached the sling to the batch of pipes, lay on the tray of the truck beside other pallets, not yet uploaded on to the building. The right leg of his denim work pants was torn and his foot lay at a strange angle.

'Me leg,' he moaned. 'It's me leg.'

He tried to reach down to it but gave a yelp of pain and fell back.

'Just take it easy, Joe,' Mike said.

Not much chance of that. A trickle of saliva ran from Joe's open mouth and dust coated his face. Mike turned to the driver. 'Can you get him a drink? I'll check the others.'

Across from the truck several other men knelt beside a figure that lay without moving. His hard hat had disappeared and blood from a gash on his shoulder was darkening his fluorescent vest. Mike began to take out his mobile but stopped when he saw Bob Kennedy, the site supervisor, already holding a phone to his ear. By the time Mike reached him he had finished.

'I called for two ambulances,' he said.

Mike nodded and gestured towards the figure on the ground. 'How is he?'

'I thought he was dead when I first got to him, but Paddy's a tough bugger. He's opened his eyes now. Concussion I'd say, and I don't like the look of his shoulder.'

Bob glanced around as if rechecking there were no other casualties. 'It could've been worse. When I first saw them fall I reckoned we likely had a fatal.'

'You were quick to get here.'

'Yeah.'

4

Bob pushed his hat back, scratched his forehead and turned to scan the site again. 'Where's Ted?'

'Ted Horton?'

'Yeah. I was comin' off the second level when I saw him watchin' them attach the sling to the pallet. I thought he must be puttin' on another of his stunts, findin' some reason for callin' the guys out. He should be here but he's nicked off somewhere.'

Mike could hear the distant sound of an ambulance siren and hoped it was coming to them. Getting through the city would be difficult and the mid-afternoon traffic would be choking the tangled knot of roads that linked the Charles Grimes Bridge with the freeway and the bayside suburbs. He spent the period waiting for the ambulances pacing anxiously between his two injured workers. When the ambulances did arrive, the paramedics appeared unhurried but took little time to check the men, provide preliminary treatment and load them on board. As Mike watched them depart a tall, lean man in his early thirties came towards him. He had the face and bearing of someone more used to an office than a building site but wore the union T-shirt with the initials BCU prominent on his left breast.

'Spot of bother here?' he said.

'And you are?' Mike replied.

'Don't you know Alan Reardon, the new assistant secretary?'

The introduction came from the missing Ted Horton, who had materialised behind Mike.

'Mike Georgiou. I'm the project manager.'

He didn't offer his hand.

'I know,' Reardon said quietly. 'I was over the road at the Riverside site when I saw the ambulances stop here. Many hurt?'

'One has a broken leg, the other concussion and a damaged shoulder as well as abrasions.'

'Someone coulda been killed,' Ted Horton said in a voice very different from the one Mike had become used to hearing him use: instead of a whining complaint, it was a sober assessment. Perhaps being a witness to the accident had put him in shock or perhaps he was deferring to the assistant secretary.

'What happened?' Reardon asked.

'Yes, what did happen?' Mike repeated. 'Tell us, Ted. I hear you had a good view of it.'

Horton seemed surprised by the question and hesitated before turning to Reardon. 'I told ya, ya should be over here rather than spendin' your time at the fuckin' Riverside site.' His voice rose to a higher pitch. 'They've got so bloody sloppy here. I told 'em they hadn't left enough clearance under the crane and now, when they didn't load the sling properly we've got blokes hurt.'

'You've contacted WorkSafe?' Reardon asked Mike.

'More urgent things,' Mike said and realised he hadn't called Ben to let him know what had happened, either. 'I'll take care of that now.'

He turned and walked back to his office.

After a delay, Ben Findlay answered his mobile. 'Yes, Mike,' he said sharply.

'Ben, we've had an accident down here. Two men taken to hospital with serious but not life-threatening injuries.' Mike drew breath to give more detail but was cut off by Ben.

'Not another problem down there! I'm about to go into a crucial meeting with our bankers. Email me all the details so I can get across them as soon as I'm clear, and be bloody careful how you go with WorkSafe. I'll be down later. Wait for me.'

The phone went dead.

Mike frowned before checking the number for WorkSafe and was about to place the call when Bob Kennedy came through the door, carrying a bundle which Mike recognised as the sling that had failed.

'What's it look like?'

Bob dumped the sling on the desk. 'You have a look.'

He rummaged in the bundle until he found the two ends of the torn arm. Strands of canvas had been drawn from both sides, confirming that it had torn right across its width. When Mike made no comment, Bob said, 'Look here, at the edge.'

He ran his finger along the side of the canvas. 'See how smooth it is. I reckon the canvas was cut at the edge and the cut widened when the load came on.'

'Cut? Why didn't they see it when they attached the sling?'

Bob gave one of his ironic grins. 'Funny you should ask. I had a chat to Joe before the ambulance arrived. He said this was the first time they'd used this sling and they did their usual check, but he also told me Ted Horton was givin' them a hard time over the width of the clearance area below the crane. They're sick of the way he keeps interferin' for no good reason. Maybe Joe told me that as an excuse for some slack checkin'.' The grin left his face. 'Or maybe that bloody pest was involved somehow.'

'You're not saying he cut the sling?'

'No, I don't think he'd be up for that, the little runt, but I reckon someone did. And I reckon Ted knew about it.'

'Just because he was being a nuisance again?'

'Admit it, Mike. We've had more than bad luck lately. Someone cancelled our concrete order. Maybe the graffiti was kids, but how did they get in? The crane drive had been regularly serviced before the gear train failed. And Ted, the delegate who swans around the site doing bugger all, has become the union rep from hell.' Bob squared his shoulders. 'I reckon we oughta get him in and put the heat on him.'

Mike again ran his fingers over the rough edge of the sling.

'It could have been faulty when it arrived on site. You wouldn't be able to see the fault unless you opened it up and looked

7

carefully on the underside. The guys from WorkSafe are sure to give it a thorough going-over. No point in getting Ted in yet.'

Bob scowled. 'You're the boss.'

'And don't you say anything to Ted.'

The scowl became a sneer. 'Don't want to upset the union, do we?'

Mike lifted his head and looked squarely into Bob's eyes. 'You're right. I am the boss. What's more, if Ted is involved somehow, I'm not going to warn him we might be on to him. Watch him carefully, but don't give him any clue you're keeping tabs on him. When we go for him, we need facts not suspicions. Now I must ring WorkSafe.'

After Mike had confirmed that WorkSafe would send an inspector immediately, he sat reflecting again on his need to pull Bob into line. The great advantage of having started with the company as an apprentice carpenter and risen to his present position was that he had a thorough knowledge of how the various levels thought and worked. The disadvantage was that a few of the long-experienced and older hands like Bob still thought of him as a kid. There wasn't a lot he could do about that except prove his competence over and over. The current problems weren't helping there. Still, he shouldn't sit there feeling sorry for himself. Best to get out on the site, talk to people and be ready for the WorkSafe inspector when he showed up.

⸺

Late in the afternoon, after the men had left, Mike was reviewing the latest version of the schedule when the door to his office was thrown open and a man in multicoloured Lycra entered. Behind him Mike could see the sky had darkened and a gusty wind was throwing dust and debris in the air.

'Hello, Ben. A training ride on your way home?'

A disdainful smile creased the handsome face of the rider.

'Serious training for me is first thing in the morning, when you're still in bed.'

He pushed back a lock of blonde hair and the smile disappeared. 'Now I've turned forty I've got my sights set on some trophies. There's an event in a few weeks' time.' The managing director of Findlay Construction dropped on to the chair across from Mike and his chin lifted.

'So Mike, what the hell's going on? Every day brings a new problem down here, but this takes the cake.'

'I've checked with the hospital and both of them are doing OK. We'll know more in a few days.'

Ben nodded. 'We need to get them back to work as soon as we can. What did WorkSafe have to say?'

'Not much. I took the inspector through what happened; he looked round the site and has taken the sling away.'

'I don't have to tell you the consequences if we're found in any way culpable in this.' Ben leant forward. 'We both know this job was a big step up for you, but Vern insisted you were ready for it and I accepted his recommendation – another piece of poor advice from him. You started OK, but the further the project goes the worse you get. Problems are breaking out all over the site, you're dropping behind schedule and now you've landed us in trouble with WorkSafe.'

Mike also leant forward so their heads were close.

'Bob Kennedy and I were talking earlier. Our problems might not be bad management or bad luck – we think someone might be getting at us.'

'And who the hell might that be?'

'We don't know, but we aim to find out. Why would anyone want this project to fail?'

Ben surprised Mike by giving a short laugh. 'The only person I know who might be happy if this project fell over would be Vern

McKenzie. He still thinks we should be building a factory and warehouse complex on this site like he originally wanted, despite the area being stuffed with underused stock and can't see how this project will lift us out of the ruck of small firms into the big league of developers.' Ben paused before adding, 'But I can't see Vern stooping that low. You'll have to invent a better story to explain your poor performance.'

Mike understood why Ben never acknowledged that Jim Findlay, the founder of Findlay Construction, was his father, but it still jarred with him when Ben called him 'Jim'. If Mike were to do the same with his father it would seem like a form of sacrilege not to use the familiar 'dad', and he was sure Demetri Georgiou would be even more appalled. 'How is your father?'

Ben glanced sharply at Mike, who was unsure whether Ben was irritated by the 'father' tag or his sudden change of topic.

'The operation went well. They wanted him to go into rehab but he flatly refused and is home now with an army of people coming in to look after him and help out.'

Mike grinned. 'We should see him pretty soon, then. When he had the first hip done, he was stomping around our sites as soon as he'd mastered the crutches.'

Ben did not return his smile. 'That was five years ago, before I came on board. I'm in charge now. All of you need to get used to seeing a lot less of Jim. The likes of you and your mentor, Vern, need to wake up to yourselves and understand the world has changed. We can't get by any longer doing what we've always done. Look where it's got us on this job.' Having begun down this path, Ben seemed unable to stop, becoming more agitated the further he went, his voice rising along with the colour in his face. 'You're simply not up to it: I should have seen that before I allowed you to be appointed. Make no mistake. If you don't lift your game I'll replace you and you won't be able to call on Vern to save you.'

Mike pushed back his chair, his face flushed.

'Let's be clear,' he said. 'Vern gave me a chance to show what I could do, but I've earned every promotion I've had in this company. I've come up the hard way – unlike some.'

'Come up the hard way? Don't make me laugh. Never worked outside this cosy, little second-rate firm that hadn't had a new idea for years until I came aboard. You were put through uni at the company's expense and, because of Vern's indulgence, fast-tracked beyond your level of competence.'

'Leave Vern out of this,' Mike demanded.

'Vern will never forgive Jim for bringing me in as MD over the top of him.'

Mike pushed himself away from the desk and stood looking down on Ben.

'Don't talk crap. They've had their disagreements, but Vern has always been fiercely loyal to Jim. Nothing will change that. And, despite the way you run him down to anyone silly enough to listen, he's been loyal to you.'

Ben also rose and they stood across the desk from one another. 'Don't speak like that to me,' he said. 'Both of you think you can't run a building project unless you've had the dirt from a site under your fingernails. You've dragged your feet in taking up the new ideas Jeff Richards has brought to this project and when I told you to get on with doing what he asks, you go your own way.'

'Dragged my feet? Whenever I point out how impractical some of Jeff's ideas are, he just waves his hands and tells me he's sure I can find a way. I've had to bust a gut to keep the project on schedule, with no help from Jeff and nothing but useless interference from you.'

'But it isn't on schedule any longer and you're leaking cash.'

'If you want to fire me for having a bad run over a few weeks, then go ahead, but don't think it will be easy to find someone who can come in and do better.'

There was a rumble of thunder and rain began to beat on the roof. 'Maybe you need to abandon your ride home.'

Ben looked away and his voice dropped, almost as if he were speaking to himself.

'Perhaps I should take over the running of this project directly and get it sorted out. That'd silence the doubters inside and outside the company. It would be a load to carry but I could do it.' He turned his head back to eyeball Mike and said, 'Triathletes aren't put off by the weather. A ride in the rain will give me a chance to think things through. But don't be surprised if I move you out tomorrow.'

He turned on his heel and began to don his helmet. The wind threw a spray of rain at him as he opened the door.

'Why would I want to abandon my ride? I'll nip down Lorimer Street and Todd Road on to the bike path along the beach and be home while you're still sitting in that VW of yours inching your way through the peak hour traffic.'

After Ben had gone, Mike remained at his desk, fuming. He had been foolish to allow Ben to get under his skin, but some kind of confrontation had been brewing for months. It was ironic he had finally snapped when Ben had been contemptuous of Vern. It was Vern who had listened to Mike's complaints about Jeff and Ben and told him to work his way around them without causing any fuss.

'We need to give Ben time to settle,' Vern had said. 'He's different from the rest of us and that can be a good thing.'

When Mike objected, Vern had tried to reassure him. 'He did very well as marketing manager at Cunnards and had a major role in making them the largest supplier of equipment to the building industry in Australia. Marketing has always been a weakness of ours. What he lacks we can teach him. Teaching your boss without upsetting him is a skill we all need. And it's up to you and me to make sure the company continues to flourish now Jim's not actively involved. We owe it to him.'

Perhaps, like the storm outside, their clash would clear the air. On the other hand, Ben might be stupid and arrogant enough to take on the job himself. Mike would find out tomorrow. Meanwhile he had to fend off this other storm. He used his jacket as inadequate cover for his head and shoulders as he ran to his car through the driving rain. When he started the car, one of his Miles Davis discs began to play, but the drumming of the rain on the roof and the thump of his wipers on their highest setting made listening to music impossible.

The low cloud and rain had aged the day prematurely and he needed to switch on his sidelights. Ben had been right: the most direct route home would be filled with traffic, slowed to a crawl by the storm. Like Ben, he should circle round via Todd Road and then back up to South Melbourne. The traffic along Lorimer Street was relatively light, although the water on the road meant every car created its own bow wave and visibility was poor. He had reached the blank stretch beside Webb dock, needing to be careful through the water-filled dips in the road, when he saw Ben, working hard to make progress against the wind blowing the rain directly into his face. Perhaps he sensed the presence of a car behind him, because he glanced back before resuming his battle with the elements. Mike was still hesitating over whether it was safe to overtake when a black four-wheel-drive came past him at speed, sending a deluge over the windscreen and blinding him for a moment. When the water cleared he could see the black car had pulled in directly beside Ben who was about to enter another dip in the road. As he did so, the car swerved so that a wall of water engulfed him. Ben was thrown into the air, falling in a crumpled heap across the kerb lining the road. Whether it was the wave alone or the front wing of the car that hit him, Mike could not tell. The black car continued to accelerate, either unaware of the harm it had caused or unwilling to admit it. Mike pulled up beside Ben and jumped from his car. Water cascaded down his face and his clothes were already sodden. Ben was on his side gasping for breath. Mike pulled off his jacket and draped it across him.

'Lie still,' he said unnecessarily. Ben was in no position to move, trapped in the mangled frame of the bike.

'There's something wrong with my chest,' he panted. 'Can't breathe.'

He gave a yelp of pain as Mike began to disentangle him from the clutch of the bike.

'Sorry, you've got some deep cuts on your legs but I don't think anything's broken.'

'Surely you saw me,' Ben gasped.

'What?'

'You drove into me as though you hadn't seen me.'

'No, that wasn't me. There was a black SUV.'

Ben looked at Mike doubtfully. 'I didn't see any other car. I looked back and saw your VW coming up behind me. Then I was sent flying. A four-wheel drive? How could it get between us? You were close.'

'It cut in between and sideswiped you. I couldn't tell whether it hit you directly or caught you with the wave it threw up. It all happened so fast.' Mike shook his head. 'I didn't get their number either.'

For the second time that day he took out his mobile to call an ambulance.

—

As Mike watched the paramedics loading Ben's stretcher into the ambulance, a patrol car arrived, carrying two young policemen.

'Are you the driver of this vehicle?' one of them asked.

'Hang on a moment.'

Mike poked his head into the back of the ambulance and called to Ben, 'I'll phone your wife and let her know what's happened.'

Briefly he was blinded by the flashing lights of the patrol car reflecting off the many wet surfaces surrounding it and stumbled into the policeman who had come behind him. The cop entered the ambulance and spoke briefly with Ben before he climbed out, the door swung shut and the ambulance turned to go back up Lorimer Street.

The policeman indicated the departing ambulance with a tilt of his head.

'He was known to you?'

'He's my boss.'

'And you ran into him?'

'Hey, no.' Mike gave a short laugh. 'It was a hit-run.'

What was it about the police? The tone they used always suggested you were the one who needed to explain yourself.

'If I could get a few details.' The policeman inclined his head towards the overhang at the entrance to the nearby warehouse. 'We'll be drier over there.'

It wasn't true – the cop was swathed in yellow waterproofs and Mike could get no wetter. It must be the paperwork he was keen to protect and, sure enough, when they were standing out of the rain, the cop produced a notebook. 'Your name and address please, sir.'

'Mike Georgiou, 14 Martin Street, South Melbourne.'

The policeman flipped back a page. 'And the victim was a Mr Ben Findlay?'

He made it sound as though Ben had been murdered.

'Yes, he lives in Brighton. I don't have his exact address but I can give you his phone number.'

The policeman was uninterested in his offer. 'Tell me what you saw.'

Mike embarked on a description of the accident, conscious of how fragmentary and incomplete his account must sound.

When he finished, the policeman, who had written very little of Mike's statement in his book, said, 'An SUV, you say, swerved towards the victim? Get a number?'

'No.'

'Odd route for you to take. Were you following your boss?'

'No, trying to avoid the traffic during the storm.'

'You knew your boss was coming this way, though?'

Mike looked into the bland face of the policeman. 'What are you getting at?'

'Better take a look at your vehicle.'

'Look, I didn't hit him. I keep telling you,' Mike said, exasperation sharpening his voice.

The policeman was already walking back to where the VW stood, the other cop waiting beside it. 'Some old scars but nothing current I can see,' this man said to his partner, who completed his own survey of the wheels and bodywork of the car before turning to Mike.

'Thank you, sir. We will now follow the ambulance to the hospital and endeavour to obtain a full statement from the victim.'

He opened the passenger door of the police car and looked carefully at Mike before entering. 'The victim recalls seeing only your car behind him before the incident occurred.'

Mike took a step towards him. For a moment it entered his mind to tell the cop about the possibility of this 'incident', as

16

he had called it, being part of the deliberate sabotage of Find-lay's that he and Bob Kennedy suspected was occurring, but he thought better of it. Instead, he watched the car depart, the twisted bicycle lying beside the road as his only company.

The storm had passed by the time Mike reached home, but the darkness had deepened into night. As he pulled into the kerb outside his cream weatherboard house, he saw his sister's battered, red Barina in front of him. Had Shane been into her again? He squelched his way unhappily on to the front veranda and paused to look into the small strip of garden that lay in front of the house. The rain would be good for the parched grass but too late for the dead blooms on the climbing roses that clung to each of the veranda posts. It was strange Lissa hadn't already dead-headed them. She used to be meticulous about how the front garden presented itself to the outside world.

Drawing in a deep breath, he entered the front door. He had taken only a few paces down the passageway when she appeared from the kitchen.

'Where have you been? And look at you, leaking all over the carpet. Go into the bathroom and take all your sodden gear off before you go any further.'

She shook her head and called over her shoulder, 'Mary, you should see the state your brother comes home in.'

Before Mike could do as he had been told, Mary came behind Lissa. 'My, you are a drowned rat.' Her face changed and she stopped her laughter. 'It was just the storm? You are OK?'

Mike sighed. 'One way and another it's been quite a day.'

'Well, get changed and you can explain to us why it's taken you so long to come home,' Lissa said. 'I'm used to you never wanting to leave the site, but we'd had no word from you, you weren't answering your mobile and the kids were giving us hell, so I packed them off to their rooms.'

Mike counted three accusations in the one sentence.

He pulled his mobile from his pocket and scrutinised it. 'After I called Jacqui Findlay, I tried to ring you, but my phone was dead. The battery shouldn't have been flat – perhaps the rain got to it.'

'Ben Findlay's wife? Why were you calling her?'

'I'll tell you all about it after I dry myself off.'

After he had stripped, towelled himself dry and dressed in a clean T-shirt and jeans, he mounted the stairs to the children's bedrooms. Leila and Jacinta were across from one another in the bedroom they shared. Jacinta was already asleep and he bent to kiss her on the forehead. She did not move, the faint rise and fall of her chest a comforting indication she was still breathing. Surely she was old enough that he need no longer have that fear. He turned to Leila, who had looked up from the book she was reading when he entered but did not return his smile and continued to eye him anxiously.

'What have you kids been up to this time?' he asked.

'It was Chris's fault,' she whined. 'He was mean to Jac and Mum wouldn't listen to us, too busy talking with Mary.'

'Jac doesn't seem to be suffering now. Time you were getting to sleep as well.'

'Aw, Dad.'

Christos was sprawled on his bed with the plugs of his iPod – a recent birthday present – in each ear. 'Hi, Dad,' he said in a loud voice and grinned. 'You in trouble with Mum again?'

'No homework tonight?'

'Finished it,' he replied complacently. When Mike showed his surprise, Christos added, 'Don't have much that has to be in tomorrow.'

'Why were you picking on Jac?'

'I wasn't picking on her. She's a pest who thinks because she's the littlest she should get whatever she wants. It's not fair.'

'A good chance for you to get ahead with your work. It's not as if you're top of the class.'

'Mum says you weren't much of a student either.'

Mike resisted the temptation to tell his son that Lissa had paid even less attention in class, more concerned with how she looked and what she would do after school, something Mike had no objection to in those days. He returned down the stairs. Lissa was working in the kitchen. Across the divide of the kitchen bench, he could see Mary on the leather couch in the family room, sipping a glass of wine.

'Now big brother it's time to tell us what you've been up to.'

Mike collected a beer from the refrigerator, enjoyed a mouthful and began by describing the ferocity of the downpour as he drove down Lorimer Street to come up behind Ben.

'Is Ben Findlay having a mid-life crisis?' Lissa asked scornfully. 'Taking on that triathlete stuff and riding to work in his rainbow Lycra.'

'Nothing wrong with keeping fit,' Mary disagreed. 'My Shane works out a lot and looks great. Would do you no harm, brother, to join him at the gym after work. It's not far over the river from where you work.'

Mike ignored her and continued with his account.

'Did you get the number of the four-wheel-drive?' Lissa asked.

'Couldn't see it in all the water thrown up from the road.'

'Pity.'

'You can say that again,' Mike agreed. 'Ben didn't see the SUV and thought it was me who hit him. I reckon the police have the same idea.'

'That's ridiculous,' Lissa interjected. 'Why would you make up a silly story like that, even if you did hit him?'

'You think I did?' Mike asked angrily.

'No, of course she doesn't,' Mary interceded.

'I had a good motive.' Mike watched them carefully as their eyes widened. 'Before he went off on his bike, I had a spat with Ben and he as good as told me I was fired.'

'As good as?'

'He was going to think about it overnight. He has this crazy idea he should replace me himself and prove to the doubters he has what it takes to be the MD of Findlay's and not just the owner's son.'

'There you are. I said he was having a mid-life crisis,' Lissa chirped.

Mary was more thoughtful. 'Apart from having an argument with him, did he have any reason for wanting you gone?'

'We've been having a bad run at the site for a few weeks. Today two of the guys were seriously injured when the load from a crane fell on them.'

'Yeah. Shane told me there were some troubles at the CityView site.'

'Shane? How did he know? What did he say?'

'Nothing specific,' Mary replied, screwing up her face as she tried to recall her conversation with her partner. 'Just you were having problems. I guess he picked up a rumour or something. He is still across the road from you at Riverside most of his time, although his new job takes him all over the place.'

'New job? What's he doing now?' Mike asked

Mary dropped her eyes.

'Not sure. He doesn't talk about it much.'

She looked up again, meeting the challenge Mike had not issued. 'It's important though,' she said with pride. 'See, working out and keeping fit doesn't just make you look terrific.'

Mike moved closer to Mary, scrutinising her carefully. 'Your friend Shane is such a strong man. Has he been working out on you again? Is that why you're here?'

Mary glared at him. 'Shane is working hard at present. He's doing overtime for Rubicon Development on the Riverside site and other places as well, including going down to the Peninsula some weekends.'

'What's he building? Not much call for a high-rise down there, I reckon,' Mike said.

'It's not building but has something to do with Rubicon. I don't know what.'

Mike was about to reply when his attention was diverted by a heap of cigarette stubs in an ashtray on the side table by the couch. He sniffed.

'Talking of keeping fit, you haven't been smoking in here, have you?'

Mary flushed. 'When you didn't come home and couldn't be contacted, we were worried about you.'

2

The call came before Vern McKenzie had finished his porridge. After many years in Australia, his insistence that porridge was essential to a good breakfast, his taste for single malt and the burr in his accent were almost all that remained of his Scottish origins.

'Vern, it's Jim. Can you come over? I need to speak with you.'

'Do I need to bring anything?'

'No, just your good self will be fine.'

Vern did not ask why Jim Findlay was calling him so early in the morning. He would know soon enough and Vern did not prolong conversations without good reason. 'I'll be with you in fifteen minutes.'

He finished his porridge, ignored the teapot and rang Freda Bradshaw, who was always the first to arrive at the head office of Findlay Construction.

'I'll be late in. The boss wants a word with me,' he told her, and she knew he meant Jim Findlay, not Ben.

Getting into his car, Vern reflected that he and Jim seldom spoke for long these days – not like the old times. Then they would argue over many things, not all of them affecting the business. Their arguments were usually contested with vigour but always resolved the same day or the day after – certainly by the end of the week. Until lately. Just yesterday he had been wondering how he could arrange to speak with Jim without Ben finding out. Now, out of the blue, he had his chance. But would Jim be receptive? That was the problem which had grown with each passing month since Ben joined the firm.

As Vern expected, the traffic flow had not yet degenerated to the peak hour dawdle it would later become so it took only fifteen minutes to reach the solid, single storey, brick house that sat comfortably ensconced within its carefully tended garden on the large block. There were only a few of these well-to-do properties left in Elwood, many having fallen under the encroaching tide of multi-storey units that were such a steady source of income for Findlay Construction.

Vern had barely mounted the steps to the terrazzo porch when the front door opened; Judith Findlay stepped out and came to meet him. Despite the early hour, she was already impeccably groomed and dressed, as if on her way to a game of bridge with her friends or morning tea in aid of one of her charities. She presented a cheek for Vern to kiss. 'Good to see you, Vern.'

'How is he?' Vern asked.

'You know he was knocked off his bike?'

'What?'

Recovering from his initial astonishment, Vern said, 'You mean Ben?'

'You haven't heard? Of course you haven't.' Judith gave an apologetic smile. 'I thought Jim would have told you. Yes, Ben was knocked off his bike on his way home from work last night. I've told him he shouldn't ride in the traffic, but he tells me not to fuss over him. Why shouldn't I? He is my son, the only child I've got.'

'How is he?'

'He has several cracked ribs along with a fair bit of abrasion and bruising. They've kept him in hospital overnight, but it could have been a lot worse, I suppose.' She did not sound convinced. 'He was fit enough to have a talk with Jim on the phone, so I expect that's why he's brought you here now.' She smiled again, a smaller one, which suggested a coyness Judith seldom showed. 'It is good to see you. You're becoming a stranger.'

'And Jim? How is he?'

'I wish he'd stayed at the Epworth for rehab, but you know Jim. He insisted on coming straight home, which is a pain for the folk who are looking after him, but they gave in to him as most people do.' Her tone changed and she looked around as though fearful they might be overheard. 'That's what I wanted to talk about with you. His heart is the real worry these days. What he needs is to rest completely for some weeks. I've found a resort at Merimbula, just right for people of our age, but he's being stubborn. You know what he's like. Now that Ben's out of action for a few days, he's even worse. Can you persuade him? He listens to you.'

'Not anymore.'

'Oh, Vern, do I have to beg?'

Vern shook his head and fingered his cheek. 'I'll try, but don't expect me to succeed.'

Judith gave his arm an appreciative squeeze and turned to lead him into the house. They walked along a thickly carpeted corridor until they reached a room at the back, where full-length windows allowed a view of the garden where thick shrubbery surrounded a kidney-shaped swimming pool. Jim Findlay, who had been sitting in a straight-backed chair with a padded seat and wooden arms, pushed on the arms and struggled slowly to his feet. He was a big man with rounded shoulders and a large head carrying a generous amount of bushy but faded fair hair. With his ambling gait, it was not unusual for people to describe him as a shaggy bear of a man, and today this image was heightened by the tan tracksuit and brown slippers he was wearing. He held out his hand to Vern and said, 'Here he is, the man himself.'

Vern shook the offered hand and nodded acknowledgement of the greeting.

'Sit down. Sit down,' Jim said, pointing at a more comfortable looking armchair before sinking back on to his.

'I'll leave you men to it,' Judith said but then hesitated. 'Tea, Vern?'

'No thank you, Judith.'

'Oh go on, Vern. I've got some,' Jim said, indicating the china cup on the small table beside him. He lifted his head to speak to his wife. 'You know how he likes it, dear – strong and black so the spoon'll stand up in it.'

When Judith had gone Jim said, 'I've heard about the accident at the site, but Ben didn't know who was hurt.'

'Paddy O'Donohue has concussion and a bad shoulder, I believe. Joe Frederico has a broken leg.'

'Poor Paddy,' Jim said. 'He's been with us for years. Which hospital? I must get in touch with him.'

'It's the Royal Melbourne, but I think they'll send Frederico home pretty soon.'

'He's only joined us recently. I know the name but I haven't had a lot to do with him,' Jim said apologetically. 'Not good.'

He took a deep breath as though drawing a line under the topic, looked into Vern's eyes and gave the open smile which, together with his reputation for honesty and reliability, had won him so many contracts. The same smile sometimes led people to think of him as easy-going, but those who knew him better were well aware of his persistent refusal to take no for an answer.

'Have you forgiven me yet, mate?' he asked.

'Nothing to forgive,' Vern replied gruffly.

'So it does still rankle. Your place in the company has always been important. It still is. Even more so.'

Vern regarded Jim through the upper halves of his dark-framed glasses. 'This has nothing to do with my place in the company.' The colour in his ruddy face deepened. 'I told you, you were making a big mistake that would cost all of us dearly – not just you – and I haven't changed my opinion.' He shrugged his shoulders. 'But it's your firm. You can do what you like.'

'You have a share.'

'A token percentage,' Vern said dismissively.

Jim leaned forward, his face now clouded. 'We've often disagreed in the past, but this is different. You sound bitter, Vern. I hate that.'

'Judith told me about Ben.'

Jim nodded and pursed his lips. 'Yeah. Actually they think he might have some internal injuries as well. He's in the Alfred and they're doing tests today. I haven't told Judy. She'd just worry and there's nothing she can do. Don't know how long he'll be off work. That's why I wanted to talk. Good excuse, really.'

Judith returned with a cup of deep black tea and a sugar bowl from which Vern took two heaped spoonfuls. Her face registered mock astonishment before she left as silently as she had arrived. He wondered whether she had overheard Jim telling him the extent of Ben's injuries. If so, Jim would cop it after Vern had gone.

'I was looking for a chance to talk with you without Ben being involved,' Vern said.

'Leave it off, Vern,' Jim replied, his normally sunny face now darkened by irritation. 'There's nothing more to be said on that score. Ben just needs a bit more time. Sure, it would have been ideal if he'd been able to come up through the ranks like Mike Georgiou is doing, but we haven't been given the luxury. Ben has to learn on the job – the top job – and you could be so much help to him if you were willing.'

'Ben's the one who isn't willing. Won't listen to anything I say.' Vern shot out his words like bursts from an automatic weapon. 'He thinks we're all out of touch. Thinks only he knows what's best for the firm, when in reality he's out of his depth. You don't see what's going on because he makes sure everything comes to you through him.'

'Vern, I'll say this once more and then we'll leave it. Ben is the MD of Findlay Construction and will remain so. The only way you can help the firm and yourself is by helping him.' Jim paused and a smile softened his face. 'I know he can be a bit prickly when he's unsure of himself, but you can deal with that. You've dealt with me for years.'

Vern wiped his nose with a white handkerchief he produced from his pocket. 'That's your last word?' he asked. When Jim nodded, Vern raised the cup to his lips, drank from it and set it down so firmly that the spoon rattled in the saucer. 'We've had a spate of problems at CityView lately,' he said.

'Yeah, that's concerning Ben too. Apparently he had a big row with Georgiou just before going home yesterday. Did you know?' Jim paused to check Vern's response, which was to give a slight scowl and say nothing. 'I didn't think you would. Ben is wondering whether we made a mistake giving Mike the job – it was a big step up for him. He's thinking of replacing him.'

'Bloody rubbish,' Vern spat at him. 'Mike's done a terrific job under a host of difficulties. The architect Ben insisted we use might have great ideas for the building he wants to create but doesn't know the first thing about construction. Until very recently Mike has kept the project on schedule and under budget despite the architect and with no help from his MD. Did Ben tell you we had to hose down our bankers yesterday?'

'No, he didn't. He had other worries.'

Ignoring the stress Jim put on his last words and despite the edict Jim had given earlier, Vern continued his complaints. 'You know how heavily we had to borrow to finance the CityView project. For a firm of our size to get such funding when we were taking on the development risk for the first time, Ben agreed to a raft of get-out clauses that I told him made us bloody vulnerable, but of course he wouldn't listen. Now we find a story is going around that we're overcommitted on CityView and we're having a lot of problems there, putting us behind schedule and blowing the budget. You can imagine how our backers liked that. All Ben could say to reassure them was to talk about how many units we've pre-committed and our forward sales estimates, when what concerned them most, of course, was our cash flow. Whoever started this story seems to know a fair bit about our problems at CityView but overlooked the rest of our business, so I was able to talk about the cash from all our other, smaller projects to buy us some time for CityView to come through.'

'You think someone is talking out of school?'

'You don't want to hear this, but there are quite a few unhappy people in the firm since you've taken a back seat and Ben has come in. Maybe someone has been sounding off.'

Jim frowned, sat back and lifted his arms to put his hands behind his head. 'There's another thing. Did you know it was Georgiou who was travelling behind Ben when he was hit?'

'No, I didn't. Fortunate, I s'pose.'

'Perhaps. It seems he was the only one nearby when it happened.'

Jim paused, eyeing Vern closely. When Vern chose to say nothing, Jim moistened his lips with a quick flick of his tongue and said, 'Georgiou told Ben it was a black SUV that knocked him over and didn't stop. Ben only saw Georgiou's car coming up behind him – no one else.' Again Vern remained silent but his eyes were fastened on Jim's. 'Ben believes Georgiou was so angry after the spat they had that he lost it when he saw Ben ahead of him and ran him down but came to his senses enough not to drive on and tried to pretend it was this black SUV.'

'What do the police say?'

'They're not saying much except that Georgiou was pretty vague about what happened and they found no incriminating marks on his car.'

'There you are.'

'Ben was going through water when he was hit. It could have been the bow wave from the car that knocked him over, they say. Look, I know your opinion of Mike Georgiou.'

'So what do you want me to do?'

'Take over, of course. You're the only one I'd trust to sort out this can of worms. Seeing I'm out of action, you have to deal with this business between Georgiou and Ben. Nip it in the bud. These personal feuds can destroy a construction team. If Ben is right, though, Georgiou will have to go – and quickly.'

'You mean if Ben is right about who's to blame for CityView's woes, or who's to blame for Ben's injuries?'

'I mean all of it. As well as sorting out Ben and Mike, you need to get CityView back on track. Hopefully I'll be back to help you soon, but we can't afford to wait.'

'OK, but before I go, there's something else I want to discuss with you.'

⸻

It was Judith who saw Vern out. 'Well?'

He shrugged. 'I think I've got him to take his time at home recovering and not rushing back to work. But he won't hear of being away from Melbourne. Merimbula will have to wait. Sorry.'

Before driving away, Vern rang Freda to tell her Jim had asked him to take over as MD and he intended to make an unannounced visit to the CityView site before coming to the office. 'I expect you would like Janine to look after you while you're acting MD,' she said diffidently. When Vern assured her that he did not intend to move office or use Ben's personal assistant but expected Freda to continue as his PA, she said blandly, 'I'll let the others know,' but was unable to fully mask the contented purr in her voice.

The peak hour had passed so the traffic did not require his careful attention, which was just as well as a torrent of thoughts was racing through his head. What was the old furphy about the Chinese symbol for crisis combining the characters for danger and opportunity? It certainly would fit the situation at Findlay's right now. He hadn't expected the freedom offered by Ben's removal from the scene, but the cloud over Mike was a worry. After all Mike had good reason to be fed up with his treatment by Ben and might have sounded off unwisely somewhere. He couldn't see him losing it to the extent of knocking Ben off his bike, though. Vern tightened his grip on the steering wheel when he narrowly missed side-swiping a delivery van parked away from the kerb. Mike would take some very careful watching and, if he was the one talking loosely, that could be useful as well.

—

The first thing Mike did after arriving on site was to ring the hospital. He learned that Joe's leg had been put in plaster and he would return home before lunch. Paddy was to be kept under observation because of his concussion and a decision would be made later on the treatment for his shoulder. When Mike asked about Ben, he was told the hospital had no patient of that name. Puzzled, he called Jacqui Findlay.

As soon as she heard who it was, her voice rasped back at him. 'You've got a cheek ringing here.'

She hung up. It was obvious any suspicion Jacqui held that Mike had run into Ben had hardened overnight into a conviction of his guilt. Perhaps Ben's injuries had not been as serious as first thought and he would soon appear on site to fire him.

Until that happened, he needed to get on with the job. He made a comprehensive tour of the site, spreading the news of Joe and Paddy and checking that yesterday's events had not fed into a slow start today. He kept Ben's accident to himself. Reassured by what he saw and heard, he returned to his office and was reflecting that he may have just completed his last tour of the site as project manager when a sharp rap on his office door was followed by it being opened to reveal the lanky frame of Alan Reardon, the union official.

'Good morning,' Reardon said without smiling.

Mike looked up from his desk. 'What brings you here?'

'I'm on my way to Riverside and thought I'd drop in and see how those two blokes who were hurt yesterday are getting on.'

'You're spending a lot of time over there. Got problems?'

'How are your men?'

Mike grinned at the rebuff. He told Reardon what he knew and added, 'I'll know more when I see them after work today.'

'You're going to visit them?' As if regretting he had shown his surprise, Reardon's lip curled and he said, 'Want to get their stories straight before WorkSafe interviews them and get them back to work a.s.a.p.?' Mike scowled at him but said nothing.

'I didn't pay a lot of attention to Ted Horton's complaints about sloppy safety. Now I'm beginning to see he has a point. Your track record's been poor, lately.' Reardon held up his hand when Mike began to object. 'Nothing as bad as yesterday, but the signs were there.'

'We suspect the sling was damaged in the first place,' Mike spat at him, getting to his feet. A voice within told him not to mention any of Bob Kennedy's suspicions and he retained enough composure to listen to the warning. 'They should have found it, but your delegate distracted them with one of his silly stunts.'

Reardon, whose height meant he continued to look down at Mike, said, 'Didn't turn out silly though, did it? Can I see the sling?'

'No, WorkSafe have it.'

'When we get right down to it, all you bosses are the same. You cut corners, skimp on safety, and when you get a problem, try to find someone else to blame.'

'That might be the way others work, but it's not our way and we have the track record over many years to prove it.'

The response came from a short, thick-set man of florid complexion now standing in the doorway, his round, pugnacious face framed by remnants of ginger hair at either side of his bald head.

Reardon turned to regard him and used the same words with which he had been greeted by Mike the day before, 'And you are?'

'If you'd been around for more than five minutes you'd know I'm Vern McKenzie,' he replied. 'What you don't know is that as of this morning I'm the acting MD of this company. But I know you, Alan Reardon, the man who had to be shifted out of WA and be found a slot in another state. Do your homework before you start throwing accusations around. Meanwhile ...' He paused to signal a change of tack. 'I'm here in my new role for a briefing from the project manager, so I suggest you get back to Riverside where I hear you're spending a lot of your time.'

'I'll take a personal interest in the WorkSafe report on this,' Reardon replied, but his voice had lost its sting. When there was no response, he pushed past Vern and was gone.

Mike sat with an amused smile as he watched him go. 'Sit down, Vern. Have you been chatting with George Fowler again?'

'You know George and I go way back. We're both survivors. He's one of the few union bosses I've ever trusted.'

Vern twisted his head and lifted his chin to indicate the departed Reardon. 'I'm told that young Turk got himself into strife in Perth and George has given him a chance here. You wouldn't think it to see or hear him, but the fire-eating state secretary of the Building and Construction Union can be a kindly soul. Watch your step with Reardon, though. I bet he's out to make a name for himself over here. I don't know why, but he's taking a lot of interest in Riverside. Best for us he stays there.'

'So you're taking over as MD?'

'Jim insisted. Just while Ben is laid up. I hope it won't be for long.'

'Have you heard how Ben is? I tried the hospital but they said he wasn't a patient.' Mike didn't mention his brief conversation with Jacqui.

'He's in the Alfred. Jim told me cracked ribs and possibly some internal injuries they're not sure about yet.' Vern scratched at the ruddy flesh on the side of his face. 'A funny business. All Ben can remember is you coming up behind him. You were the only one to see what happened and, from what I've heard, were pretty vague as well, although you say there was a black SUV involved. You must have seen more than you told the police.'

'It was pelting with rain and happened so quickly,' Mike replied defensively. Vern was starting to sound like one of the cops.

Vern regarded him carefully. 'Come on, Mike. Best you tell me the truth. I know you'd had a row with Ben. Did you see the chance to let off some steam and give him a fright but got too close? Was that how it happened?'

'No, I've told you what happened and that's the truth, although the family seems to have decided it was me. Have you come to fire me?'

Vern scowled at him. 'What are you talking about?'

'You already know Ben and I had a row yesterday before his accident. I reacted when he said I wasn't up to the job and only got it in the first place because I was your favourite.'

'He said that?'

'Not quite in those words, but that's what he meant, and he said quite a bit else, including that he was thinking of taking over here himself, and would decide overnight. If he believes it was me who ran him down that'll settle it.'

'I'm not here to fire you.' Vern gave a small, uncharacteristic smile and added, 'Not yet anyway. Now tell me about the faulty sling.'

Mike was part way into an account of yesterday's accident when Vern interrupted. 'Let's get to the point. I made sure you were made project manager so we would have someone on site who I could trust to make up for the lack of any real construction experience in our MD and our architect. But you've been plagued by blunders lately. What's going on?'

'We think we're being got at.'

'What do you mean?'

'The sling had been tampered with and we think some of our other recent problems were the result of someone trying to sabotage the project. We also think Ted Horton is involved.'

'The union delegate?'

'Yeah.'

'Bullshit.'

Mike blinked at the strength of Vern's response. 'George Fowler vouched for him when he came on to this project. You sure you're not trying to cover up your own mistakes? Maybe Reardon was right.'

Vern gave a deep sigh. 'I told you I didn't want to take over. Particularly, I didn't want to be saddled with this project. It's the wrong option at the wrong time and we've borrowed heavily on it, putting the whole company at risk. Now, when our backers are getting nervous, the man who dreamed up the project and insisted it was our great leap forward, gets himself into hospital.'

'But Ben told me last week it's selling well.'

'You've seen the figures,' Vern scoffed. 'Off the plan sales have been steady but not spectacular. The budget was always too tight and by taking on the development as well as the construction risk we're more dependent on the money men than ever before. You should know that. What do you sit in on the finance meetings for if you don't pay attention? Now with some competition ...'

'What do you mean?'

'I mean Riverside.'

'But they're upmarket from us. That's the beauty of this project, feeding off them.'

Vern shook his head. 'You've really swallowed Ben's pitch, haven't you? Always the salesman. What if Riverside comes down to meet us? Have you thought of that?'

'What have you heard?'

Vern sat back as though retreating. 'Look, I'm not saying we shouldn't get into the development game. We could have put our toe in the water with a smaller project, a safe one like those we built the company on, not this one, the first high-rise residential we've ever done. Now we have a man with little experience leading us down the most ambitious road we've ever tried, putting at risk the company we've spent years building.'

Vern's voice dropped and Mike was unsure whether he was continuing to address him or had lapsed into a reverie of his own. 'Jim was a fool to bring Ben straight in as MD and now we're in trouble he wants me to sort things out for him like I've done so often before. Why should I bother? It's a pity whoever put Ben in hospital didn't put him properly out of action. Perhaps having him out of the way for a while will give us a chance to put things right, but he'll be back ruining things again.'

Mike could not believe what he was hearing. Never before had Vern voiced the slightest criticism of Jim to Mike or anyone else and, despite the provocation, had adopted the same stance towards Ben. Vern looked up to see Mike observing him and passed his hand across his lips as if wiping them clean. 'But I was talking about Riverside. They have a totally different set-up. Angelo Rossi, he knows how to do it.'

'The boss of Rubicon Development?'

'Yeah.' Vern nodded and screwed up his eyes as if focussing on a distant scene. 'One time Angelo's company was a small construction firm, smaller than us. He didn't jump into the Riverside project straight off like Ben's trying to do.'

'Come on Vern,' Mike objected. 'Riverside is huge. CityView is not even the size of one of their towers.'

Vern paid him no attention, his gaze still far off. 'Angelo started small and had no need to find backers with big money like we've had to do. Then, when he'd reached the stage where he needed that kind of support, he hit the jackpot, married into it.'

Mike laughed. 'Is she rich as well? Angelo and Carla, the glamour couple of the building industry. Lissa showed me an article on them in *New Idea* about six months ago. They had photographs of the pair of them at their holiday pad, the other side of Flinders. Quite a place! My dad was over with us at the time and he said she reminded him of Sophia Loren, the Italian actress all the men of his age get randy about.'

'Don't know about that,' Vern growled. 'I do know Carla's the daughter of Mario Mancini, the owner of Mancini Transport, who's made a bundle from real estate, as well. He looks and acts like a pillar of society these days but it wasn't always that way and they say he still has his finger in many pies, from the highest level of government down. Mario had the money and the connections to set Angelo on his way to the top. That's how he got control of all that land in the Docklands and funded the Riverside development. He's done very well.'

Mike had never heard Vern speak of anyone in the admiring tones he was using to describe Angelo Rossi. Vern's admiring tone persisted.

'And Angelo never stands still. So what would you do if you were in his position?'

'What?'

'With the gloss gone off the luxury end of the market, I bet he's holding quite a few unsold units in the last completed tower and the next stage is starting to come out of the ground already. So I'd also bet he'll be looking to revamp that stage to appeal to just the punters we're pitching to. If Ben can see an opportunity I'm damn sure Angelo will see it too. That's why they've slowed the work over there.'

Mike went to explain he had noticed the slower tempo in the sounds he heard when he walked past the site but Vern had not finished. 'It wouldn't surprise me if that's why Reardon is spending so much of his time over there.'

'Has George Fowler told you this?'

'Our only hope is if we can finish CityView before Riverside takes the market away from us. So you'd better get your act together and have this site humming along to completion ahead of time, before Riverside can change course. And ahead of budget, before our bankers have any more second thoughts. Meanwhile, I'd better check on our other sites. At least we know what we're doing with them and I don't see any problems.' He turned to leave, tossing over his shoulder, 'Make sure you let me know the minute there are any new developments.'

Mike sat trying to come to terms with the sudden change Vern had undergone. Everyone knew Vern and Jim did not always agree, but Vern's fierce loyalty to Jim meant he never mentioned a word of those differences to anyone else. Not anymore. What had caused the turnaround? And the way he poured the bucket on Ben? Mike was brought from his musings when Bob Kennedy poked his head in the door. 'Got a minute?'

'Only if you've got some good news.'

'Good and bad. Depends how you look at it.'

He sat down opposite Mike, who stared at him enquiringly.

'You told me to keep an eye on Ted Horton. I thought I'd go a bit further and recruited a few of the blokes I trust.' Seeing the concern on Mike's face, he hastened to add, 'You know Rocko, Matt and Bluey; they've been with Findlay's a long time and they're rock solid loyal to the firm.'

He gave a small grin. 'Actually it's really Jim Findlay they'd go to the wall for – he's always treated us like one of the family. Bit early yet, but maybe they'll feel like that about you one day. I can't see Ben'll ever make it. Anyway, when I hinted at my worries about Ted, they opened up to me. Just lately, he's been bad mouthin' all of us as well as tryin' to stir up trouble. They're pissed off with him, but I told them to play along and see what they could get out of him. That's what they did in the pub after work yesterday.'

'What did he say?'

'Not much. Not to them. They told me he seemed pretty shaken up by what happened to Joe and Paddy – sort of as though he was somehow to blame – but when they tried to press him, he started goin' on about safety on the site – the usual stuff he's been pushin'.'

Mike showed his frustration by squaring his shoulders and drawing in a deep breath.

'Hold on,' Bob continued. 'He took a call on his mobile and the first thing he said to the caller was that two of our blokes were in hospital. Whatever the guy on the other end said brought him up sharp and he went into that smarmy routine of his – agreein' a lot with whatever was said to him. Finally he said, "OK, Bruno, six o'clock at the Hibernian." He left soon after and the guys gave me a call to tell me what happened. I know that pub, it's not far from my place, and I reckoned it might be interestin' to see who the shit was meetin' up with. I got there in plenty o' time and waited across the street for him to arrive. It was bucketin' down and I was worried I'd miss him, but I didn't want to wait inside in case he saw me. Anyway, I did spot him and went in after him. It was pretty crowded so I could get quite close to him where he had his back to me. He had to wait a while but eventually the other bloke turned up – a stocky thug with a shaved head and tatts; looked like he was in one of them bikie gangs. I couldn't hear what Ted was sayin' because he had his back to me and was talkin' soft. No problem with Bruno. He was really gettin' stuck into Ted. "Yeah, well I was fuckin' busy knockin' over a sittin' duck," was the first thing he said. "You'll hear about it tomorrow".'

'Did he mean Ben?' Mike asked.

'Ben?'

'Oh, you haven't heard? Ben was hit by a car, when riding his bike home last night. A hit-run. He's in hospital and Vern McKenzie is acting as MD. I was coming along behind and saw the SUV that did it. Didn't get his number though.'

Bob scratched his chin. 'Yeah, well, I guess it might have been this Bruno bloke. He didn't say any more about that, but gave it to Ted. Told him he was piss weak and had no guts. I don't know what Ted said back but Bruno threatened him – somethin' about he'd been well paid and if he tried to get off now he'd end up in deep shit. You can see he's a lovely guy for Ted to be playin' with.'

'Where's the good news?' Mike asked impatiently.

'I'm just gettin' to that. The guy said somethin' about being on a roll, no time to stop, and asked Ted what they could do next. Again, I couldn't hear Ted, but Bruno said, "Yeah, you don't need to get worried some fucker is goin' to get hurt and I know where we can get bloody good cash for stuff like that. Tomorrow night. I'll meet you here at ten." I couldn't tell what Ted said but I don't reckon he was too keen because the thug said, "Can't be that much to set it up. You've got all day tomorrow, ya bludger." Then he gave Ted an evil grin and said. "Don't let me down, Ted. I'd hate to lose you, ya little arsehole".'

'I wonder if they're after our electric cable. We've just had a delivery ready for the sparkies to get moving on the lower floors.'

'Yeah, you could be right,' Bob said. 'Don't forget the fittin's. I hear there's a good market for that stuff these days. We need some extra security on the site. Those patrols are just too easy to avoid. Look what Ted and his pal have done already with security seein' nothin'.'

'No. If we do that Ted'll find out. You know how rumours spread around here.'

'So, what are you goin' t'do?'

'*We* are going to wait for them to arrive and catch them at it.'

'You don't think we should have one or two of our guys with us?'

'No, we have to keep this tight or we'll warn them off.' Mike grinned and added, 'Worried about handling Bruno, are you?'

He knew this would stir Bob, who was said to have been a good boxer in his youth and still boasted he could handle any of the guys on site who tried to give him lip.

Bob shrugged his shoulders. 'It wasn't me I was worried about.

I can handle the bikie, no problem. I guess you can look after Ted – the little runt.'

He stood up to leave, but turned to face Mike again. 'I had to make some changes in the crewin' so we could keep on with the southern crane. Weasel-voice wanted it shut down until Work-Safe finish their investigation, but I told him to get stuffed and, for a change, he didn't argue back. Backs up the idea he had a hand in yesterday's sling failure and feels bad about it.'

'You can ask him after we nab him tonight.'

——

Vern McKenzie was sitting at his desk, reading the phone messages Freda had presented to him on his return to the office, when his mobile rang. He did not recognise the number of the caller. 'Yeah,' he said irritably.

'Pity about your MD being put out of action.'

Vern's face soured further. He didn't know this voice and he was careful to give his mobile number only to a select few – mostly key people at Findlay's – and never to strangers.

'Who is this?'

'You can call me Ivan.'

Vern did not imagine a burly Russian was speaking to him. This man's voice was higher, his slight accent more middle European and the rhythm of his speech somehow conveyed to Vern a picture of a short, rather fastidious person.

'I have a strong interest in the affairs of Findlay Construction. You're going through a very bad patch – questions from your bankers, problems at CityView and two of your workers and your MD himself, all in hospital. Now you are in charge, an overdue recognition of your talent.'

'What do you want?'

'It would be in all our interests, particularly your personal interest, for us to meet. I have some proposals to put to you.'

Vern nodded and a smile came on to his face. He hadn't expected things to move so fast.

'I suggest you ring my secretary and she'll fix a time for you. As you'd expect, I'm pretty busy.'

'Tonight at five. Take a cab to the Crown Towers Hotel. You will be met there and brought to where we can have a discreet conversation.'

'Why should I play these games with you?'

'These are not games. You have much to gain. You also have much to lose.'

'Five's no good. Can't make it until around six.'

It was a small, probably silly gesture, but he'd done it now.

'Best, of course, you keep our appointment to yourself.'

Ivan was gone. Vern immediately made another call. 'George, it's Vern McKenzie.'

'How are you, Vern?' the state secretary of the BIU asked.

'Fair. Only fair, George. Remember we were chatting about our neighbours across the road. You told me your new boy, Reardon, was spending quite a bit of time at the Riverside site'

'Yeah?'

'Heard any more recently?'

'Nah, I haven't. To tell the truth, Vern, Reardon's holding out on me. Don't know why. When I chased him for an update yesterday, he said he'd stopped most of the scams they've been trying on but was now on to something bigger. Said he couldn't tell me more yet but he would as soon as he was sure what he had.'

'Is a bloke called Ivan involved?'

'You're a ripper, Vern. There is a guy called Ivan Sarac who was behind the problems at Riverside. He has a few enforcers who were the ones Reardon was trying to nail to start with. I just asked him if it was Sarac he was after now.'

'What did he say?'

'Nothing. Just gave me a blank stare and said he didn't think the problem was just on the Riverside site. Buggered if I know what he meant and I couldn't get him to open up to me.'

'Thanks, George.'

'Hey, not so fast. What've you got for me?'

'Like your boy Reardon, nothing yet. If I get anything I think might interest you I'll be in touch.'

Having closed off the call, Vern used his forefinger to push his glasses up his nose. Sarac already knew he was MD when very few others had been told. Had Mike tipped him off?

3

Whenever Mike entered the foyer of a hospital he became dispirited, but this afternoon was worse – the first time he had been back to the Royal Melbourne since his mother died. He well remembered the long walk along the concrete floored tunnel from the car park with the thick blue strip painted down its centre. The arcade of shops surrounding the foyer made it look more like a down-at-heel shopping mall than a hospital. The woman at the enquiry desk scrolled through the list on her computer before telling him Mr O'Donohue could be found in Ward 4 South, and pointed to the nearby set of lifts. He knew where they were; the intensive care ward was at 2 South. He had been the one to instruct the doctors to remove his mother's life support. The stroke she suffered had been severe and the doctors were surprised she clung on through the ten days the family had searched for a sign of recovery from the small figure embedded in tubes, electrical cables and softly beeping instruments. His father knew it was time to let her go but could not bring himself to say the word and implored Mike to do it for him.

When Mike entered Paddy O'Donohue's ward, the world changed. Several helium-filled balloons on multicoloured streamers formed a jigging canopy above his bed. Below them, his back to Mike and his bare shoulder swathed in bandages, lay Paddy, deep in conversation with a woman who sat on a narrow metal chair beside the bed. Her blonde hair was long and bouffant, her lips a bright red which matched the colour of the miniskirt drawn tightly around her, revealing all but the uppermost reaches of her plump thighs. Above the skirt she wore a white singlet that was hard pressed to contain the fullness of her breasts. As Mike came closer to the bed she looked up and gave him the full examination he had just given her.

Paddy turned his head and exclaimed with a laugh, 'Well, the saints be praised, it's the boss 'imself come to visit poor Paddy.' When the woman gave Mike a welcoming smile, Paddy added, 'Now, Sheena, stop flutterin' those lashes at the man. This is Mike Georgiou, the project manager at CityView.'

He turned further so that he could face Mike directly.

'Boss, this is Sheena, the best barmaid ever to grace Pugg Mahone's pub.' He waved his good arm in the direction of the bed across the ward. 'Grab the chair from Jimmy's bed. The poor bugger won't mind – too drugged up to notice.'

After Mike had brought the chair across and sat down he asked, 'And how are you, Paddy? Are they looking after you?'

'Just fine. They wanna keep me cooped up in 'ere for a bit 'cos of the bang on me head. I keep tellin' them I never had any brains to start with, so there can't be any damage, but they pay no mind to me.'

'What about the shoulder?'

'Had far worse in me time. Need an op when they can spare me the time – not now. I just want to get out. I was just tellin' Sheena they're a bit short on the beer round 'ere and the nurses aren't a patch on 'er.'

Sheena gave a giggle that travelled down her body.

'I 'spect you want to chat about what happened,' Paddy said, his face serious for the first time since Mike had arrived.

'Not really, but WorkSafe will want to interview you some-time, I guess.'

'Still, p'raps we'd better have a word,' Paddy insisted. 'Sheena, me dear. D'ya mind? The boss and me need a private chat.'

'Right,' Sheena said cheerfully and jumped to her high-heeled feet. She leant over to kiss Paddy and turned to smile at Mike. 'Remember, now. Any time you're in Carlton you'll be welcome at Pugg's – I'll see to that.' Turning back to Paddy she said, 'See you tomorrow. About the same time OK?'

Paddy nodded and both men watched Sheena sway her way from the ward. When she had departed Paddy said, 'She's a good lass, Sheena, and she meant what she said about makin' you welcome at Pugg's. But don't get me wrong, it's not every boyo she says that to.'

'Sorry to barge in like I have.'

'No. No. Good timin'. Maureen's due in shortly. She's only lately moved in with me and, while the colleen is an understandin' type, I don't know she'd 'it it off all that well with Sheena.' He winked at Mike. 'That's why I put on the palaver about needin' to talk.' He paused and gave Mike a quick glance. 'Still, I guess you were wonderin' how I came to be where those poles came down on me?'

'Not your usual spot.'

Paddy sighed. 'I guess I could blame it on the gee gees.'

'What?'

'Joe Frederico's often good for a tip, livin' near the track and spendin' 'is time there. Hadn't seen 'im for a bit and thought I'd have a chat on me way back from a break. Coulda picked a better time. First he was arguin' with Ted Horton and after 'e'd seen Ted off he was in such a stew he wouldn't give me the time o'day – a moody bugger, Joe. I was jist walkin' away when he started the lift and then it 'appened: poles rainin' down like God was throwin' javelins at us. Won't go down well with the boys from WorkSafe, will it?'

—

Mike left the hospital in a far better mood than the one he had carried in with him. It would be fun to see how Paddy conducted himself when Maureen and Sheena met up, as seemed sure to happen at some stage, though it wouldn't surprise him if Paddy had dealt with such situations before. Some of Mike's cheerfulness evaporated as he crawled towards Flemington in the sunbaked peak hour traffic. He had trouble finding Hope Street where, contradicting their address, few of the old houses showed the optimism of similar homes in South Melbourne. Several boys reluctantly halted their game of cricket on the roadway to allow him to pass and were not pleased when he parked at square leg, just outside number twenty-four, the home of Joe Frederico. It had a rickety front fence, a parched and straggly strip of garden and drab, brown weatherboards from which some of the paint was peeling.

He knocked and waited, listening to the sound of Coldplay coming from the back of the house. When no one came to the door, he tried again more loudly. This time he heard Joe's voice through the window of the front room. 'Carol. Someone at the door.'

'Orright. Orright,' came from within and Mike heard footsteps on bare boards. The door was thrown open and a spare woman in torn jeans and a tie-dyed T-shirt confronted him. 'Yeah?' she said in a challenging voice.

'My name is Mike Georgiou. I've come to see Joe.'

'You from Findlay's?' She made no attempt to invite him in, standing with legs apart in the doorway.

'That's right. I'm the project manager at the CityView site.'

'Just the man. What you goin' to do for Joe now he's laid up?'

'He'll be on full compo for the time he's off work, of course.' Mike tried a diplomatic smile. 'How's he getting on?'

Still his way was blocked. 'That ain't good enough. What

about 'is job at the track? He can't do that. And who's goin' to look after the kids while I'm at work? I'm waitin' on 'im hand and foot in the day, but I've got me cleanin' job at night. I gotta get out to that. We need all the dough we can get just to survive. Even more, now he's on his backside all bloody day.'

Mike looked more closely at the woman. It was hard to see why a three-income family should live so poorly and be so stretched. Her chalky skin, the dark rings under her eyes, her unkempt and straggly hair suggested an illness or perhaps a habit they could not afford.

'For Christ's sake, Carol, let the man in. I need to talk to 'im.'

At last Joe had reacted. Carol turned and, without another word, clomped down the corridor to the back of the house, leaving Mike to find his own way into the front room where Joe lay on a threadbare couch with his legs along its length, the right leg sheathed in plaster below the knee. Beside him was a small table, which carried a pack of cigarettes, a full ashtray and four stubbies, three of which had already been emptied. When he saw Mike he switched off the television set he had been watching.

'Don't mind 'er,' he said. 'She worries a lot.'

'I didn't know you worked at the track.'

'Yeah, well, Flemington's just down the road and I go there a bit, sellin' tickets, a bit of security, cleanin' sometimes. Pay's nothin' special but I like the 'orses.'

'Paddy says you give him tips.'

'Always after easy money is Paddy,' Joe observed dismissively. 'You won't find easy money backin' 'orses, though.'

'How's the leg?'

Joe shrugged. 'Gives me a bit of pain. They say the itchiness will be worse when it starts. They say the break's a pretty clean one but will still take a fair time to get fixed.'

'You'll be covered for all the time you need, and the medical expenses too, of course,' Mike said, thinking again of the woman who had met him.

Joe waved a hand as though dismissing the subject. 'Y'know it wasn't my fault?'

'The sling was faulty,' Mike replied noncommittally.

'Yeah, they'll want to say I shouda seen that, but I checked it. No problem I could see.'

'I hear Ted Horton was hassling you over the size of the no-go area under the lift.'

'Bloody rubbish,' Joe exploded. 'It was Mick Reilly who's to blame.'

'Why the crane operator?'

Joe leant forward as if taking Mike into his confidence.

'That's it, you see. As soon as he began the lift I could see the sling was skew-whiff and I called Mick to stop, but the silly bugger must've been dreamin' an' just went haulin' away. Then, when I sang out, he stopped it so sharp the line swung around, bashed into the buildin' and the pipes went all over the place. If Mick'd stopped proper when I told 'im, even if the sling dropped the load, they all would've fallen from much less height, well within the zone and no one woulda got hurt.'

Joe frowned and gazed gloomily at Mike. 'Much easier for the WorkSafe blokes to tell me I shoulda checked the sling. They don't like complicated answers. I'm not takin the blame for this, though. There's a tip you can back in.'

———

The cab pulled under the portico of the Crown Towers Hotel at five past six. As soon as Vern stepped out, a tall, fair-headed man left his position at the side of the entrance and came directly towards him. He was dressed in dark jeans and a deep green T-shirt which displayed his muscular arms and strong torso.

'Vern McKenzie?' he asked.

'And you are?'

'Follow me.'

The man entered the lush coolness of the marbled foyer and led Vern across it to a side door which brought them on to the crowded concourse beside the Yarra. Some of the crowd were still dressed for work, but the majority wore the casual clothes and the expectant expressions of people on their way to dining at one of the restaurants or trying their luck at the casino. Vern's guide navigated his way through them towards the King Street Bridge until they reached two men in similar T-shirts and jeans, each with his back against the building. One, strongly built, with a shaven head and prominent tattoos on his arms, was looking past them, as if searching for others who might be following. The other man, taller, with a faded baseball cap on his head, was watching those who came towards him from the direction of the bridge. Vern's guide turned sharply between these sentries into a narrow alleyway which was concealed by a box hedge and led to what appeared to be an electrical services cabinet with two head-high, grey doors. He opened the left hand door and gestured Vern through. The door closed behind him as he mounted a short, narrow staircase and entered a softly lit room suitable for board meetings or private dinners. A man rose from his seat at the head of the mahogany table dominating the room and held out his hand.

'I'm glad you could join me, Vern,' he said. He was taller than Vern had imagined but his neatly tailored, pinstripe suit, precisely knotted tie, slicked down dark hair and mottled complexion matched Vern's other preconceptions.

'Hullo, Mr Sarac,' Vern replied without enthusiasm.

Sarac nodded as though Vern had told him a not very amusing joke and gestured for him to take a seat at the corner of the table. Vern glanced around the room. Apart from the table and its accompanying dozen chairs, the only other item of furniture was a sideboard which ran along most of one wall and carried a vase of red roses. Original abstract oil paintings hung above the sideboard and along the opposite wall. There were two doors, the one through which Vern had entered and another at the other end of the room – both of them now closed.

'I trust you will join with me in a dram? Dram – that is how you Scots describe it, I believe.' Without waiting for a reply, Sarac opened the bottle beside his elbow and filled two tumblers. 'You take it neat, I understand.' He raised his glass as if making a toast. Vern ignored the invitation to clink glasses and took a sip.

When he could not restrain himself from nodding his approval of the whisky, Ivan said, 'I thought you'd enjoy it. Glenkinchie.'

Vern responded in a bored tone. 'At least you didn't arrange to blindfold me before leading me here. You said you were not playing games. Can we stop whatever it is you call this pantomime and get to the point?'

Sarac took his time over enjoying another sip of his drink before saying, 'I know that, regardless of the support you have given him over many years, Jim Findlay has turned his back on you and your advice is ignored by that Johny-come-lately, Ben Findlay. You have every reason to feel bitter. I also know the company is suffering a number of difficulties, none of which is down to you, but you're the one they expect to sort out the mess. I have an alternative you will find financially rewarding, and satisfying in other ways as well.'

Vern regarded Sarac over the top of his glass. 'Are you offering me a job?'

'What I have in mind …'

Vern did not let him finish. 'Wait,' he ordered. 'I want to talk with the man running Rubicon, not his messenger. Anything further you might want to say I want to hear from him.'

Again Sarac appeared to find Vern amusing. 'Ah, yes, you

know of my interest in the Riverside project so you want to speak with the boss of Rubicon. I can arrange for you to speak with him if you wish. I hope you are free on Sunday. Angelo would be happy to entertain us at his Flinders property – a very handsome place where we can enjoy his hospitality and talk without any concerns we will be interrupted. I'll arrange transport for you.'

'No. I'm happy to make my own way there. As you have my number you can text me with directions. That way no one else in the office will know.'

Mike glanced at his watch. There was just enough light for him to see that it was a quarter past ten. Earlier he had picked up Bob, driven to the site and parked on the far side behind a couple of company vehicles which were left there overnight. It was on this spare land they hoped eventually to build stage two of the project.

'Car approachin',' sounded in the earplug of the crane intercom unit he was wearing.

The alert came from Bob who was positioned on the second floor with a good view of the entry to the site, while Mike remained at ground level covering the back and side fences. Headlights swept the fence and a small van stopped in front of the gate. A man in uniform peered into the dimly lit building, inspected the padlock on the gate and pushed a card into the mesh, before getting back into his van and departing. Until the vandalism, Mike had not given much thought to site security – there hadn't been a need. He must tell Vern that whatever he was paying for the service was not money well spent. 'Sorry,' Bob said.

Silence returned. There was very little traffic down here at night – the occasional transport and the odd car. Mike went back to replaying the conversation he had with Lissa just before he came here. She had given him a twisted smile and said, 'You're not having an affair are you?'

He knew that smile – the one she used to signal a joke when she wasn't joking. 'What?'

'You used to get home regular as clockwork, but lately I never know when you're going to arrive and now you say you're heading off to the site but won't tell me why.'

'Opportunity'd be a fine thing,' Mike said, intending to match her jokey tone but hearing the words come out a touch ruefully.

There had never been anyone other than Lissa for him. Since he was quite young he had cheerfully gone along with the family assumption that one day the boy from the greengrocer's would marry the girl from the bakery down the street. After all, the families were both Greek, marriage was many years away and he did find her very attractive. When he reached the age for rebelling against family assumptions, it wasn't the one he chose. Rather he rejected the idea he would follow his father into the greengrocery business his grandfather had founded. When he told his parents he was leaving school to take up a carpentry apprenticeship, it was his father who was most upset. His mother was disappointed he would not stay at school and perhaps go on to university. At least she eventually got what she wanted. His father never gave up and continued trying to persuade him to come into the business, which had expanded to three shops – the original in Port Melbourne, one in Albert Park and another in South Melbourne. After Mike finished his degree in building, his father appeared to accept that he would stay in the construction industry but recently he had begun to press Mike again.

Lissa had to choose a different option for her rebellion – her mother's serious illness, which coincided with the end of school, cut off her escape from the bakery and forced her to take over her mother's role of serving in the shop and helping her father with the baking. Lissa chose instead to dump Mike, telling him she found him too dull, and began a series of passionate and short-lived affairs, which were not all that different from the way his sister, Mary, lived her life. Shane was the third bloke she had lived with and there had been other men along the way, every one the love of her life – for a while. Perhaps that was why Lissa and Mary were now such friends. While Lissa was living it up, he had other girlfriends, not as many and not with the intensity of Lissa's romances. One day, not long into their twenties, unexpectedly and without explanation she took up with him again. He didn't ask her what had happened to change her mind, happy to resume where they had left off. Perhaps she was tired of her superficial and hectic love life. Perhaps she had come to long for the stability and security he could give her. Only quite recently another possibility occurred to him: marriage and children provided her escape from the bakery, perhaps the only escape she could find.

After their marriage, he'd come across some veiled offers and Celia, one of Lissa's friends, had left him in no doubt she was available, but he wasn't interested. Several times lately, though, he had wondered what it would be like to have an affair. Was this idle curiosity or was he becoming bored with Lissa? Like Lissa had said of Ben, he was a bit young for a mid-life crisis, wasn't he?

'Two pedestrians this time.' Bob spoke without excitement but his voice startled Mike, as though he had been caught in some wrongful act. 'Doubt it's them. They'd need a vehicle if it's the cable or the fittings they're after.'

Shortly afterwards Mike saw two figures, both wearing hooded jackets, approaching the gate. They paused and the taller one held out his hand to the other, who took a key from his pocket and handed it to him. He unlocked the padlock and they slipped inside, closed the gate and reset the padlock.

'Here they are, Bob,' Mike mouthed into his microphone. 'Watched the patrol leave and used their own key to open the gate, the cheeky buggers. Better come down, but do it quietly.'

The pair passed under one of the lights and Mike recognised the frame and walk of Ted Horton. His partner was taller and much more solidly built – Bob was bigger but might still have a problem if he needed force to subdue the man they knew as Bruno. Mike moved his position so that he could more easily watch them while remaining hidden. He sucked in an anxious breath when they continued past the containers and headed directly to the back of the site. Where were they going? Did they have some other target in mind? Surely they weren't making for his car? Were they going to check it? Why? The headlong flow of Mike's thoughts ended abruptly when the pair stopped beside the cabin of a battered ute, one of the company's old survivors.

'I've lost them,' Bob hissed in his ear. 'What are they doing now?'

Before Mike could reply there was a spluttering roar as the motor of the ute sprang to life, followed by the thump of clos-ing doors, and it moved slowly forward, travelled across the site and stopped beside the container where the fittings were stored. They hadn't brought a vehicle because Findlay's had provided one for them!

'You were right, Bob. They're going for the fittings.'

Ted, who had been in the passenger seat, was first out. He reached on to the tray of the ute and lifted out a small crowbar, which he handed to his accomplice who was now standing beside the door of the container. At least Ted hadn't been able to get a key for the lock on the container, although he had made sure he wouldn't be stymied by that small detail. It took very little time for his partner to prise open the door and enter. Ted looked around, as though checking for any observers, and followed Bruno inside.

'I'm across from you,' Bob whispered. 'Let's bail them up while they're in there.'

'No. Let them bring out some of the gear. They haven't actually taken anything yet. When I reckon it's time to get them, I'll try to wait till Bruno is inside and Ted is by himself. I don't expect much of a problem with Ted so I should be able to help you with the thug if you need it.'

Mike's voice dropped as the thieves came out, each carrying an armful of cartons which they dropped into the ute. After returning inside, Ted was first out, staggering a little under the load of a larger number of cartons.

'What ya doin', ya weak bastard?' his accomplice complained as he arrived. He tossed his load into the ute, lifted half of Ted's and threw those cartons in as well. After they again returned inside, Mike said, 'Get close to the side of the container.' He scuttled forward to take up a position beneath and to the front of the ute's bonnet. On his left he saw the shadow of Bob, crouching beside the container.

As Ted reappeared with another load, Mike stood and walked along the side of the vehicle to confront him. Mike feigned surprise.

'Hullo, Ted. What are you doing here?'

Ted's head jerked up. He let slip his grip on the cartons and several clattered to the ground. For a moment he froze, as if unable to decide whether to answer Mike or run. His head spun to the other side when Bob appeared from around the corner and stood at the door. This gave Mike time to grab Ted firmly by the arm. The remaining cartons tumbled down as Ted wriggled in Mike's grasp, but he made no real effort to escape, apparently still in shock from Mike and Bob's unexpected arrival.

'Down,' Mike commanded, pushing Ted so that he pitched forward among the cartons in the dirt beside the truck. The ground, still soft from last night's deluge, allowed him a softer landing than he would otherwise have had but smeared him with dirt.

There was a roar from inside the container. Bruno, head down, came barrelling out into Bob, sending him sprawling on to the ground and taking the wind out of him. As he struggled to get up he was again felled by a swinging hook to the jaw followed by a boot to the ribs. Bruno turned to face Mike.

'You're next,' he snarled as he headed straight for him.

Mike swivelled, trying to get out of his path, but a blow to his shoulder made him stagger before tripping over Ted and falling heavily on his hip. Bruno, having missed Mike with his first charge, turned and looked down on him sprawled before him. A nasty grin cracked his face as he unhurriedly came towards Mike, his intention clear – he would finish him off with his boots. Mike desperately tried to get to his feet by pushing with his hand in the soft dirt but struggled to free his legs from their entanglement with Ted. He got to a kneeling position. His hand closed over something cold and hard – the shaft of the crowbar, abandoned when its job was done. He glimpsed a boot speeding towards him and flung up his arm, holding tight to the crowbar. The rigid metal tool deflected the boot so that it scraped his ribs, instead of burying itself in his stomach.

Bruno yelped in pain and stumbled forward. Mike's flailing arm, the impetus of his attacker and the unyielding crowbar had combined to inflict a heavy blow. Bruno's jeans had been ripped at the knee and even in the poor light Mike could see a damp stain spreading into the fabric. Behind him Bob, still on his knees, was fighting for breath.

'You bloody prick,' Bruno gasped and began coming towards Mike again before giving another sharp cry of pain and reaching for his knee. Spurred on by adrenalin and elation at his escape Mike scrambled to his feet, still brandishing the crowbar. His voice had gained extra power.

'Get down there next to your mate,' he commanded the thug.

Bruno eyed the crowbar and spat into the dirt. 'You'll keep,' he said and began to hobble away.

Ted, freed from the burden of Mike's weight, began to clamber to his feet. Mike took hold of his arm and poked the crowbar into his ribs.

'Don't you move any further,' he said.

Bob, still unsteady on his feet, finally came to stand beside him 'Sorry,' he gasped. 'I blew it and now he's walking away. I'll go after him.'

Mike suddenly became aware of his own shortness of breath and the pain spreading from his shoulder, hip and ribs. Mary was right: he needed to be as fit as Shane if he was going to take part in any more of these escapades. He shook his head and tightened his grip on Ted, although his captive made no attempt to pull free.

'No, Bob. Leave him. Even with a crook leg I reckon he's too much for either of us to handle in our state. We've got the man we really wanted and I'm sure he can be persuaded to tell us what we want to know.'

They watched as Bruno reached the gate, took the key from his pocket to release the chain, opened the gate and went through it, leaving it wide open.

'Time to talk, Ted,' Bob said. 'You can start by tellin' us who your mate is and how you got linked up with him.'

Ted shook his head. 'Can't do that. You seen what he's like. I'm not goin' to end up in a gutter somewhere with me 'ead bashed in.'

'Why have you been trying to sabotage the site?' Mike asked 'I aint done nothin'.'

Mike took out his phone and found the number he needed. There was a long delay before a gruff voice said, 'Yeah?'

'Vern, it's Mike Georgiou. I'm at the site. Bob Kennedy and I just nabbed Ted Horton, trying to pinch a batch of electrical fittings.' There was a long silence, causing Mike to ask, 'Vern, are you there?'

'Was he on his own?'

'No, he had a mate, not one of ours. He got away.'

'Pity.'

'I'm about to call the police.'

This time the response was immediate. 'Don't do that.'

'What?'

'Let Ted go, clean up the place so it looks as close to normal as you can make it and then go home. Tell Bob Kennedy he is to speak to no one about this. And you, neither.'

'But …'

'Just do it. And be in my office by seven-thirty tomorrow.' The phone went dead.

4

The plain, two-storey, brick building that housed the head office of Findlay Construction had a desolate air. The receptionist, who usually sat behind the curved wooden counter in the entry foyer, had not yet arrived and there were no sounds of activity from anywhere in the building. Mike mounted the stairs that led to the offices of the senior staff and found Freda Bradshaw alone at her desk. Vern had employed Freda soon after he joined the company and over the years she had become not only personal assistant to Vern and Jim Findlay but also the gatekeeper, consulted by all other staff when needing to know how they should approach either of her two bosses.

Freda, a small woman, with short brown hair and a kindly face, had changed little during her years with the company. The young girl, who seemed prematurely to have outgrown the fancies and frivolity of youth, was now a woman whose clear skin and dress sense belied her age. The confidante of many in the company, she could be relied upon to keep her own counsel. At a Christmas party one year she had told Mike she felt a sisterly connection with a former First Lady of the United States who had said she spent her life pretending to know things she did not know and pretending not to know things she did know.

When he became managing director, Ben employed his own personal assistant, Janine, a glamorous creature with long dark hair and longer legs, well suited by the current fashion for minimal skirts. Janine, who Ben decreed would look after Jim as well as himself, was neither efficient nor proactive on behalf of her bosses, but was often saved by Freda's intervention. She was insistent that, as the personal assistant to the chairman and to the managing director, she outranked Freda, who outwardly seemed indifferent to this imposed downgrading.

'Good morning, Michael,' Freda greeted him primly. 'A busy night I understand.'

'You could say that.'

'He's very keen to see you,' she said and Mike understood the warning. 'Go straight in.'

When Mike entered Vern's office, the acting MD had his back to him and appeared to be contemplating the patchwork of tiled and iron roofs, the ranks of aged brick chimneys and the occasional interloping second storey improvement, which was all that could be seen of the houses lining the rear of the property. He swivelled in his chair and said, 'Sit here,' indicating the wooden chair in front of his paper-strewn desk. 'And tell me exactly how you came to be at the site last night, doing the job we pay the security firm to do for us.'

'A good place to start,' Mike replied. 'I don't know what you're paying for that security firm to swan up to the front gate a few times a night, but it's a waste of money.'

'Answer my question.'

When Mike began by repeating his suspicions about Ted, Vern scowled and said, 'You've already told me this.' When he described Bob's initiative in having a few of the men try to pump Ted, the scowl deepened but Vern said nothing. It was only when Mike moved on to the conversation in the Hibernian that Vern sat forward and began to listen attentively. Encouraged by having finally engaged his boss's interest, Mike gave an account of what had happened at the site, omitting much of the detail of the fight. Piqued by the sly grin Vern gave when he described why he had allowed Bruno to escape, Mike finished by demanding, 'So why did you tell me not to involve the police? Ted gets the sack, of course, but the thug gets away scot free.'

'Was anything taken?'

'Thanks to our actions, no.'

'Apart from a padlock, anything damaged?' Vern asked.

'What difference does that make?'

'I don't want a bunch of police poking around the site, starting all sorts of rumours, when there's no chance of them making an arrest.' Vern sat back, lifted his shoulders and took a deep breath. 'And we're not sacking Ted.'

'What? We confirm he's working with a thug, trying to sabotage the site, and then we catch him breaking in and trying to pinch a stack of electrical fittings.'

Vern's face twisted into a grin, but there was no humour in his eyes. 'Poor little Ted. He does his best to make sure the site is a safe one, battles against the inept and callous project manager, who plots to get rid of him by hiring a thug to threaten him and lead him into a carefully laid trap. When the trap is sprung, the thug is allowed to go but the framed union official gets the sack.'

Mike could not contain his anger and attempted to stand, stumbling over the leg of the chair as he did so. 'You can't believe that,' he shouted

'Sit down and shut up. I bet it's the line George Fowler will take on Ted's behalf and they're due here in a few minutes.'

He looked up as Freda opened the door and stood in the doorway.

'They've just arrived,' she said. 'Three of them – Mr Fowler, Ted Horton and a tall, lightly-built man. I put them in the conference room.'

'Thanks, Freda.' He turned back to Mike. 'You speak only if I tell you. And take that surly look off your face.'

When Vern and Mike entered the conference room the three

men were sitting together on one side of an oblong teak table which took up the bulk of the small room, once used to store unused furniture and old files. After his arrival, Ben had it fitted out with new carpet, curtains and the table with its eight matching chairs. The only other times Mike had been in the room were for the company finance and planning meetings, which had been held in Jim Findlay's office before Ben took over.

The three shifted in their chairs but did not attempt to stand. George Fowler, the state secretary of the Building and Construction Union, kept his eyes firmly on Vern; Ted Horton had his head down, apparently studying the polished surface of the table, and Alan Reardon had pushed his chair back so that he sat slightly apart from the other two, giving the impression he had come as a spectator.

'Good morning, gentlemen,' Vern said without warmth. 'I think we all know one another.'

'Yeah, I've spoken to Georgiou once or twice,' Fowler replied.

Mike had no recollection of this and doubted it was true. Vern made sure that all of George Fowler's dealings with the company were with him, an arrangement Fowler seemed very happy to accommodate. He was about the same age as Vern and shared his short, thick-set build and his lack of hair, but differed in his accent, speaking with the flat vowels of a man from south of the Scottish border.

Vern sat across the table from Fowler and waved his hand to indicate Mike should sit to his right. 'As I told you, we have a problem with Ted and need to hear what you're going to do about it,' Vern began, glancing across at Reardon before returning his eyes to George.

'No,' said George, half rising from his chair as he leant across the table to confront Vern. 'You have a problem and that problem lies squarely with Georgiou.' He paused but, when the only reaction from the other side was for Mike to suck in a breath and thump his elbows on the table, he continued. 'I told you Ted Horton was a man of integrity who would make a good delegate for your site and you accepted him. Recently the safety standards on the CityView site have slipped and slipped badly. Ted has pointed this out to Georgiou many times and the only response has been hostile rejection, reaching a crisis the other day when two workers were badly injured.'

'What's this got to do with last night?' Vern asked.

'We know Georgiou hired a hit man, who threatened Ted and, when he refused to compromise on his concern for the safety of our members, forced him to attend the site so he could be accused of attempted theft.'

Vern gazed earnestly at George. 'That's a very serious charge, George. Before I ask Mike to account for his actions, have you got any proof for your accusations?'

'Ted can give you all the proof you need. Just ask him.'

'Do you know the name of the man who threatened you?' Vern looked directly at Ted who squirmed uncomfortably.

'Never gave a name,' he answered hesitantly. 'Made 'is threats bloody clear, though.'

Vern shook his head sympathetically. 'Nasty. And he told you Mike had hired him?' Ted hesitated again, before nodding. 'Strange,' Vern continued. 'Mike's a simple builder. If you were ignoring his threats, then the simple thing for him to do was to carry them out – have you beaten up – not this scam to frame you. You don't know where this man comes from or any of his pals, do you?' Again Vern's eyes were fixed on Ted who, this time, immediately shook his head. 'No, I didn't think you would,' Vern said. 'But these are very serious charges and the police are sure to want more from you than you've been willing to give us.'

Ted shot a puzzled glance at George. 'You said no police.'

'Call the police if you want,' George said in a tone much milder than he had used so far. His face tightened and he added, 'Of course we will deny any of this happened – a fabrication intended to discredit a union official blowing the whistle on site safety.'

Vern nodded understandingly. 'This is how I see it, George. I accept that Ted is the good man you've told me he is. I accept he was coerced by a thug we can't identify to act in ways Ted regrets. I'm not sure his regrets include actions beyond the attempted theft the other night, but we don't need to go into that. I also don't think we need to sack Ted.'

Vern glanced sideways at Mike, who had drawn in an angry breath and seemed on the point of voicing his objection. He reached over to put a restraining hand on Mike's forearm before continuing. 'On the other hand, it will be awkward for Ted to remain on our site and it seems to me that, as a gesture of recipro-cal goodwill, you might arrange to transfer Ted as the delegate on another site not associated with Findlay's. He'd go, of course, with our good wishes.'

Mike felt he was observing the playing out of a well-rehearsed script. George nodded his agreement, Ted looked mightily relieved, but Alan Reardon's lips were taut with disapproval. Obviously he was not privy to the deal George and Vern had cooked up.

'We'll need an assurance Georgiou will lift his game on safety,' George said.

Vern made no reply. Apparently this went beyond the done deal. He got to his feet, closely followed by George and the others. When Vern ushered them out of the room, Reardon hung back so that Fowler and Horton were already descending the stairs when he said to Mike, 'I've been to see the WorkSafe people about the sling. I'd like a word.'

Vern frowned his disapproval, but Mike saw an opportunity

to vent some of his annoyance with him. 'Of course. Come back in here for a minute.' He turned and walked back into the conference room but did not sit at the table, preferring to stand just inside the door. 'What did WorkSafe tell you?'

'Officially nothing. They wouldn't let me look at the sling and said the investigation of the accident was ongoing. All I got, and all I needed, was a hint that could later be denied.' Reardon lifted his head and a small smile flitted across his lips. 'The sling was faulty all right. I'd say they don't know whether it was damaged at the supplier's end or yours. I'm also pretty sure the reason they're being so secretive is because they think the damage may well have been deliberate. They're nervous about the fuss such a finding will create when the damage to the sling is all they have and there's nothing to suggest who might have done it or why. So they revert to their usual bureaucratic response – say nothing, drag their feet and hope something will turn up to save them from having to make a tricky decision.'

'It was Ted's pal, the one he won't tell us anything about,' Mike said with conviction.

'You think so? Ted's not the first union official to be threatened.'

'Have they been having the same problems at Riverside? Is that why you've been spending time over there?'

'I'd like to know why you've been targeted. It could tie in with the investigation I've got on now.'

'What investigation?'

Reardon blinked his eyes and gave a straight-lipped grin. 'Can't tell you that I'm afraid, but if I find out anything that might interest you I'll let you know. We should stay in touch.' He took out a business card and handed it to Mike, who felt inside his wallet for one of his own. Reardon glanced at it before looking questioningly at Mike. 'Our bosses have a very cosy relationship, don't they?'

'You don't like that,' Mike replied, eyeing him carefully.

'Always good practice, when you've stitched up a deal on the quiet, to go through the negotiation in front of witnesses. Saves exposing yourself to the claim you're in the pay of the boss.' He paused and tilted his head to one side. 'I'm pretty new around here, but if I didn't know George to be straight, I'd suspect you had him on a retainer.'

'You think that?'

'Don't play the innocent with me. You know it goes on. Maybe not as much as where I've come from, but we all know how much easier your life would be if you had someone in the Building and Construction Union looking after your interests. A good investment, I'd say.'

'You're wrong.'

'Sure I am.' He managed a tone that left Mike uncertain whether he was agreeing or asking a question. 'But watch your back. I certainly have to watch mine. And remember, none of this conversation took place. I've risked enough by speaking with you. I've only done it because I think there's a connection between your problems and mine. I'm not sure what that is.' He turned to go with Mike following him. Freda Bradshaw stood in the doorway.

'If you have finished, Michael, Mr McKenzie would like to see you.'

This time, when Mike entered Vern's office, he was not contemplating the houses at the rear but standing in front of his desk with his face set and his arms folded across his chest.

'You've been taking your time with that beanstalk. What are you two up to?'

'He's been to WorkSafe. He thinks they reckon the sling was tampered with and are worried about making it official without any evidence of who did it or how they managed it. It'll be a good while before we hear from them.'

'Is that all you talked about?'

'Are you bothered that if I speak with a head office guy from the BCU and you're not there to hear every word, it'll somehow upset this cosy arrangement you have with George Fowler?' Vern started to object but Mike continued. 'Stop treating me as though I came down in the other day's downpour. You and George had the transfer of Ted all worked out and you were happy to leave me like a bloody shag on a rock.'

'Now, Mike, calm down. We've sorted everything out without any boats being rocked. You're free to get on with the job and save the company. Concentrate on that and leave the union to me. I've told you already, Reardon has form.'

'You told me yesterday our backers were getting nervous. What are they worried about?'

Vern did not answer immediately but sat examining Mike carefully.

'Interesting question. They'd heard a rumour CityView was in trouble. You know anything about that?'

'No. It could be the same people who are trying to sabotage the site.'

'These money men are always hearing rumours,' Vern scoffed. 'They're paid to be paranoid. I sorted them out the other day.'

'I'm not paranoid, but I sure as hell believe someone is trying to get at us.'

'Mike, I'll tighten security on the site so you don't need to worry. Not about that anyway. What you do need to worry about is driving the project along now I've cleared the decks for you.'

'And you're not worried someone is out to make trouble for us?'

Vern shook his head. 'If you really want to know, I think that thug you let go was working a protection racket. He'd recruited Ted as his inside man with a combination of cash and threats

– more threats than cash after Ted started to get nervous. He was about to approach us for payment to stop the trouble at the site, but we've scotched that now. Back a bit, there was a lot of this going on. In those days it was the union officials, not outsiders, who ran the racket. No way would George be part of that.' Vern raised his eyebrows. 'But Reardon? Where he comes from there's still a lot of it going on.'

When Mike began to respond Vern waved his hand dismissively. 'Not for you to worry about. Get back to work and tell Bob Kennedy the gag I put on you last night stays. You can tell anyone who asks that the union has shifted Ted to another site – end of story.'

———

Mike had barely returned to his office when Bob Kennedy put his head in the door. 'Well? What happened? Did Ted spill the beans?'

'Vern and George Fowler stitched up a deal between them. Ted has been transferred to a non-Findlay site with nothing to be said about what happened here.'

'You're kiddin'.'

'I wish I was. I don't know what Vern and George have going between them.'

He thought of his conversation with Alan Reardon and checked himself. 'I can tell you the new deputy secretary, Alan Reardon, wasn't happy about it, either. We're all sworn to secrecy. Vern wants you to know the gag he put on us last night stays, and you are to tell anyone who asks that the union has transferred Ted to another site.'

Bob gave a disparaging laugh. 'Is there somethin' about bein' MD that makes their brains go soft? Vern's been around the traps so long he must know he can't stop the word gettin' out.'

'You mean you've already been talking?'

'Those guys who tipped me off Ted was meetin' someone at

the Hibernian were at me first thing to find out what happened. Ted was missin' from the site and despite our cover up they knew somethin' had gone on here last night. What could I say?' Bob pursed his lips. 'I'm really sorry I let you down last night, leavin' you to deal with the thug on your own. I've never had it in the bread basket that hard before. It still aches. And me jaw is sore as well.' He reached out an arm to Mike. 'But what about you?'

'Just a bit stiff.'

'You were great. The way you laid into him with the crowbar when you were on the ground was somethin' to see. Gave me a new picture of you.'

'Just a lucky break my hand closed over it.'

'Let's hope your luck holds.'

Bob hovered over Mike in a manner bordering on the paternal. 'I hope you told Vern what that thug said to you before he slunk off. You'll need to watch your back, I reckon.'

'Don't worry. You're the second person to tell me that this morning.'

Mike didn't explain it was Alan Reardon, not Vern, who had warned him and that his warning concerned a very different threat.

'By the way, Vern thinks Bruno had us lined up for paying protection and we've put an end to that.'

'Protection? Used to be a union stunt. Bruno's not a member, is he?'

'No way. Now let's get back to our real jobs, making this site hum the way I like to hear it.'

After Bob had gone Mike stood up and stretched. Fortunately his bruises were out of sight and he could camouflage the pain. Lissa, who had waited up for him, had been shocked when she saw his battered state. It was good to have her fussing over him, recalling happier days. She had laughed when she was rubbing the ointment into his side. 'If you are having an affair, she certainly plays rough. Does she bring out the caveman in you?'

'No, having you massage me does that,' he replied.

It was a pity the pain prevented him delivering on his claim. Lissa seemed disappointed, too. She lay silently beside him for a few minutes before saying, 'Oh, I forgot. Mary rang.'

Mike struggled to sit up. 'Not again. Is she badly hurt this time?'

'No, nothing like that. Your good friend Shane has invited us out on Friday night – you, me and your dad.'

'What's this all about?'

'Apparently he has to work at the weekend and won't be around for your dad's name day feast, so he's taking us all to Café Filipo. They say it's very upmarket.'

'It'll make a change for Shane to do something kind.'

Lissa turned on to her side and looked into Mike's eyes. 'You know, you're very hard on Shane.'

'You know what he does to Mary.'

'Yes, I do. But Mary still loves him. She says that it's only rarely they have a falling out, and afterwards he's very apologetic and treats her in ways that make up for it. It's not the way I'd want to live but maybe it's preferable to leaving your differences unresolved and festering in silence.'

Mike knew he was expected to reply but couldn't think what to say and settled for, 'Maybe,' before yawning and rolling on to his side so that he was facing away from her.

5

When Mike took an early morning stroll around the site he was pleased with the productive sounds coming from all parts and surprised by the greetings he received. Everywhere he went the men gave him a cheerful wave or an appreciative grin. He was never one of those project managers who cast a chill wherever they went, but this was extraordinary. When he arrived on one of the lower floors where the sparkies were running electric cable and mounting fittings, one of them called out to him, 'G'day, boss. Don't need to worry. No one 'ere's goin' to pinch anythin',' and his mates grinned knowingly.

Higher up, where several of the men were having difficulty levering into place a column suspended from the crane, one of them broke off when he saw Mike approaching and offered him the crowbar he was using.

'Come on, boss. I hear you're good at this. Got a strong arm, they say.'

'Careful,' one of his mates laughed. 'Let 'im grab hold of that thing and 'e'll take a piece of ya.'

Mike turned away but was still close enough to hear another mutter, 'Got more balls than I thought.'

The further he went the more he felt he was making a form of triumphal tour so that, when he saw Bob Kennedy, he drew him into a secluded corner and demanded, 'What the hell have you been saying about me?'

'Me? Say about you?' Bob feigned innocence with a smile designed to disarm him.

'Yes, you! I can't walk around here without being treated like

I'm the new heavyweight champ. You told me you'd spilt the beans to a few of them, but this is OTT and then some. What have you said?'

Bob nodded and spread his hands placatingly.

'They all wanted to know what happened and I had to tell them somethin', so I concentrated on how you saw off Bruno. To cover my weak effort, I might have made him seem even tougher than he was and you know how word gets around.' Bob winked at Mike. 'Won't do you any harm though, I reckon.'

Mike hurried back to his office, trying to avoid any more encounters with his men. He was embarrassed, that was true. But surely he shouldn't be ashamed that this embarrassment gave him a warm feeling and made it hard not to smile as he replayed some of the comments he'd heard. Besides, the sun was shining, it was not overly hot, the breeze was mild and the site was operating smoothly without any problems needing his attention. Why shouldn't he smile?

It was only later in the morning, when Vern appeared in his office doorway with a concerned look on his face, that Mike's contentment wavered.

'Are you OK?'

Vern's voice indicated much greater interest in the reply than was usual with such greetings.

'Couldn't be better.'

'You don't need to pretend with me. I didn't notice anything the other day, but Freda did; she's good like that. She said you were moving stiffly. I told her you were just miffed with me, but she was right.'

'What?'

'You didn't tell me how close you came to being beaten up by the thug Ted had with him. I hear you did a pretty good job of looking after yourself, though. Quite a performance.'

Usually such words coming from Vern would have been delivered with a sarcastic tone and smile. Not this time.

Mike sighed. 'I'm sorry we couldn't keep the whole thing quiet and now it's become ridiculous.' He sat behind his desk and waited for Vern to revert to normal and complain about Mike's failure to prevent the story spreading.

'No, of course. I should have given you a better story to tell, rather than try to gag the two of you. My mistake.'

Mike was bemused. He had not met an apologetic Vern before and didn't know how he should respond.

'I thought I should take you out to lunch. Can you spare me an hour?'

This was not the first time Vern had offered lunch to Mike, but the relatively few previous occasions had been restricted to celebrating the completion of a qualification or a promotion.

'Yes, of course. Thank you.'

'Let's be off then.'

Mike expected Vern to lead him to his car. Instead, he headed through the gate and across the road.

'I thought we'd go to a place I know on the river. Good day for a stroll.'

They made their way across a bare patch of ground and began walking towards the city on the paved pathway that hugged the Yarra. Vern turned to gaze downstream at the Bolte Bridge with its lines of slowly moving cars and trucks.

'You know, Riverside will go all the way to the bridge by the time they finish. A massive project.'

As he spoke, he turned back and lifted his head to take in the height of the latest tower, rising beside the river.

'Does seem a bit quiet, doesn't it?' Mike replied.

He considered telling Vern about the significance he placed on the sound of a building site but thought better of it. He gestured instead at the still incomplete frame of the Southern Star Observation Wheel, jaggedly reaching into the blue sky across the river.

'Do you reckon they'll ever get that thing up and running again?'

'Glad we haven't got the job,' Vern replied and strode ahead, apparently more intent on reaching his destination than enjoying the stroll he had suggested.

They reached the two completed towers, separated from the river by a lawn on which wooden tables and benches stood among flowering shrubs. Vern, wearing his usual tweed suit, was starting to labour in the warm sun, the colour in his ruddy face deepening. They crossed a footbridge that brought them to a marina where a flotilla of expensive craft lay murmuring in the wake of a passing tourist ferry. The bulk of the ANZ Bank building across the river stood in dark contrast to the gleaming white cabin cruisers, speed boats and yachts in the marina. Mike was surprised when it appeared Vern was headed for Bistro Vite where diners sat on cane chairs overlooking the marina. A beer and a pie in a pub was the usual extent of Vern's infrequent hospitality. But they passed the bistro and went under the Charles Grimes road-bridge to reach the single storey building that had replaced the line of tin sheds that for years had clung to the wharf on this side of the river. The buildings of the CBD were plainly before them and Mike was beginning to think Vern intended to take him all the way to the casino when his boss turned to enter the door beneath a sign proclaiming Highland Steak. Inside, only a few diners occupied the black, metal framed chairs set around matching pedestal tables. A bar ran along one side, its base covered in tartan fabric. Above it, the dark head of a bull poked from the wall.

'All the meat here is good,' Vern said. 'And the beer's OK as well.'

He pointed to an unoccupied table and Mike decided Vern's reference to the beer was probably intended to signal that the large array of whisky bottles behind the bar was off limits this lunchtime. The bottle of malt Vern kept in the bottom drawer of his desk was renowned for its quality and the rarity of its appearance in company.

After they had ordered a T-bone each and the waiter had brought them bottles of Becks, Vern leaned forward and stared at Mike over his glasses.

'Look,' he said awkwardly, 'I've been thinking about what's happened in the past few days and reckon I should have told you more than I have. For a start, you were right about Ted Horton. George Fowler has never let me down before, so I couldn't believe he had this time. Perhaps it's a sign of age – stuck in my ways. I should have put you in the picture before we met with the union people. There was no point in bringing in the police – having them around the site would only bring us a heap of disruption and get us nowhere. I knew Ted Horton had to go, of course, and started to think how we could get something positive out of it. That's when I got the idea: if we didn't sack Ted but allowed George to move him, George would not have to go into bat for him, would save face and owe us big time. You were right about George, letting me know what was going on at Riverside. He's been useful to me in many ways in the past and now he's sure to be useful in the future.'

Vern paused and scratched the side of his face as if considering what he had just admitted. Or perhaps he was weighing up what else he might say.

'The trouble is, when it comes to Riverside these days, George is being kept in the dark by Reardon. That beanpole is on to something at Riverside and has uncovered some dodgy practices there. But now George suspects Reardon is angling for a pay-off from Rubicon to keep quiet about what he's found and is freezing George out.'

Vern took a draft of his beer as though needing to lubricate his voice. Mike could not remember Vern speaking for so long or being so candid.

Apparently refreshed, Vern continued.

'I said to be careful around Reardon. But you seemed to be getting on pretty well with him the other day and we might be able to use that.' Vern nodded and a conspiratorial smile crossed his face. 'After all, you both have bosses who tell you nothing of the deals they stitch up between one another, and I hear he was hinting he might be open to an offer at the right price.'

Mike shook his head vehemently, partly to deny Vern's accusation and partly from irritation that Freda Bradshaw had heard and passed on the tail end of his conversation with Alan Reardon.

'No, you've been given a bum steer there. Actually, he was saying he thought you might be slinging something George Fowler's way.'

There was a time, a very recent time, when Mike would not have dared to speak like this to Vern, but that had changed or, as Mike watched for Vern's reaction, he hoped it had.

Vern smiled again. 'If you say so. Keep in touch with Reardon and see what you can find out from him. If nothing else, it'll give you some experience of how to cultivate a union official. I won't always be around to do it.'

Mike noticed yet another change in Vern's attitude. Until now he would never countenance any dealings with the head office of the union that did not go directly through him.

'But why this focus on Riverside? Do you think they're behind these attempts at undermining us?' he asked

Vern shook his head vigorously. 'No, nothing like that. I told you the thug you call Bruno was trying to mount a

78

protection racket. I also told you Reardon is very familiar with that kind of stunt. Perhaps he's the link to Bruno. Could be. No, I've been thinking about the company more than the site, Rubicon rather than Riverside. I think Rubicon could be a saviour for us.'

'What?'

The waiter returned with two plates crowded with large steaks, topped with tomato and onion and surrounded by hefty servings of chips.

'Another beer?' he asked.

'Yeah,' replied Vern after consideration. 'Need something with the steak.'

Although Mike had drunk most of his first bottle while he listened, Vern's was still half full. Mike waited for Vern to continue what he had been saying, but he was more intent on dealing with the steak and they ate in silence until the waiter brought the second round. Vern finished off his first beer with a long draft and licked his lips, looking around as he did so, as if checking he could not be overheard.

'I told you the other day I'd been thinking about the company. Since then I've done a lot more thinking. Jim's as good as gone – nothing more than a figurehead. Ben's a disaster, with big ideas and no detailed understanding of what we need to do if we're going to achieve any of them. You might say he can learn over time, but he's already put us in a position where we don't have any time left. I've tried to counsel him, but he's too arrogant and too impatient to listen or learn.'

Vern broke off to dispatch some more of the steak and sip his beer before continuing in a voice which began in a self-deprecating tone but soon became assertive.

'I'm only an accountant but I've been in the industry a long time, I know how it works, I've had the experience of turning

Jim's ideas into viable projects and I have valuable contacts. I also know our financial situation backwards. I can tell you we haven't got anywhere near the financial backing we'll need to take us down the path Ben has in mind for us, yet the rest of our business, the projects that are all ticking along very nicely for modest gains, are a nice little cash cow, which would be attractive to a purchaser.'

'A purchaser?'

Mike's surprise was obvious.

Vern dropped his voice so that Mike had to lean forward to hear him clearly.

'What we need is an arrangement that covers our weaknesses and uses our strengths. The best way forward for us is not to try to leap into the big league by some kind of frontal assault. We have to become part of a bigger outfit that could enhance and build on our strengths. Someone like Rubicon. The fit with them is great. For a start, there is the synergy between the sites – Riverside and CityView. Our other projects would give them the cash flow they will need if I'm right about them being over-committed with Riverside, and they have access to the funding sources we lack.'

'Have they approached you?'

'Angelo Rossi is a smart man and he has the knowledge and experience to do the same analysis I've done. He mightn't have got around to it yet – busy with other things – but I wouldn't be surprised if he did.

'Have you discussed this with Jim?'

'No, not yet. You're the only person I've mentioned it to.'

'Why me?'

Vern nodded encouragingly as though Mike had at last asked the question that mattered.

'It was Jim who first suggested we should look within our

own workforce for people with the potential to rise higher in the company if we gave them the opportunity. Like many of Jim's ideas, he left it to me to implement. We've had some successes over the years and we've had our share of failures, but you stood out. You need more experience yet and maybe you'll fall short, but you were my best bet for leading the company in some years' time, when I expected Jim would be hanging up his boots. That's all changed now. I reckon Rubicon would give you the chance you need.'

Mike fought unsuccessfully to prevent a self-conscious grin coming on to his face but dismissed it quickly and frowned.

'There's no way Jim would agree and I wouldn't blame him, even if it does make it harder for the firm to survive. He's spent a good deal of his life developing Findlay Construction and to see it disappear, even if it was part of a bigger firm, would be devastating for him. You know that better than I do.'

Mike raised his glass to his lips and thought of his own father who must one day, possibly soon, face the same dilemma. Would he be willing to sacrifice his own career – the one Vern had just described in such glowing terms – to prolong the life of the family business? He finished his beer and added, 'I'll just keep giving this job all I've got. Only yesterday you said I owed it to Jim and you were spot on. If it wasn't for him, and for you, I'd probably be a foreman carpenter somewhere.'

'I told you things have changed. Jim has all his funds tied up in the company. He needs to release them. And when Ben thinks about it he'll see the advantages for himself as well. It'll give him the opportunity to lead the marketing effort of a much larger outfit, and that's an area he does know something about.'

'Vern, you can't tell me Jim would ever agree to what you're suggesting. We've got to stay as an independent firm whatever the risks.'

Vern looked at his watch. 'We should be going.'

He signalled to the waiter for the bill and leaned forward so his head was close to Mike's. 'I said I hadn't mentioned any of this to anyone else. Let's keep it that way. If Angelo isn't as switched on as I think he is, it may all come to nothing. A pity, but I don't see any other contenders I would want to deal with.'

He looked at his watch again.

'I've arranged for a cab to pick us up out the back of here in a few minutes. I'll drop you off on the way back to my office.'

—

Back in his office, Mike closed the door and sat at his desk staring at the drab wall opposite him. What a change-around! Was Vern really serious about encouraging, even possibly initiating, a takeover of Findlay's? It was so hard to see him as a defector to Rubicon, but that was pretty much the way he sounded. He hadn't said anything about his own place in any new structure. Was that what this was all about: a way to secure a future for Vern? Why would he try to recruit Mike to the idea before at least floating it with Jim? That wasn't the way Vern worked – wasn't the way he *had* worked. And it was so out of character for Vern to be so forthcoming. Perhaps this was an illusion – just like Mike's new standing with Vern and with the men on the site was an illusion. Maybe there was a lot more going on than Vern had told him.

Mike opened the booklet of business cards he kept in his desk drawer and reached for his phone. After punching in a number, he waited until hearing Alan Reardon's voice.

'Alan. Mike Georgiou here.'

'Hi, Mike. How's it going?'

'Fine. Things have settled down again on the site, I'm glad to say.' He paused but, when Reardon said nothing, Mike went straight to the point of his call. 'You said you thought our problems here might be linked with those at Riverside. It could be the sabotage here was the lead up to coming at us for protection money. Is that what's on at Riverside as well?'

'Haven't come across anything like that here. If I do, I'll give you a call. Now I have to go.'

It was clear, despite his approach to him yesterday, Reardon wasn't yet about to confide in Mike any further.

6

Lissa gave him an appraising look.

'Why are you wearing a suit?'

Mike returned the look and decided the short skirt of the green silk dress asked questions of the wearer's legs that Lissa was well able to answer.

'Hey, you look good. I haven't seen this before, have I? Still got good legs.'

Mike thought the rich tone of the dress suited her dark colouring, although the fit could have been more accommodating – she was starting to thicken across the hips.

Lissa smiled her appreciation.

'I'm glad you like it. I thought it was time for something new. You're looking very smart yourself. But why so formal?'

Mike had hesitated when dressing. Few of the diners at Café Filipo would be wearing suits, but his father was sure to be one of them.

'Not every day Shane takes us out for dinner,' he offered by way of explanation 'When is Jessica due?'

'Any minute.'

Lissa frowned and touched the back of her hair uncertainly. 'I do hope Christos will behave. He thinks it's an affront to his manhood to have a sitter. I told him she was here for the girls, but he's convinced he should be allowed to do the job.'

'That'll be her now,' Mike said as the door chime sounded.

He brought in the tall young woman with dark plaits, who was carrying her laptop and several university texts. Lissa delivered her usual briefing before they kissed the children and walked into the street, where the night was fast taking over. Across the road and along the next street they came to an imposing house on the corner. A white picket fence and a formal fringe of box hedge and lawn ran across and down to the side fence separating the front of the house from the garage and back garden. The house itself was entirely white – wooden block walls, galvanised roof and cast iron lacework along the surrounding veranda – like a wedding cake in the twilight.

They were mounting the steps when the front door opened and a well-built man with a full head of silver hair came out to embrace them. As Mike had expected, Demetri Georgiou was dressed in a neatly pressed navy suit and white shirt with a colourful tie. It made a stark contrast to what he was happiest wearing – his daily outfit of jeans and green T-shirt with 'Georgiou the Greengrocer' in red letters across his chest. He donned his suit for the occasions he deemed important – family events such as weddings, funerals, baptisms or name day celebrations – or for what many might see as less significant functions, such as a school parents' evening or the annual general meeting of the long defunct South Melbourne Hellas Soccer Club.

'No sign of the taxi,' Demetri said with concern.

'Should be here any minute, Dad.'

When Mike first suggested it, Lissa had said there was no need for a taxi and one of them could drive, but Mike had insisted. He knew that anything hosted by Shane would include a lot of alcohol and he found he always drank more when in Shane's company – often sipping a drink avoided the need to respond to one of Shane's provocative comments.

They had hardly settled themselves in the large sitting room when the sound of a horn announced the arrival of the cab. Mike shepherded Lissa and his father into the back of the car and sat beside the driver, a young Indian who nodded when Mike said, 'The casino, please. The hotel entrance.'

The short trip from South Melbourne was taken up with Lissa answering Demetri's questions about the health of the children and their progress at school.

When they reached Clarendon Street the driver swung left away from the hotel entrance as though intending to take them across the river.

'Hey, I said the hotel entrance. Straight ahead.'

The driver smiled at him anxiously. 'The casino is just here, sir.'

He gestured at the front of the casino across the street and swung the cab in a wide turn, which brought them to its doors.

'The other end is where we want to be dropped,' Mike insisted.

'Mike. We can walk from here,' Lissa said.

Demetri opened the door and began to clamber out, so Mike paid off the cab driver and they entered the casino. He asked directions to the restaurant from one of the security men stationed at the entrance and was told, 'Bear left when you enter the casino, continue through the food court and up the mall. It's at the hotel end; quite a walk. Pity you didn't come in there.'

Mike muttered some ungracious thanks and they entered the casino where they were immediately surrounded by the flickering lights from the long banks of poker machines and the TV screens rising above them. As background to the electronic beeps and rattle of the poker machines, Mike could feel the bass thump of a poorly reproduced band playing slow rock music.

Conscious of how the three of them stood out among the casually and, in many cases, poorly dressed players, Mike's mood darkened, but his father shared none of his embarrassment, striding along with an easy gait and gazing about with the confidence of a celebrity walking among admirers. His father had an air of distinction about him, whether wearing his suit or serving in the shop, similar to that which defines a good headwaiter. Mike wondered whether he shared this distinction. Earlier, when knotting his tie in front of the bedroom mirror, he had seen a younger version of his father examining him – the same build, the same open face with the deep shadow of a well-shaven, heavy beard and the same thick hair. Just the other day he had seen a couple of silver strands among the dark waves.

They walked beyond the blackjack tables and entered the food court where he could hear the plaintive call of a country and western singer – Mike's least favourite form of music. They passed a row of ATMs and entered a wide corridor, which became increasingly elegant the further they went along it. Large, glossy, black and white paving tiles formed a pleasing pattern on the floor, recessed lights shone from above and, to one side, boutique shop fronts displayed exclusive brands while stylish restaurants appeared opposite them. Mike's mood lifted.

'This is more like it,' he said. 'Café Filipo should be along here.'

'Café Filipo,' his father repeated. 'I didn't know we were going there.'

'Didn't you? Very upmarket. Shane's sparing no expense,' Lissa told him.

The further they went the more hesitant Demetri became, the confidence he had earlier displayed ebbing away before the opulence of their surroundings.

When they arrived at Café Filipo, his father hung back, signalling with his hand that Lissa and Mike should precede him. The restaurant was not large, but given a spacious air by the reflections from the full-length windows, which looked out over the Yarra. The other walls were covered in a soft white fabric that matched the crisp coverings of the tables, where small silver vases carrying single red roses stood in the midst of the settings. This otherwise severe decor was softened by colourful abstract paintings on the walls and boxes of indoor plants separating the tables. For Mike this was but indistinctly perceived background for the sound of Thelonious Monk playing *Round Midnight*. Monk could capture him at any time, but the quality of the reproduction and the dampening acoustic allowed the sound to transcend the buzz of the other diners without appearing to intrude. Thelonious was never a background musician, but in Café Filipo he pulled it off with great success. Mike was brought to his senses by his father bumping into the back of him and the sight of Lissa, turning to find what had become of him. A waiter dressed from head to toe in black approached them.

'A table in the name of Shane Francis,' Mike said.

'Certainly, sir.'

He did not hesitate but turned and began to lead them to where Mike could see Shane rising from his seat and Mary waving a hand. Already the table carried a glass of sparkling wine and a tankard of beer. Just as Mike was beginning to look like their father, Mary was growing increasingly like their mother. She had her dark good looks, more angular than their father and more subtle – a beauty, Mike would have said, more suited by discreet rather than blatant display. To judge by the neckline of her blue dress, Mary did not agree with him. As expected, Shane was jacketless, a yellow cotton shirt tightly enclosing his strong shoulders and chest, the short sleeves revealing his muscular, tanned arms. Reluctantly, Mike understood how attractive he would be to some women. Mary was obviously one of them.

The greetings complete, they moved to take their seats. Shane, clearly in charge of the evening, insisted that Demetri sit at the head, facing into the body of the restaurant, flanked by Lissa and Mary with the men opposite their partners. 'Now that's settled, what will you have to drink?' Shane asked.

'Some bubbly, please,' Lissa replied and she and Mary grinned at one another.

Mike waited for his father to order and, when he did not speak, Mike turned to look at him. Demetri was staring fixedly across the restaurant as though finding something of intense interest. As Mike focused on him, he dropped his head and appeared as if trying to sink into his chair. Mike turned to see what had caused this strange behaviour. A tall, heavily built man was making stately progress among the tables, any waiters in his path nodding a welcome and adroitly stepping away to allow him an uninterrupted passage. A navy polo neck smoothly followed the bulk of his torso. A cream jacket hung from his shoulders. He had a wide forehead, an aquiline nose, full lips and the expression of a man who was well used to the deference the waiters were paying him.

Mike noticed none of this. His attention was taken by the woman who followed behind. For an instant he suffered the discomfort of seeing someone he thought he knew but could not recall. Then he realised who she was – Carla Rossi did indeed have the face and figure of the film star his father remembered with such fondness. Glossy dark hair, cut quite short, framed her oval face with its high cheekbones. Her sleeveless, high-necked dress, in crimson satin, embraced the contours of her body, and a wide silver bracelet clasped her right wrist. Earlier the restaurant had been merely a setting for the music of Thelonious Monk; now it was a backdrop against which Carla shone. What transfixed Mike was not only her beauty, but also the serenity of her expression, her stillness and the straight-backed grace with which she held herself, like a ballerina, gliding effortlessly between the tables.

Mike would have continued to stare had not the man leading Carla hidden her as he changed direction to come straight towards their table. The man was smiling broadly, his eyes on Demetri. When still several paces away, his voice boomed out, 'Demetri, my old friend. You will not speak with me but you come to my restaurant. You cannot hide from me here.'

He held out his right hand but, when Demetri made no attempt to stand or to take the offered hand, he spread both arms wide and spoke to the whole table as though addressing a meeting he had called.

'I must apologise. My name is Mario Mancini. Demetri and I knew one another back in those distant days when we were together at the market, the Wholesale Market.' He looked around the table and smiled indulgently. 'We first met before any of you were born.' He swept his arm around in the manner of a master of ceremonies introducing the next performer. 'And this is my daughter, Carla.' He paused and managed to look almost apologetic. 'I welcomed you to what I called my restaurant, but it is really hers now. It was an ordinary Italian trattoria in my time, but she has transformed it into what you see today.'

Carla bobbed her head and offered a tranquil smile, her eyes staying with Mike until Mario turned to speak directly to Demetri. 'Unlike you, I have no son to follow me, but Carla is my son; she has taken over a number of my interests. I retain my transport business – not something she wanted to take on, regrettably.' He turned back again to address the whole gathering. 'And my son-in-law, Angelo.'

Mike focused for the first time on the third member of their party. Angelo Rossi was also a handsome man with rugged good looks akin to those of Shane, although he was dark and Shane fair. However, he lacked the presence of his father-in-law and the elegance of his wife.

'Angelo runs Rubicon Development. It has the superb Riverside project just down the Yarra from here,' Mario said. 'I like to think that each of us played a part in bringing the Riverside complex to fruition, but Angelo no longer has need of us there.'

His attempt at maintaining a jokey tone failed to hide the feeling that he missed being involved with Rubicon. And, Mike wondered, was he using the royal plural or did he mean Carla was on the outer as well?

Mario looked enquiringly at Demetri who belatedly struggled to his feet and spoke hesitantly to Carla and Angelo, ignoring Mario as he went round the table. 'I am Demetri Georgiou. This is my family – my daughter Mary, my daughter-in-law Lissa, my son Mike and Mary's partner Shane.' The word 'partner' brought Mike's eyes away from Carla and to his father, who had often complained about the casual nature of Mary's liaisons and never before acknowledged her relationship with Shane in the way he had just done.

'Hello, Shane,' Angelo said.

Shane nodded an acknowledgement but looked rather awkward, as if caught out doing something wrong. Mike had not seen him look like this before – Shane was usually full of bluster when accused of any wrongdoing. 'It's Demetri's name day on Sunday. We're here to celebrate,' Shane said as though offering an excuse.

'Ah, Sunday,' Angelo said knowingly. 'You hadn't told me you were part of the Georgiou family.' Shane looked even more embarrassed.

Mario considered he had been out of the conversation long enough. 'Your name day? I offer my warmest congratulations and good wishes.' He paused and his tone changed. 'You don't have your son with you in the business?' he asked, sounding too unbelieving for his enquiry to be anything more than a chance to have a gentle dig at Demetri, a challenge that brought an immediate response.

'My son will lead the business when we are ready for him to take over from me. Already, he is involved.'

'Ah, when you retire, perhaps.' Mario became thoughtful and spoke earnestly, leaning forward towards Demetri. 'My offer to you would be so helpful in securing your future.' He paused to glance across to Mike before returning his gaze to Demetri. 'Particularly if your son prefers to stay where he is and not commit all his time to the business.'

Demetri sat stony-faced and Angelo spoke, this time to Mike. 'I believe you're Findlay's project manager at CityView – one of our rivals.'

'I doubt we have anything like the size we need for you to consider us a rival.'

'Don't be so sure,' Angelo said.

Carla touched her father lightly on the arm in an unspoken reminder.

'Yes, of course,' Mario said. 'We must go to our dinner and let you get on with yours. It has been a pleasure to meet you all. I hope you enjoy yourselves to the full tonight.'

The commanding figure continued on his way, his retinue behind him. He paused to speak briefly to one of the waiters and then disappeared through a door beside the entrance to the kitchen.

The Georgiou family sat in awkward silence until Mary giggled and asked, 'Do they eat in the kitchen?'

'No,' Shane replied quickly. 'There's a private room up a few stairs.'

'You seem to know this place well,' Mike said.

Before Shane could reply, a waiter arrived, carrying several champagne flutes and a large bottle. 'Mr Mancini asks you to accept this Moët et Chandon with his compliments.'

'Yeah. Some of us would like to order something else to drink, and how about some menus, mate. We'd like to eat sometime.' Shane had become his old, aggressive self.

'Of course, sir.'

'Pay no attention to him,' Lissa said gaily. 'Some of us would certainly like some of that champagne before you go any further.'

———

By the time Mike had returned from seeing their baby-sitter safely home, Lissa was in bed but not asleep. As Mike hung up his suit jacket, she said, 'That was a funny kind of celebration.'

'You thought?'

'For a start, did you know your dad was an old pal of Mario Mancini?'

'I wouldn't say they were pals,' he replied as he began to undo his tie.

'You're right there. More like old enemies circling one another. What was that about an offer Mancini had made your father?'

Mike waited until he had fully removed his shirt before replying. 'It was the bit about me taking over the business that got me. I've told Dad a million times I'm not interested, but he won't give up.'

'And why was Shane so coy with his boss?'

'Was he?'

'Of course he was. Seemed like he was apologising for being there and ashamed of being called a member of the family.'

Mike removed his socks and shoes before stepping out of his trousers. 'Shane certainly hit the grog tonight. I'm glad Mary persuaded him to take a taxi home. He was in a wild mood. I hope she'll be OK with him tonight.'

Lissa sat up revealing to Mike that she was wearing his favourite, black nightdress, the lacy one with the shoestring straps. 'You were hitting it pretty hard yourself. Your dad was the only one to hold back. He seemed quite dispirited after speaking with Mancini.'

Mike hung up his trousers. 'You had your eye on all of us tonight; didn't miss a thing.'

'You didn't notice because you couldn't take your eyes of the lovely Carla.' Lissa raised an eyebrow, a trick Mike had always found enticing but never mastered himself. 'I don't blame you, though,' she lied. 'She's gorgeous.'

'A bit cool for me,' he lied in return as he removed his jocks. 'I like a woman with a bit more bubble.'

Lissa, content to believe or willing to forgive him, smiled and gazed at his nakedness. 'The champagne was delicious. And the food was very good, too. But it wasn't the celebration I was expecting.'

Mike clambered into bed beside her. 'We'll just have to have our own celebration,' he said as he embraced her, crushing her to his chest.'

'What's got into you?'

'I liked that restaurant,' he said.

'If this is the result, you'll have to take me there again soon.'

They kissed, his tongue searching for hers, and she reached down for him. He wondered if Angelo and Carla were making love. What would she be like in bed? He would have to be more restrained than he was now, fearful she might break in his hands.

Afterwards, with Lissa asleep beside him, Mike could not settle. What was it about Mario Mancini that had turned his father, renowned for his affability and courtesy, into the man he saw in the restaurant? His father had never mentioned Mancini before. And what was the offer Mancini mentioned – an offer that promised him security in retirement? Surely it had something to do with the business. Why would he reject it out of hand, without even mentioning it? Mike smiled ironically in the darkness. After all, his father claimed he was involved in the running of the business. And Lissa had been right about Shane.

Angelo seemed to know him a good deal better than he would have expected, but Shane had clammed up later on when Mike tried to get him talking about the job he did for Rubicon.

Mike turned on to his side. He must get to sleep. Tomorrow would be a busy day, preparing for Sunday. To judge by the music in the restaurant, Carla liked jazz, too.

7

When Mike came slowly awake his head was fuzzy, the light streaming in the window hurt his eyes and there was no sign of Lissa. He levered himself from the bed, put on his cotton dressing-gown and wandered into the kitchen. There he found Lissa fully dressed with a mug of coffee in her hand.

'Ah, lover-boy, just the man I need.'

'In that case why didn't you stay in bed?'

'Oh no, that's not why I need you now. You have to help me prepare for the feast tomorrow. Make food, not love.' Mike who, in his rather fragile state, found Lissa's robust good humour hard to take, was relieved to see her become more serious. 'Mary just called. She's not well.' Lissa watched him carefully as she gave him the news, but he had the good sense to remain silent and look enquiringly at her. 'It appears you are not the only one with a hangover, but she has bad period pains as well. I guess they're not troubling you, which is just as well because, without Mary, I need you to help me out. Have a shower – that should help you rejoin the human race – and I'll get you some breakfast. We need to be off to the market in twenty minutes.'

Slightly rejuvenated by the shower if not the breakfast, Mike sat beside Lissa as she drove her Forester into the car park above the South Melbourne Market. She took out and assembled the four-wheeled trolley with practiced skill.

'There you are. That's your responsibility,' she said, and set off with Mike trailing behind her.

Usually Lissa shopped on a Friday, so it had been some time

since he had come with her to the market and he enjoyed the cosy proximity of the stalls lining the concrete floored aisles. On another day he might have been tempted to browse at The Merchant of Fairness, the second-hand bookstall, but Lissa moved straight past it and was not delayed by the display of colour at the neighbouring florists, either. When they reached the lower end of the market, where the meat and delicatessen stalls clustered, Mike was struck by the number that carried the first name of the proprietor: 'Theo's Deli', 'Steve's Deli', 'Tony's Meat Supplies', 'Ralph's Meat Company', 'Jim's Fresh Fish'. He had not noticed this before and was amused by the thought of such an approach in the construction industry. Somehow 'Jim's Construction' and 'Angelo's Development' didn't strike the right note.

Lissa was not diverted by such musings, but moved confidently from stall to stall, collecting hefty quantities of pork and lamb, on the bone and minced, substantial supplies of pita bread, walnuts, almonds, spices, flour and eggs, and a range of cheeses. As the silent trolley-wheeler, Mike was able to observe a side of Lissa he had forgotten. Each of the stallholders greeted her with the warmth due to an established customer, yet appeared slightly edgy, as though undergoing some kind of test. Certainly she let them know if they offered anything she considered not up to her standard. When the man in the delicatessen, after searching through the shelves of the cheese room at the side of his stall, told her he had the fetta and kasseri she wanted but was out of graviera, she left him in no doubt he needed to do better in the future.

The detailed knowledge and the easy authority she brought to her task sat well with her. Showing none of the irritability she sometimes displayed at home, she demanded and most often received high quality, attentive service. On the odd occasions it was lacking, she expressed her disappointment as if schooling children in how they should behave. She also took careful note of the amount she spent at each stall, something Mike had not seen before.

Returning to the lift for the car park, they bypassed the fruit and vegetable stalls.

'Come on,' she said cheerfully, 'we still have to pick up my order from the Palace of Georgiou.'

For Mike, the wide expanse of these stalls lacked the magic he still encountered in his father's shops. After stowing their purchases in the back of the Forester, it took only a short time to reach the shop in Bay Street where she pulled into the only vacant spot – one marked in red letters as LOADING ZONE. 'I would like to have made my own selection but your dad rang yesterday to ask what I wanted and said he'd have it all ready for me. If you go in and collect it, I'll stay here and watch out for the parking narks.'

On entering the shop Mike immediately enjoyed the pleasure of returning to well-loved territory. As a young child he had seen it as a magical cave abounding in treasure: golden bananas, ruby plums, polished apples, amber grapefruit, silky green cucumbers and zucchini, lush tomatoes. The mingling odours of earth, spice and sweetness enriched the atmosphere of the cave, presided over by the antique figure of his grandfather. How could anyone not be enchanted? It was in his blood and among his earliest and most indelible memories – nature and nurture working together.

All other fruit and vegetable shops or stalls were drab in comparison with the richness of his memory. There had been changes over the years. Customers were no longer attended by the staff but served themselves. They took their red plastic baskets to the front counter, where modern technology removed the need for suspended scales to weigh their purchases or mental arithmetic to calculate the bill. But Mike unconsciously ignored these changes. When he rebelled in his teens, it was not to reject the shop – he would never do that. What he rejected was the idea his life should follow exactly the same path – the same rut as he thought of it then – as his grandfather and his father. As if his memories had taken on a present reality, his father stood in the middle of the shop, where memory said his grandfather stood to chat amiably with the customers, assist them to make their selections and encourage them to feel the shop existed only to serve their needs.

A small queue stood at the checkout where Gail, the most recent of his father's assistants, was billing and packing. Demetri was bent in conversation with a tiny old lady in a black coat and headscarf, who obviously came into the shop for more than fruit and vegetables. He winked at his son and tilted his head to signal he should go to the back of the shop. Mike pushed through the curtain of plastic strips to find Peter Roberts, Demetri's longest serving employee, busy opening cartons of apples.

'G'day, Peter,' Mike said. 'I thought you were running Albert Park.'

'He wanted me back here to give a hand. Didn't he tell you?' This time it was Peter who sounded surprised.

'We don't talk much about the business,' Mike replied.

'P'raps you should,' Peter said and then bent to pick up a tray of apples. 'I'd better get these out in the shop. Your stuff is over there.' He pointed to a collection of boxes in the corner.

'Yeah. I'd better get moving too. Lissa is illegally parked. I'll catch you tomorrow.'

On the way home Mike thought about Peter Roberts' brief comment. It was odd his father hadn't mentioned Peter's return to Bay Street. Some five years older than Mike, Peter was the eldest son of a woman abandoned by her husband, who left her with five children. Knowing her plight, Demetri found a need for a part-time position that Peter was able to fill after school and at the weekend. By the time Mike was spending some time in the shop, Peter was working full time and became a friend and a hero to the younger boy. Though they rarely saw one another these days, Peter was always keen to know about Mike's successes from Demetri, who passed on to Mike any news of Peter.

After they had unpacked the food, Lissa said, 'Thanks for coming with me. It makes it so much easier for me to concentrate on what I'm buying when there's someone else to look after the trolley. As your reward I'll make you a coffee and allow you to sample some of the walnut cake I made yesterday. It's a new recipe I'm trying. Then you can return to normal duties. Leila is due at ballet at eleven and Chris has a match at two. I'll be busy preparing the marinades and baking some of the pastries for tomorrow. Don't dare ask me to provide any lunch for you or the tribe. Without Mary I'll be flat out.' Lissa sounded pleased, though.

—

The ballet classes were held in a dusty hall attached to what had once been a Congregational church. The classes were taken by Mrs Johnson, a short, sturdy woman in her late fifties who remained remarkably flexible and light on her feet. She also had a voice and manner with the children which reminded Mike of an army sergeant-major. She was assisted by a mousy woman known to all as Elsie, who banged out the required pieces on an out-of-tune piano in a manner Mike found hard to bear. There were twelve children, all girls, and an equal number of parents, only two of them men. After the girls in their pink leotards and ballet shoes were assembled, the parents were banished to a corridor where they could listen but not watch the lesson proceed. It was Mike's opinion that most of the students, like Leila, were sufficiently lissom to meet the requirements of Mrs Johnson but showed few signs of the special aptitude required to become a dancer; before long they would move on to other pursuits like netball or cello or boys. His favourite two were a couple of ugly ducklings destined to turn into ugly ducks, who could be heard clomping their way through the moves prescribed by Mrs Johnson. They were the type who in later life would insist on wearing the shortest of skirts above their chubby thighs. He admired their refusal to be inhibited. For Mike, the least favourite were the pair with a natural talent that marked them as possible future stars of the dance, and knew it. He shouldn't blame the girls; their self-important parents were even harder to take.

Carla looked as though she might have been a dancer. He had no idea what she was like as a person. The music at the restaurant last night, suggested she favoured his kind of jazz. John Coltrane had moved in after Thelonious Monk was done and Miles Davis dropped by later. There had been others, more recent performers, perhaps, he did not recognise, but all were interesting. Did Carla choose them? To judge by the whole atmosphere of the place, she had very good taste. But maybe when she got home the calm reserve dropped away and she became as bitchy with her husband as Lissa could be at times. Unlikely, he would say, but you never know. And that was it – he would never know. The chances of them meeting again must be close to zero, although she and Angelo might turn up at one of those bunfights the industry ran from time to time. He hated them but perhaps should try a few more now he was more senior – with Lissa of course. What he should do, though, was forget all about Carla and get on with his life; he had plenty to occupy him right now. He rose to his feet ready to go but found the ballet lesson was not yet over. The curious eyes of the other parents followed him as he sank back on to his seat.

——

Mike was relieved the clouds that built up during the morning had not yet led to rain. If the ground became wet and muddy, Chris's matches lost any appeal as a spectacle and degenerated into a closely-packed swarm of twenty boys surrounding a sodden ball as it meandered up and down the field while at either end the goalies stood trying to keep warm. Today his team won 2-1 and Mike thought Chris did well – not that his opinion mattered to Chris. The trouble was that Demetri loved to regale his grandson with tales of his glory days at South Melbourne Hellas, the stories becoming more mythical in their content and plausibility with each telling. Chris loved them and saw himself as heir to a great family tradition. He pitied his father, the son of a champion, born without any ability at football, and saw Mike's praise as merely the opinion of someone who was neither a student nor a hero of the game. A pity for Demetri that Chris was not his son – he probably would have stood a much better chance of persuading him to go into the business.

It occurred to Mike that his father and Jim Findlay had that much in common. He had not before thought of them as being at all alike, but both desperately wanted their sons to follow them. Initially both had failed, but Jim prevailed at a cost that had yet to be calculated. Perhaps he should use this as a cautionary tale the next time his father raised the topic. No, it would do no good and only prolong the awkwardness.

Still, it had been a good week for Mike's standing with his son. Lissa told him that when she had explained to Chris why his father had been moving so gingerly at breakfast on Wednesday morning and wasn't willing to talk about it, he had said. 'What? Dad caught a thief at the site? And they had a fight? He must have won. Cool!'

When they returned home they were greeted by delicious smells from the kitchen. A note from Lissa informed them she had gone to Demetri's house to check it out. Demetri had a woman who cleaned for him, but Lissa was unconvinced she would have the house the way it should be for tomorrow's feast. As a postscript she reminded Mike he needed to pick up the drinks. This was no big deal as all he needed was a range of good quality beer and various soft drinks – Demetri insisted that only the wine from the well-stocked cellar he had built up over many years would do for his name day.

Mike and the children combined to suggest to Lissa, who normally provided all their meals and had a righteous hatred for all forms of fast food, that fish and chips would give her an opportunity to rest after all the work she had done.

When they had finished their fish and chips, Mike took the drinks he had bought over to his father's house. Sitting in the darkening back room, each with a beer in hand, Mike glanced at his father and said, 'You never told me you were an old pal of Mario Mancini.'

Demetri shifted uneasily in his chair and frowned. 'We are not pals. Never pals.'

'He seemed to think so, and you do go back a long way, together.'

Again Demetri wriggled uncomfortably and then he sighed. 'Perhaps I should tell you. I am getting old and he will not go away.'

'What?'

Demetri took a long draft of his beer and sat forward.

'Alright, I will tell you.'

He stared straight in front of him and spoke as if to himself.

'I was very young when I first went to the wholesale market. I went with my father who was convinced only he had the knowledge and the skill to make the right choice of fruit and vegetables. As I got older he insisted I continue to go with him but would never let me do more than hump the loads on to our van. I was resentful and I was bored.'

Demetri came out of his reverie to glance across at Mike and give a gentle smile.

'A dangerous time, the later teens. A time for rebelling against your parents. Christos is not many years away.' He turned away to resume his monologue. 'I got into bad company, and there was plenty of it at the market in those days. Still is, I s'pose, but it was much worse back then. All kinds of rackets were run out of the market and there were standover merchants who extracted money by threat. Mancini was one of them. That's how he got his start.'

Again Demetri turned to Mike, but there was no gentle smile this time, his face set as though Mike had interrupted to disagree with him.

'He might be a respectable businessman now, but back then he was a merciless thug. I saw that eventually. But, at the start, I was stupidly impressed by him and wanted to thumb my nose at everyone the way he did. Fortunately, I came to my senses after I'd had a few run-ins with the police – nothing too bad but the kind of thing which can lead on to serious crime. To tell the truth, I didn't so much come to my senses as get scared of what I saw Mancini do. Anyway, I broke away from him and we saw little of one another for a few years. Perhaps he spent time in jail or was away somewhere else. I can't remember now. I was just happy to be shot of him.

'When he returned to the market I was in my twenties and doing all the buying, while my father looked after the two shops we were running by then. Mancini now had his own gang and ran various scams where they fleeced the growers unmercifully. They also continued to demand protection money from many of the traders. Anyone who tried to ignore them, or worse still reported them to the police, was very likely to end up in hospital. One man was killed. No one was tried for the murder although the word was Mancini had fought with him and killed him.

'Mancini didn't threaten me at first but tried instead to recruit me for his gang. I knew that when I refused to join him there would be hell to pay so I prepared for it. When he started to sound off about how he was going to treat me I led him on, suggesting he was more hot air than a real threat. It was a risky thing to do, partly triggered by my embarrassment at ever having been impressed by him. But it paid off. Well, I thought so at the time. He became more threatening and more boastful, telling me he had killed the man I mentioned. I don't know if he was telling the truth or whether he was making it up, but it sounded real and was damning. These were the old days, long before every kid had an iPod hanging off their ears. It never occurred to Mancini that I was recording every word he said. After he was done I made some copies and gave one to him, telling him I'd arranged for another copy to go straight to the police if I or anyone associated with our family or our business was hurt.'

Demetri sighed and bowed his head as if apologising for what he had done.

'It worked, but with every passing year I become more ashamed that I protected myself, and continue to protect myself, by letting a murderer go unpunished. Now you can see why I want nothing to do with the man.'

Mike was still adjusting to a new version of his father, a father with a troubled past that until now he had kept secret.

'Dad, why didn't you tell me earlier? Did Mum know?'

'No one knew. I told you. I was – I am – ashamed.'

'Mancini cut an impressive figure last night. Do you think he's reformed, or is that just a pose?'

'I have no idea but I wouldn't trust the man a millimetre.'

Mike wanted to ask, 'And what do you think about Carla?' But he did not, keeping to himself the questions of whether the businesses she ran were legitimate or if she also had criminal links.

Demetri broke into Mike's thoughts.

'I'm sorry I told him you are involved in the business. That was foolish. It was just the way he gloated about his daughter running some of his.'

'You did more than that: you told him I would be taking over.'

'I'm sorry. He has that effect on me.'

'Please give it up, Dad. You know it's never going to happen and pretending to others that it is makes it embarrassing for us all.'

Demetri shook his head sorrowfully and Mike thought he had not seen his father look so sad – even defeated – on the many occasions they had this discussion before.

'But what am I to do? I made a solemn promise to my father that the name of Georgiou would always be maintained in Bay Street. He made the same promise to his father and he kept his promise. You have your career, I know that. Christos is too young; I cannot wait for him. But how else can I keep my promise if you will have nothing to do with the business?'

8

This time when Mike awoke, his head was no longer fuzzy and the light streaming in the window did not hurt his eyes. But again there was no sign of Lissa. Already she was in the kitchen packing boxes with the food she had prepared and the ingredients she would need at Demetri's house today.

'Ah Mike, my love, could you see to the kids, get them some breakfast and dressed. They know what they're wearing today. At least the girls do. Will you have a look at Chris and see he's respectable. Then come over and give a hand laying out the place for the feast. I thought Mary might be here by now. Probably she's gone straight to your dad's.'

'I'll give you a hand with these boxes. You really have been busy.'

Lissa gave him a grateful smile.

'Lots more to do yet, but I reckon it's going OK. A good start.'

—

It was another hour before Mike arrived at his father's house with the children. It was not Chris who delayed him; Jacinta kept changing her mind over what she would wear. Mike was used to such to-and-froing; Lissa often displayed uncertainty over her choice of clothes, but he had not seen Jac like this before – an inherited trait he had no hope of arresting. Then the balloons for the front veranda had to be found. When Mike tried to maintain these were unnecessary – everyone who was coming had been before and well knew where their grandfather lived – the children were unmoved.

Mike first sought out his father, who was at the rear of the house, to give him name day greetings. The day was surprisingly warm and perhaps the heat, or an acceptance that these occasions no longer required such formality, had led Demetri to forgo his suit coat. Mike had gone even further, wearing a broad-checked, open-necked shirt and moleskin trousers. His father seemed rather ill at ease and Mike wondered whether it was concern over his attire or the memory of last night's confession that had unsettled him. Lissa had been intrigued when he told her about his father's early links with Mancini and he made her promise not mention it to him. The arrival of Christos spared him the need to create a conversation.

'Christos, how good to see you.' Demetri embraced the boy and hastened to say, 'Sorry I couldn't be there yesterday. Opening on a Saturday afternoon is a real pain we didn't have when I played, thank goodness. How did you go?'

'We won 2-1,' Christos replied cheerfully before frowning. 'I didn't play too well, though.'

'I thought he was good,' Mike interjected.

Demetri waved his hand as if dismissing the views of an unreliable informer and draped his arm around his grandson's shoulder. 'You must tell me all about it. Did you take your chances? That was always the key question when I was at Hellas.'

Mike sauntered into the kitchen where Lissa was peeling vegetables. 'No sign of Mary?' he asked.

'No. I wonder where she can be.'

'I'll give her a call.'

'I've already done that. Both her mobile and her home phone go through to message bank.'

Mike frowned.

'When she rang yesterday, saying she was ill, did she say anything about bailing out today? Surely she would ring if she was still sick. And to miss Dad's name day!'

Lissa glared back at him. 'I don't know. What I do know is that Mary had agreed to work with me on this and now I have to cope on my own, so if you don't mind, or even if you do …'

'Ah Lissa, Mike, there you are.' A full bosomed woman in her late sixties swept into the room and embraced them both.

'Brioni! So good to see you.'

Mike had never heard Lissa greet his aunt so enthusiastically. 'I'm getting a bit behind and could do with some help.'

'That's why we're early. I always like to lend a hand. Now, Mike, leave us. This is women's business. Go and join Kostas and your father. They'll be complaining to each other about the price of vegetables.'

Brioni was right. Mike found Kostas, who had grown vegetables at Werribee for almost as long as Demetri had sold them, and had been married to Demetri's sister for only a few years less, sitting sharing a beer with his father.

'It's the middle-men,' Kostas declared. 'Them and the supermarket chains. I get nothing for growing the stuff and you get nothing for selling it. We're both being screwed.'

—

Vern sipped the mug of sweet, black tea and looked out from the Flinders Village Cafe at the falling rain. It had been sunny and warm when he left Melbourne and it was only at this end of the Peninsula that he ran into squally showers from broken clouds that raced across the sky between bursts of sunshine. The drive down had taken less time than he expected, so he had stopped for a cup of tea and found himself among a crowd of people enjoying a leisurely brunch.

A large, black SUV travelled past the cafe sending up a spray from both sides. Was this the car Mike had claimed to see, now making its way to Angelo Rossi's place for the meeting? Fanciful to think so – black SUVs were the vehicle of choice on the roads around here. But now he was here, it felt more like going into the lion's den than it had before. Perhaps he should have told someone he was coming down but he was reluctant to let anyone else know what he was up to. Taking Mike into his confidence was a calculated risk. He needed to know where Mike stood; he was a key player in his plans. Vern took another sip of his tea and gave a rueful smile. If he did get into strife today, having someone know he was here wasn't going to help him.

—

The guests were beginning to arrive: cousins with their spouses and children, neighbours and old friends from the area, some of the other past and present traders from Bay Street, all the employees from Georgiou's three shops, together with their families, and a few remaining fossils from South Melbourne Hellas. Demetri stood in the hallway beside the front door welcoming his guests and accepting their congratulations and good wishes. Mike stood further back, looking out for Mary who had still not arrived nor phoned.

At last he saw her, although for a moment he was not sure it was her. She had a new hairstyle, which pulled her hair forward across her forehead and down one side of her face, and she approached her father with the diffidence of someone unsure of their welcome. As Demetri grasped her in his bear hug, her head held so that Mike was looking directly into her face, she winced and the lock of hair fell away, revealing a bruise running from her eyebrow to the side of her head. When free of her father's embrace, her hair back in its covering place, she tried to walk straight past Mike, saying, 'Sorry I'm late. Must get into the kitchen to help Lissa.'

'Not so fast,' Mike ordered, sounding to his ears like a movie gangster. He grabbed her arm swathed in the long sleeves of her dress and she yelped in pain. 'Not just your face, then.'

'Stop. You're hurting me,' she hissed.

She tried to pull away but Mike retained his grip. He steered her along a corridor to the second bedroom, which was seldom used for anything but storage these days. Once inside, he shut the door, let go of Mary and stood with his arms folded.

'OK. What happened?'

Mary stood rubbing her arm and glaring at him. 'You always make such a fuss. It was nothing really.'

Mike continued to stare at her and the sharpness in her voice softened.

'We were both drunk and got into a silly argument. I started it by saying that taking us out like he'd done didn't make up for missing today and he should tell them he couldn't make it. Shane said it was important for him to be there but wouldn't tell me where he was going or what he would be doing. It was my fault. I should have let it go, but I goaded him, said he was making it up and just wanted a weekend away with his mates. He's apologised. In the morning we'd both sobered up and could see how stupid we'd been.

'Can't you just let it go?' she pleaded. 'It mustn't spoil Dad's day. As it is I've let Lissa down badly. Not a good way to start our partnership.'

'What do you mean?'

'Hasn't she told you?'

Mike made no reply. It was the second time this weekend he'd been told a member of his family was keeping something from him.

———

Bruno drove the black Land Cruiser into the carport beside Angelo's Porsche and cut the engine. The four men stepped from the vehicle almost simultaneously and the sounds of slamming car doors were like a volley of shots. When Shane raised his arms to stretch his large frame, the stiff breeze, carrying the tang of salt water, ruffled his long, fair hair. Another man, even taller than Shane, also stretched, but his baseball cap, apparently a permanent attachment to his head, withstood the wind's grasp.

'Rick, do you stick that cap on with glue?' Ivan asked and hunched his shoulders against the wind. 'It's a lot warmer up in town,' he complained as he pressed the button on the security system beside the front door. At first there was no response, except for the arrival of the next shower, blown in on them as they huddled under the inadequate overhang. Bruno nudged Ivan aside and pressed the button with great force.

'Come on, you bugger,' he grunted.

Eventually the door opened to reveal Angelo Rossi, the collar of a red linen shirt showing above a white cashmere jumper.

'Come in,' he said without enthusiasm. 'You caught me at the other end of the house.' He led them down the steps to the spacious living room, where a curved wall of glass allowed an uninterrupted view of low cloud and scudding rain.

'Doesn't look like we'll be eating outside today. We can still use the barbecue – it's under cover.'

'Just as well,' Ivan replied.

Angelo shook his head and made a sound, which could have been a cough or a scoff. 'There's nothing else here,' he said. 'Beside the grog, of course.' He looked away from Ivan to the others and said, 'How's the knee, Bruno? Back on your feet, but I see you're still favouring it.'

'It's OK,' Bruno growled.

'A nasty business. I hear it was Mike Georgiou who did it.' He grinned. 'Got to be careful with builders. They can surprise you at times.'

'I'll surprise the fucker any day now.'

Ivan glanced at the digital watch on his left wrist. He had

abandoned his pinstripe suit for a navy turtleneck skivvy and matching chinos.

'He'll be here in about half an hour, I reckon.' Ivan looked across at Angelo. 'You know what to say.' It was an order not a question.

'Like a drink?' From Angelo's expression it was unclear whether this was what Ivan had instructed him to say or whether he was making him an offer. Shane walked behind the bar that stood along one side of the room.

'Yeah, let's all have a beer,' he said. He spoke with the confidence of a man who knew he had no need to wait for his host and began taking stubbies from the fridge. Angelo drew in an irritated breath before a mocking smile came to his face.

'How did you enjoy your meal at Café Filipo the other night?'

'OK,' Shane replied, turning away.

'You hadn't told me you come from the same family as Mike Georgiou.'

Shane looked up quickly from peering into the fridge to find the other four carefully watching him.

'Not in the family. I live with his sister. She's a very different type to that bastard.'

Bruno took several steps towards Shane but Ivan gestured for him to stay. 'Angelo, how did this interesting news come to light?'

'Friday night. The whole family, celebrating old man Georgiou's name day with dinner at Café Filipo, courtesy of Shane.' Angelo turned to face him directly. 'I hope you didn't think Carla would give you a free ride. It's only free in the private room when you're with me. When the old guy introduced you he sure made it sound like you were part of the family.'

Again Bruno stepped towards Shane and said, 'Did you tip off Georgiou I was goin' there with Ted Horton the other night? Someone did and, when I find him, I'll kill the fucker.'

'Yes, Shane, you do have some explaining to do,' Ivan smoothly intervened. 'But before you do, bring us those drinks and we will sit here quietly while you tell us all about your links with Mike Georgiou.'

Angelo walked to the bar, picked up one of the stubbies and removed himself to sit in one of the three leather armchairs occupying the far end of the room. Ivan, Bruno and Rick took their places around a low wooden table closer to the bar and Shane carried the remaining bottles to the table. After downing about half of his, he began. 'I met Mary about three years ago. She's an attractive woman and we've had this on-again-off-again thing going. She can be a bad-tempered bitch at times. Maybe it runs in the family because brother Mike is a right bastard. I hate him. The old bloke tries to pretend they're one big, happy family but more like one small, unhappy family I'd say. Mike walked out on his father's greengrocer's business years ago and hasn't been forgiven. He and his wife are always having digs at one another. At least when Mary and I fight, it's out in the open.'

Shane looked around at his listeners and perhaps it occurred to him that he was showing too much knowledge of the Georgious. 'I steer clear of them as much as I can, but Mary talks about them.'

'And, seeing you're in the same business as Mike Georgiou, you never have a chat with him about what we're doing?' Ivan asked.

'Never. Not even his sister. Got into strife with her on Friday night when I wouldn't tell her where I was coming today and what I'd be doing.'

'So she was fishing?' Ivan continued his questioning.

'No way. Just a curious bitch who wants to own all of me.'

'You'll have to tell her that it's me that owns all of you,' Ivan said. 'I hope you've been straight with us, Shane. We have a lot riding here and you know how nasty Bruno can get.'

——

When the women brought the food there was hardly room on the tables for it all. The children had been press-ganged into carrying around plates of appetisers: deep fried tiganita, fava puree, Cretan dakos salad and grapevine packets of dolmadakra with pitta bread. On most days these would have made an adequate lunch but today they were merely the precursors to the dishes of moussaka, the slow-baked lamb kleftiko, the pork apaki and the fried ketedakia accompanied by a variety of salads. Mike was kept busy seeing all the diners were well provided with drinks: his father's vintage wine, beer for the less refined palates and soft drinks for the ever-thirsty children. After a short recovery time, which was all Lissa allowed them, the tables were cleared and replenished with desserts and pastries: sticky katafi, deep fried loukoumodes, rich baklava and more of the walnut cake Mike had enjoyed the day before. When Lissa came from the kitchen bearing pots of thick coffee it was the signal the meal had reached its final phase. Mike wrapped an arm around her shoulders. 'That was a superb meal you turned on,' he enthused. 'Your best ever, I reckon.'

'Yeah, it does seem to have gone well.'

'Dad is stoked. Get ready for a crushing hug.'

'Thanks for the warning,' she said drily. 'Are you proud of me?'

'A pity your mum and dad couldn't make it down from Coff's. They would have been really proud.'

'They taught me. I didn't learn it anywhere else.'

Mike took his arm from her shoulder and drew back a little. 'What's this partnership between you and Mary?'

Lissa's cheeks deepened their colour. 'Oh, that,' she laughed. 'Not really a good start with Mary out of action until the last moment.' She paused as he continued to look enquiringly at her. 'I've decided to go into catering – lunches and dinners for people in their own homes or businesses. Mary and I are going to be partners.'

'Full time?'

'Not at first. We need to see how it goes.'

'When did you decide?'

'I've been thinking about it for the past year, I guess. The kids don't need the attention I used to give them. I haven't got a career to take up. I only ever worked in Dad's bakery and that's well gone. But I reckon I can cook and Mary says I should have a go.'

Mike could see there would be many issues in setting up and operating such a business, but now was not the time for mentioning them.

'Great. I'm sure you'll go really well.'

He could hear the doubt in his voice and Lissa heard it, too. She tossed her head, but as he was about to explain he had no doubts about her ability, he was cut off by his aunt.

'Lissa. A wonderful meal and so traditional. You have gone to so much trouble with such little help.'

She was joined by others who offered their thanks and Lissa went to the table to dispense the coffee. Mike walked though to the rear of the house where he found his father in the sun-room, deep in discussion with Kostas. They stopped abruptly when he came in and Kostas said, 'Your wife has put on a great meal.'

'Yes, she has,' Demetri agreed and got to his feet. 'I must go to thank her.'

'Sit down with me, Mike,' Kostas said, patting the seat Demetri had just vacated. 'I would speak with you.' Before Mike was properly settled Kostas began. 'It is time you followed the family calling. You have stayed away too long and your father is no longer young.'

'Did he put you up to this?'

Mike began to rise from his seat but Kostas put out a restraining hand. 'Hear me out, Mike. Demetri does not put me up to anything. That is not the way we are with one another. But he does tell me about the business and his ambitions for it. Any fool, certainly this one, can see you are needed. You owe it to your father.'

'Rubbish.'

Brioni, who seemed to have developed a talent for breaking into fraught conversations, had entered unnoticed and now stood over the two of them.

'It was your mother's dearest wish you should make use of your brains, go to the university, not be a gardener or a grocer. A great tragedy she died before she could see you reach the heights you have. An even greater tragedy if you throw it all away because of the pleas from these foolish old men. Come, Kostas, you have been drinking too much. You need coffee.'

Kostas spread his hands and gazed at Mike before rising and following his wife.

—

Vern turned off the main road, through a brick-pillared gateway and along a gravel driveway that wound through thick trees and brush. There was no sign of the house, well protected from the view of anyone who might pass. Mike had described the property he had seen in the magazine as 'quite a place'. Perhaps Mike hadn't seen it in a magazine at all but had been invited down, just as Vern had been today. No doubt he would soon come to a view of the sea, which the trees denied the cars on the main road but preserved for the Rossi family and their guests.

Suddenly he came clear of the trees and found himself on a paved area with no view beyond an extended carport, which looked much like the overflow car park at a three star motel.

He pulled into a vacant space beside a Porsche and a black Land Cruiser. Could it be the black SUV? His ageing BMW looked quite humble in comparison with the other two. Humility would not serve him well today. The clouds had moved on and the sun was warm, so he took off his jacket and left it in the car. He was wearing one of his golf shirts with the Kingswood insignia on the breast pocket. He had played poorly yesterday, probably thinking too much about today and where it would lead. His regular partner, Paul Jones, was having a bad day as well, not helped by their opponents trying to pump him for his take on the latest scandals in the police force. As an assistant commissioner Paul Jones was far too experienced and shrewd to be caught out there but, like Vern, he considered golf a serious business with any chatting to be done in the bar afterwards.

Vern strolled over to the Land Cruiser and inspected the front passenger side. There were streaks of mud from the wet road but the duco was flawless – too flawless. Not conclusive, but an indication that the side panel could have been replaced recently.

He walked to the large, wooden door that divided the carport in two, the other section sheltering a quad bike and an empty trailer. Vern pressed the button beside the door and stepped back. The brutal facade made it clear to him that the house had been designed by one of those trendy architects who delighted in creating controversy. What would he find inside? Would the brutality continue with the bare forms of construction revealed for all to see? Or would the interior be full of architectural artifice, clamouring for attention? He had no truck with this kind of gimmickry. Give him a builder's house every time. One like Jim's that sat in plain view without pretension, solid and functional – an honest building.

Vern was not surprised when the baseball-capped man he had seen beside the Yarra opened the door and led him down some steps into the house. What he found there did surprise him. His first sight was of natural clay tiles that flowed across the floor, beyond a curving glass wall and out to a swimming pool surrounded by a rockery with low shrubs that presented the pool as a natural water-hole and took the eye on to the land beyond. There, grassy dunes stood before a small bay guarded by ochre cliffs and wave-swept rocks that sparkled in the clear sun. Thick trees and scrub covering the upper part of the block continued down either side to the cliffs, framing the entire picture. It was hard to tell where the house ended and the view began.

'You're seeing it at its best,' Ivan said and rose from his seat at a small table near the bar, behind which his blond henchman stood. 'When we arrived, all you could see was cloud. You found us alright?'

'Your directions were fine,' Vern replied.

He saw no sign of Angelo – not until he glanced to the other end of the large room and saw him sitting in one of the leather chairs with stubbie in hand, carefully watching him.

'Come and meet Angelo,' Ivan said. 'That's why you're here, after all.'

It was only when they were almost upon him that Angelo stood up.

'I'm Vern McKenzie. I doubt you would remember me, but we met at an industry do, once.'

'I remember you, Vern. How is Jim Findlay getting on? I hear he's been in hospital.'

'Yes, it runs in the family at present, but Jim's making a good recovery from his hip operation.'

'What would you like to drink?' Angelo asked.

'That will be a good single malt,' Ivan said before Vern could respond. 'Can you manage that, Angelo?'

'There's several bottles at the bar. Don't drink whisky myself so I'm not sure how good they are,' he replied defensively and Vern became conscious of a tension between the two of them

'Fortunately I thought to bring a bottle, just in case. I know Vern enjoys Glenkinchie,' Ivan said. He looked directly at the blond man. 'Shane, will you get it? I left it in the car.'

As Shane opened the door to go outside he was met by a shaven-headed man who Vern guessed might have been the one involved in the failed burglary the other night. As the man came down the steps Vern noticed he slightly favoured one leg. His eyes were firmly on Ivan and he gave him a confirmatory nod.

'Thank you, Bruno' Ivan said. So he was the one – Bruno. Had he been seeing whether Vern had brought some friends, or checking out his car? Ivan sat down and, with a wave of his hand, invited Vern to take the chair on the other side of Angelo. They sat in silence while Shane, having returned with the bottle, poured some of its contents into a tumbler and brought it to Vern.

'Time for you guys to fire up the barbecue,' Ivan called down the room to his men. 'You know where everything is.' The three trooped from the room and Ivan turned to Vern. 'Business first and then we eat,' he said, as though the meal would be some sort of reward. He nodded at Angelo and sat back.

Angelo raised his stubbie to his lips, looking all the while at Vern with what seemed to be troubled eyes.

'We have been taking an interest in Findlay Construction and understand why you would feel frustrated and aggrieved with the way you've been treated while the firm slides further and further into trouble,' he said.

'Yes, I've already covered this with Vern,' Ivan said impatiently. 'Explain our proposal to him.'

Angelo shot an angry glance at Ivan before turning again to Vern.

'The Riverside project has changed direction. Our next

tower is being revamped right now to provide cheaper options, similar to those at CityView. There isn't the demand in the area for both projects to come on line together, so one has to be held back. We're offering you the chance to join us in making sure Riverside is the one that goes ahead. You'll be well rewarded for helping us and afterwards you will have a new career with Rubicon.'

When Angelo hesitated, Ivan gave a click of his tongue.

'Angelo has trouble cutting to the chase, so I will. Findlay Construction is finished. After the way Jim Findlay's treated you I can't imagine why you would stay loyal to him, but if you do, you'll go down with him. It will be a little easier for us and so much better for you if you join us.'

Vern took his time before replying. He had already achieved one of his objectives. He knew Sarac was merely an enforcer but he had not known the extent to which Angelo was involved. It was now clear to him that Angelo was an unwilling accomplice and had very little say in shaping their schemes. Vern needed to get to the man who really called the shots. But before that he needed to shake up Sarac. Vern fixed his eyes on him as he spoke.

'If you think you can put Findlay's out of business without me, you're more deluded than I thought. Look what you've achieved so far. First of all, you arrange to disrupt the CityView site but your muscle-man, Bruno, is so incompetent the project manager down there catches him red-handed and deals with him. I see Bruno's still limping. If it hadn't been for me the police would have charged him by now.'

Vern was pleased to see the complacency disappear from Ivan's face. He thought he knew about Findlay's operations but the idea Vern had already played a role in covering for him was a surprise. 'You try to scare off our bankers so ineptly that the incompetent Ben Findlay is able to reassure them without me giving him any help. And then you botch running him down. I suppose it was Bruno who mucked that up as well?' Ivan glared at him but said nothing. 'If you aim to wreck Findlay's, the last person you want to put out of action is Ben Findlay. Leave him there and he'll do it for you. If you haven't much time we might need to help him along, and I can do anything that needs to be done without being the MD.'

Vern glanced across at Angelo who was watching him carefully. The ghost of a grin flickered across his face when Vern added, 'You're going about this totally the wrong way.'

'All right, smart man, what do you suggest?' Ivan demanded.

Vern sat silently for a moment, partly for effect, but also absorbing the significance of Ivan's challenge. It seemed they had no inkling of the scheme he had put to Mike on Thursday. What was more, Ivan hadn't denied Bruno was the driver of the black SUV.

'I told you the other day I wanted to speak to the man calling the shots and he's not here.' Vern turned to nod an acknowledgement to Angelo. There was no point in putting him offside – he might need him before he was finished. 'You're a good builder, I know – one of the best – but the idea to undermine Findlay's didn't come from you, did it?

The frown that Vern's earlier words had brought to Angelo's face softened, but Sarac was not going to allow him to reply. 'Let's get back to the point,' Sarac said. 'What are you suggesting?'

'I'm telling you I'm not going any further until I meet your boss. If we're going to work together I have to deal with him direct, not through the hired help.'

Sarac's face flared, but he brought himself under control.

'Ah, difficult. He's a man who likes to stay in the background. He only deals directly with people who've shown they have what it takes to work with him. You've shown us nothing. You're very free with your opinions, but we haven't even heard whether you're coming on board.'

'I've already started.'

'What do you mean?'

'I've told you, you went for the wrong man – Ben Findlay poses no problem, but Mike Georgiou does. He's a bloody good project manager who has kept CityView on track despite having to deal with a dud architect, an incompetent MD and your puny efforts to disrupt the site. What's more, he's rock solid loyal to Jim Findlay and I haven't been able to shake him. I need to take him out for a while.'

'We can do that for you,' Ivan said with an unpleasant grin, showing all his teeth. 'Bruno is looking for an opportunity to even the score.'

'I don't want Mike harmed.'

'Getting squeamish are you? What is it they say about not being able to make an omelette without breaking eggs?'

Vern sighed. 'Yeah, violence can be effective, but only when it's properly applied, and what I've seen of Bruno's efforts so far tells me he doesn't make omelettes, just an untidy mess that others have to clean up. Properly handled, Georgiou can be an important asset for us. We don't want Bruno's petty need for revenge to get in our way.'

'You got a better idea?'

'Of course. I've already set him up to be charged with bribery.' Vern was pleased to see his announcement had caused Ivan to glance sharply at him as though having discovered a new side to him – another objective achieved. 'I've also heard that young Reardon has been giving you grief and you haven't been able to shake him off. He must be taking good care that Bruno and his mates can't get close to him.' Vern waited for Sarac to pour scorn over him, but he remained silent, so George Fowler's suspicions were wrong – they hadn't paid off Reardon. 'I guess you won't mind if I stitch him up at the same time as I fix Georgiou.'

Unwilling to show himself grateful to Vern for anything, Sarac pursed his lips and frowned as if considering a difficult problem. 'Yeah, if you can deliver on those two, my man might be willing to consider meeting you. But he'll want more than you've given me so far. Tell me what you have in mind that's so much better than our ideas.'

'OK. You'd be stupid to put Findlay's out of business when it's much easier to take them over.'

'What?'

Vern settled down in his chair with a confident smile.

'I'll sketch it out for you. I can arrange for industrial strife on the CityView site any time I want. That will be even easier now that Ben Findlay will be back tomorrow.' Vern was pleased to see the surprise return to Ivan's face; here was another thing about Findlay's that he didn't know.

'Oh, yes, Ben is making a good recovery. You couldn't even run him down effectively. Then I can really put the wind up our bankers. I am the accountant for the firm after all. When they panic and escape to safety, along comes your boss with an offer too good to refuse. He will take over the financial backing for the company providing he's given a controlling interest in the firm.'

'And Jim Findlay will cheerfully hand that over?' Ivan scoffed, just as Vern hoped he would.

'Do you know who owns Findlay Corporation? I see you don't. Given your limited ambitions I guess you didn't bother to check. I have a ten per cent share Jim offered me when he first brought me into his tiny company. Cash was a problem back then, too. When your boss comes along to save us from our crisis, and wants only forty-five per cent, Jim will be delighted. It gets him out of a hole, provides him with funds for his retirement, and

126

he retains control through my loyalty – it won't occur to him to question that. That's when I get my reward for all those years of unappreciated service. Money is only secondary to me.'

'And why do you think we would want to own a company on the verge of bankruptcy?' Ivan asked.

Vern noticed Angelo had remained silent and wondered whether he was still deferring to Ivan or had begun to see where Vern was heading.

'But it wouldn't be. You've focused too much on CityView and not thought about the rest of the company. It has a substantial number of small, profitable projects that provide a good cash flow and will continue to do so. Just the cash flow you lack, the source of the problem for your boss.'

Ivan shot him a dark glance while Angelo's eyes suggested a more thoughtful appraisal. Vern turned to face Angelo.

'You made a bad mistake when you put all your eggs in the Riverside basket and stopped going after the smaller jobs. I guess Riverside was a massive step up for you and, with Mancini's backing, you didn't need to worry about cash flow. Now though …' He shook his head and turned back to Sarac. 'Once you have control of Findlay's you have the cash flow you need, you can proceed with CityView, giving you more cash, complete the rede-sign of Riverside and bring it back on after CityView.'

Angelo spoke for the first time since Vern had begun. 'He's right. It makes good sense.'

'You're s'posed to be the brains around here. If it's so good why did we have to wait for him to suggest it?' Ivan demanded.

Angelo gave a humourless smile. 'You came along and told me what we were going to do whether I liked it or not. You didn't want to know about any alternative.'

While the two men continued to glare at one another, Vern decided to press Sarac once more. 'Now you know the outline of my plan you'll understand why I must know who I'm dealing with and whether he can deliver what I need. In any case, if he wants to stay in the shadows and take your advice on a deal like this without having a look for himself, he's a fool and I want nothing to do with him. Is that how you got into this mess in the first place?'

'Vern's right again.'

Angelo leaned forward, no longer the passive spectator. 'We have to explain why we're changing tack and he will want a lot more detail than Vern's given us today, including all the financial details. You won't get to first base without stumbling and you know how he'll react to that. He'll want to see Vern, and you need Vern to explain how the whole thing will work. This isn't your show any more, Ivan. Vern will be the one making the running, not you.' Angelo looked happier than he had throughout their conversation.

For the first time since he had met Sarac, Vern saw him hesitate.

'Yeah. OK. I'll need to talk with him. I'll call you during the week.' He stood up and, looking down on the other two, resumed his confident air. 'Those boys should have the steaks done nicely by now. You sticking with the whisky?'

Vern nodded. He had achieved all his objectives.

———

The crowd had thinned out when Peter Roberts came to Mike and said, 'Spare a minute?' He didn't wait for an answer and led Mike through the back door into the garden where two of Peter's children were jumping on the trampoline Demetri had insisted on erecting for his grandchildren several years ago. Peter showed no interest in supervising the children, his attention fixed on Mike. He began hesitantly. 'I don't know whether I should be telling you this but I think you need to know.'

'What is it, Peter?'

'You were surprised to see me at Bay Street yesterday. I've been there for a few months.' He paused and took a deep breath. 'It's your dad. He's finding it hard going these days.'

'He seems OK to me. Looked very chirpy with all his old mates, here today.'

'Yeah, he hides it well when he needs to, and I don't think he's seriously ill or anything like that, but he finds the grind of the shop hard to take. That's why he got me back. I'm really running the business for him these days. Not that I mind. Great for me, but not so good for him, hanging about the shop like a ghost from the past. They hardly ever see him at South Melbourne and Albert Park. They're all right – I see to that.'

'Why are you telling me this?' Mike asked, pretty certain he knew the answer.

'He wants out, I reckon, but can't figure out how to do it. He needs help from you.'

'Not you too. Are you all ganging up on me? You know I'm not coming into the business.'

'I know and he knows. But with all the changes in Bay Street – the changes that have occurred and the ones that are rumoured to go ahead – he's obsessed with ensuring the Georgiou name stays on in the street and doesn't know what to do. He needs your help.'

Peter shook his head and smiled sheepishly. 'You know how I feel about your dad, but I've got some self interest here, as well. All of us who work there do. The competition from the super-markets gets fiercer every week. We need to change the way we go about things, alter our range. Some people sell flowers along with the fruit and vegetables, sweets and chocolates as well. He won't hear of anything like that. I didn't want to lumber you with this, but you are his only son.'

9

'Shane, it's Mike.'

'Hullo Mike. Mary tells me the party went well yesterday. That wife of yours certainly knows how to put on a good feed.'

Hearing Mary's name, Mike's grip of the phone tightened. 'We need to speak, Shane.'

'I thought that's just what we're doing right now.'

'Don't play funny buggers with me. I don't want to do this over the phone. We need to meet.'

'Do we, pal? Now why would that be?'

Shane continued to affect a bantering good humour, but Mike could detect the wariness in his voice.

'You know why. I want to see you today without fail, so name your time.'

'Gee. Difficult. I'm really tied up today. Matter of fact they need me right now. I'll call you back.'

Mike frowned as the line went dead. He hadn't wanted to wait until the afternoon but he knew Shane was almost certain to be at Doherty's Gym after work. If he had to confront him there, that's what he would do. There was plenty to keep him busy until then.

As Mike put down his phone the door to his office was thrown open and Ben Findlay stood in the doorway. Mike started from his chair. 'Ben, I didn't know you were back on deck.'

'Thought you'd be surprised.' Ben did not smile and his eyes bored into Mike. 'It takes more than knocking me off my bike to get rid of me. Or for me to forget what happened last Monday.'

He turned to look out over the site. 'I've heard about some of your adventures while I've been away. It doesn't suit me to take over from you right now, but you'll need more than a day or so of heroics to change my mind about you. Meanwhile, I'm here to have a good look round, so take me on a tour of inspection and make it thorough.'

After farewelling Ben, Mike reflected on the difference in atmosphere when accompanying his boss around the site, compared with the reception he had been given last Thursday. Today the crew appeared totally immersed in whatever they were doing and completely ignored the visitors. No sign of the good-natured ribbing or the admiring glances he received then. At a number of points Ben went up to one of the hands to ask a question. They were reasonable questions, although some of them displayed an ignorance of construction methods that must have surprised the men on the job. The real problem was that he seemed incapable of asking his questions without underlining he was the boss and putting his men on the defensive. How could a son of Jim Findlay so lack the common touch? Perhaps that's what you get when you send your boy to Melbourne Grammar. It was good to see him leave. Mike also wondered how Vern felt now Ben was back. Was he still thinking about a merger with Rubicon?

The sound of his phone broke into Mike's thoughts, although he had not properly disengaged from them when he answered, 'Georgiou.'

'Michael?' He didn't know the voice, but the two note motif the woman made of his name was so musical compared with the amputated 'Mike' he usually heard, he was charmed.

'Michael?' There it was again. 'This is Carla Mancini.' Even in his flummoxed state he noted she used her maiden name. Was that her practice or did it signify a change of status?

'I'm sorry. I didn't recognise your voice. You didn't speak on Friday night.'

The music continued as she said whimsically, 'When with my father, there is little opportunity to speak.' Her voice remained light but became brisk. 'Actually, that is why I've rung you.' He could hear the businesswoman speaking. 'I would like to speak with you about our fathers.'

'Our fathers?'

'Yes. They cannot speak with one another so we must do it for them.'

'I don't understand.'

'You do not?' she sounded surprised, surprised and a little disappointed. 'All the more reason we should speak. I apologise for the short notice, but would you be free to have lunch with me tomorrow?'

He stopped himself from replying, 'Of course,' and instead said, 'Yes, I could make that. What time?'

'Shall we say one o'clock at Café Filipo? When you arrive give your name – you will be expected.'

'I shall look forward to it.' She wouldn't read it as more than politeness, surely.

'Until tomorrow.'

Mike sat staring at the blank wall of his office. What did she want? Was it really to do with their fathers or was this an approach from Rubicon? He still thought the most likely explanation for the attempted disruption of CityView had its origins at Riverside.

Mike needed to be home in time for the concert Jac's recorder group was giving late in the afternoon, so did not walk to Doherty's Gym but took his car. As he drove across Queens Bridge, the righteous anger he had felt in the morning began to ebb. What did he hope to achieve by confronting Shane? What could he say that might make him change? He would need to be careful not to make things worse for Mary. If he did stir Shane up, he might well take it out on her. He was fortunate to find a parking spot a short way up Queen Street. Across Flinders Street was the brick facade of the railway viaduct bearing the sign DOHERTYS 24/7 GYM and underneath the words WE NEVER CLOSE. He crossed with the lights and entered the gym. Immediately inside the door was a counter attended by a fit-looking young guy in a black T-shirt. Behind him a long gallery with an arched ceiling stretched into the distance. Three women jogged on treadmills that faced a line of TV screens. Beyond them four men rode stationary cycles in front of a long mirror. Through the window at the far end Mike could see people walking along the path by the river.

'G'day,' the attendant said.

'G'day. Is Shane Francis working out here today?' Mike asked.

'Shane?'

'Yeah. A big guy with blond hair.'

'Could be on the weights.'

The attendant nodded towards an archway in the right wall. The gym consisted of a series of linked parallel tunnels, like a set of whitewashed catacombs, with different equipment in each gallery. Mike went through the archway and found a man in a grey tracksuit contorting himself on a metal frame bolted to the floor. Further along, two men were exercising with barbells in front of another mirror, their brief shorts displaying bodies rippling with overdeveloped muscles. Beyond them he could see Shane raising hefty weights by pulling down on the levers of a machine constructed from metal bars, wire ropes and pulleys. The effort showed in his tense muscles, set face and heavy breathing. When he noticed Mike approaching he let go of the levers, sat back and wiped his face with a towel.

'Come to work out with me, have you?' he said with a cheeky smile. 'I reckon it'd do you a lot of good.'

Mike went directly to the point. 'No, I've come to tell you to stop beating up Mary.'

Shane stiffened for a moment and then rose to his feet. He was not tall enough to look down on Mike but, standing close beside him, the difference in bulk and strength was apparent. He shook his head and said, 'No, Mike. You've got it wrong. It was an accident. We were both pissed.'

'Don't give me that,' Mike spat with sufficient venom to make the bodybuilders look around at him.

'Have you spoken to Mary?' Shane asked.

Mike took a deep breath. Shane's relaxed attitude was getting to him. 'I didn't need to. I could see what you'd done, even though she tried to camouflage it.'

'But did she tell you how it happened?'

Mike was not going to cause Mary any further trouble with Shane by telling him what she had said. 'No, I told you I could see for myself.'

Shane nodded his head as though Mike had made a concession to him. 'Well there you are. She wouldn't say anything because she was embarrassed. Like I said, we were both pissed and, to tell you the truth, the sex got out of hand. That sister of yours is really something when she gets going, and likes to experiment. This time her crazy idea ended up with me falling right on top of her. I was too far gone and couldn't help it. Sorry you got the wrong idea, but you can see why she'd be shy about telling.'

Shane's sleazy smile infuriated Mike. 'Bullshit,' he shouted and pushed Shane away. 'I know what you did, and if you do it again I'll kill you.' This time it wasn't just the bodybuilders, but several other men who had come into the gallery, who turned to look at them.

'Don't get physical with me.'

The menace in Shane's voice went as quickly as it had come, and he laughed. 'Calm down, mate. I hear you fancy yourself as a street-fighter these days, but I wouldn't try it on in here. They take a dim view of any rough stuff.' He leant down to pick up his towel. 'Time to go. A run along the river back to my car and home. Mary's cooking something special tonight. She tells me Lissa gave her the recipe.'

Mike stood glowering at Shane. He shouldn't have lost his temper. He wouldn't get far with Shane that way. He had more confidence these days that he could handle any rough stuff, but it was not the sensible way to go, no matter how satisfying it might be to take the smile off Shane's face.

'Are you coming?' Shane asked but did not wait for an answer before walking towards the entrance. When he reached the counter, the attendant stared at him enquiringly. 'OK?'

Surely, Mike thought, he hadn't heard his outburst up here. Perhaps someone had alerted him. This place wouldn't run to closed-circuit TV.

'No problem,' Shane replied. 'Just a little family disagreement. All good now.' As if to offer proof he put his arm around Mike's shoulder and said, 'Come on, mate. I promise you we'll be more careful in future.'

Mike would have liked to break free from Shane, but his grip was strong. Still holding him firmly, Shane piloted Mike through the door on to Flinders Street. 'You and I should get on better,' he said affably. 'After all we're members of the same family. That's what your dad said on Friday.' When Mike attempted to shrug his arm away, he let go and added, 'From what I hear you've got a few people gunning for you. I'd worry about them rather than me.'

It came as a welcome relief to Mike when his phone sounded and he could turn away and lift it to his ear.

'Mike, it's Alan Reardon.'

'Oh, hi, Alan.'

'Can you speak up? There's a lot of noise at your end.'

Mike lifted his voice. 'Yeah. I'm in Flinders Street with a lot going past on the road and the footpath. It's hard to hear you as well. Is that better?'

'Still no good. Go somewhere quiet and give me a call as soon as you can.'

'OK. Talk to you soon.'

When Mike rang off, Shane, who had been carefully watching and listening to Mike asked, 'Everything OK?'

'Sure. Just a work matter. I must go.' He saw the lights begin to blink red and hurried across Flinders Street.

'Take care,' Shane called after him, still maintaining his pretence of brotherly concern. He turned to make his way towards Docklands unaware he was being watched by a tall man sitting at a table in the kerbside cafe next to the gym, a baseball cap pulled well down on his head. Although he was close enough to see and hear the two men, neither had realised he was observing them. Mike had never met him and Shane was too attentive to Mike to notice Rick, his mate in Ivan's gang, among the patrons of the cafe.

When Mike reached the car, he immediately called Alan Reardon.

'Mike Georgiou,' he said.

'That's better. We need to meet. There's something I want to show you.'

'What is it?'

'We need to meet somewhere we won't be seen. Do you know the Lord Nelson? Could you be there in say half an hour?'

Still angry with himself over the way he had mishandled Shane, Mike was in no mood for dealing with a secretive and anxious union official. 'The Lord Nelson?'

'Yeah. It's a pub in Nicholson Street, Fitzroy. We should be safe there.'

'Safe? Safe from what?'

'I'll explain when we meet.'

If Alan was going to be so mysterious, Mike was not going out of his way to accommodate him. 'I can't be there in half an hour. In fact the earliest I could make it would be eight o'clock.'

'I'll see you then.'

Mike arrived in Fitzroy early and had no difficulty finding the Lord Nelson. It was a quiet night, perhaps not unusual for this pub. The bistro was closed and the only movement in the bar came from a bank of TV screens filling the back wall and displaying current betting odds as well as the running of a horserace. Where would they be running at this time of night, Mike wondered. The bar room was U-shaped with the bar itself filling the void of the U. Along one arm sat or stood about a dozen nondescript individuals, their eyes on the TV screens. A small group of pensioners clustered together at the end of the bar, looking to Mike as though the Fitzroy Youth Club from Peter Temple's *Jack Irish* novels had abandoned the Prince of Prussia and come to the Lord Nelson instead. It was hard to imagine Alan Reardon was a regular here, unless he was an addict of the TAB and this was the nearest one to where he lived. Mike knew almost nothing about him.

He bought himself a beer and took a seat at a table in the empty arm of the room. Earlier he had done his duty and sat through the torture of six young girls blowing on their recorders. He hated the recorder as a musical instrument and agreed with the comedian he remembered describing it as an ill wind that nobody blew good. The girls were in tune with this description, if nothing else, although their teacher expressed satisfaction and the parents affected delight in their performance, adding to his pain. He found it difficult to hide his feelings from his family and envied Lissa's ability to appear genuinely thrilled with the poorly coordinated squawks they heard from their daughter. Lissa had been less thrilled when he told her he had seen Shane.

'You must leave Mary to sort things out, not go barging in making even more trouble for her,' she hissed at him.

'But you saw her on Sunday. It's got to stop.'

'You're right there, and I told Mary that on Sunday.'

'You talked about it with Mary on Sunday?' he asked, unable to keep the surprise from his voice.

'Mary and I are good friends; haven't you noticed? That's what good friends do — they talk with one another. They don't just talk past each other like some people do. Shush. They're about to start the concert.'

He had long admired Lissa's ability to toss such barbs at him and get away before he could think of a reply.

Just after eight Alan Reardon entered the bar, nodded to Mike and said, 'G'day. Is that a heavy?'

'No, a light. I'm driving.'

'I take cabs these days. A bit safer, I reckon.' He went to the bar and returned with two glasses, sat opposite Mike and said, 'You weren't followed here?'

Mike shook his head impatiently. 'For God's sake stop this cloak and dagger stuff. You love to keep everything to yourself, but it's time you started telling me what's going on. Why come to this out of the way pub? What are you doing at Riverside? What is it you're going to show me?'

'OK, OK. But, before I begin, I want your word you will tell no one of our meeting and keep strictly to yourself what I'm about to tell you.'

'That's a bit steep when I don't know why I'm here and what you're going to tell me.'

'I can't risk it getting out. If that's your attitude we may as well go our separate ways. Sorry.'

Partly swayed by Alan's intensity, partly out of a desire not to have wasted his own time and partly from curiosity, Mike weakened. He waved a hand as if dismissing Alan's ultimatum. 'OK, OK, you have my word. Can we get on with it?'

'Thank you. All this started when George asked me to look into Riverside. We'd heard whispers the firm was putting off some of our members without their full entitlements and were cutting corners on a bunch of work practices. What I found was a rash of attempts to short-change some of our members. There aren't many sites that don't try these dodges when cash flow is a problem. It was the intimidation I found unusual.'

'Riverside has a cash flow problem?'

'There's a guy called Ivan Sarac who has come into the company and doesn't mind bending the rules if he can get away with it. As soon as I started making a pest of myself, and began calling up their employee and pay records, he tried to put pressure on me.'

'How did he do that?'

'He has a few heavies he uses to threaten people. That's why I take a lot of care over my safety – what you call "cloak and dagger". I persisted and the problems are pretty much sorted out, at least for now – the problems for our men at Riverside, that is. From being around the site I began to build up a picture of what was going on. For a start, the sales of the units in the latest tower at Riverside are going badly and Rubicon has slowed down construction while they revamp the design to go for the middle rather than the top end of the market. This is where the cash flow problems come from and it's where you come in.

It puts them in direct competition with CityView and explains why they would try to disrupt you.'

Mike nodded. So Vern had been right about the threat to CityView from Riverside and he had been right about the problems on the site coming from the Rubicon people.

'Sarac is just the man for the job,' Reardon continued. 'I bet it was one of his heavies who was leaning on Ted Horton and making a nuisance of himself at your site.'

Mike gave a frustrated sigh. 'I'd pretty much worked that out for myself, and we've seen off Ted and his mate. Why get so excited that you have to drag me up here and swear me to secrecy?'

'OK, I was just getting to that,' Alan replied defensively. 'Yesterday I took some shots you might like to see.' He took a set of photographs from his pocket and placed them, one by one on the table, like a dealer at a card game. In the first one the thug, Bruno, looked up at Mike. The picture was slightly fuzzy, as if shot from a distance with a telephoto lens, but Bruno was unmistakable, as was Shane, standing beside him to tend a barbecue. The second was a wider shot, which covered a group, consisting of Bruno, Shane, a taller man with a baseball cap and a fourth man whose arms were raised as if he were addressing the others. 'Do you know any of these guys?' Alan asked.

'The one on the left is Bruno, the hood who gave us trouble at CityView. I don't know his surname, but the blond guy next to him is Shane Francis.' Mike noticed Alan glance quickly across at him. 'He lives with my sister. I don't know the other two.'

'With your sister? You must have some interesting chats, swapping notes on the doings at Riverside and CityView. I wonder if Sarac knows you and Shane are members of the same family.'

'Hardly that. I just spent some time this afternoon telling Shane to lay off my sister. When he gets drunk he beats her up.'

'Yeah, that sounds like Shane. He still works on Riverside as Sarac's man on the spot and obviously has some extra off-site duties like cooking the steaks. He's not as scary as the man you call Bruno but not far behind. By the way, Bruno's surname is Kordic. The one doing the talking is Ivan Sarac, the guy I mentioned earlier, and the one with the cap is the third of Sarac's heavies. His name is Rick Jennings.' He paused and Mike had the feeling Alan was about to play his trump card. Down on to the table went a group sitting at a table, eating. There were six of them: the four from the previous shot, Angelo Rossi and Vern McKenzie.

Mike felt a surge of annoyance, partly with Alan for the theatricality with which he presented his revelation, but more with Vern for associating with these people. 'They're at his house at Flinders, aren't they?' he said.

'How do you know he has a place at Flinders?'

'More interesting, who tipped you off they were going to be there?' Mike replied.

'But what about our friend Mr McKenzie? What was he doing there?'

Mike wondered how long they could go on batting unanswered questions at one another. 'I'll have to ask him.'

'Don't do that.' Reardon's tone had lost all its lightness and his words came down hard, demanding obedience.

'Why not?'

'I don't want him to know he's been seen, you dickhead,' Reardon scoffed. 'And remember your promise to me.'

'I understand. You can trust me.'

'Can I? I hope so. There are very few I do trust. You have no idea why he would be there?'

'Not a clue,' Mike lied. He had been doing quite a bit of that lately. Perhaps Reardon shouldn't trust him. Already it seemed he had divided loyalties in various directions: Alan Reardon, Vern McKenzie and Ben Findlay as well.

'How do you get on with McKenzie?'

'I owe a lot to Vern and he's been Jim Findlay's loyal offsider for years,' Mike replied quickly and then hesitated, his tongue flicking his lips. 'Only recently I've realised how bitter he is about Jim bringing his son into the firm.' Mike felt the pain of his admission, an admission he had trouble making to himself and now to a man he hardly knew. 'Ben Findlay is a bit of a liability and hard to take – the other day I had a major run-in with him, myself.' Mike could hear himself desperately trying to find some form of vindication for Vern. 'I still can't see Vern ever doing anything to harm the firm.' It was true. Mike hadn't liked the plan Vern put to him last week, but he said it was the way to save Findlay's. 'So what do we do now?'

'I'll continue digging. There's something brewing, which goes far beyond some shifty practices on the Riverside site. I need to discover more and you need to keep your eye on McKenzie – find out why he's meeting with Rossi and Sarac.' Alan downed the remnant of his drink. 'I'll call a cab. Where's your car?'

'It's just up the side street a bit.'

'I'd stay clear of the side streets if I were you. Bruno Kordic is a nasty type and it wouldn't surprise me if he was looking to pay you back. Sure you don't want to share my cab?'

'I'll be fine.'

Alan called a cab from his mobile and Mike continued to mull over what Alan had told him. 'Have you told George Fowler what you're doing?'

'I prefer to keep this to myself at present. Safer that way.'

'But you've told me?'

'Yeah, I have. I need to get a better fix on McKenzie.'

They sat looking at one another awkwardly until Mike asked

him about his time in the west. 'Had a few problems,' he said guardedly. 'But I've put all that behind me now. I'll just go and stand where I can see the street. I don't want the cab to nick off if I don't appear immediately.'

Alan rose from his seat and patted Mike gently on the arm. 'Take care.'

Mindful of Alan's warning, a warning which echoed the one from Shane, Mike scanned the street carefully from the doorway of the pub and found it deserted. Almost to his car, he passed into the darkness under one of the spreading trees that lined the street when a figure stepped from behind the tree and he found himself facing a snarling Bruno. 'I said you'd keep, you bastard.'

Mike tried to duck past him, but Kordic shot out a hand and grasped his jacket. Mike pushed at him but could not get free and Bruno brought his other arm up to take him in a bear hug. Slowly the pain built as the thug squeezed the air out of him, until it reached a crescendo and Kordic swung him off his feet into the side fence of a cobbled lane running off the street. Darkness enveloped him as his head hit the edge of a fence post, splitting his eyebrow. He felt the ground rushing to meet him. He stretched out his hands to cushion his fall but they got caught in the gaps between the bluestone pitchers, bending his fingers so that he scraped his knuckles and added to his pain.

Winded and only partly conscious he heard Bruno's footsteps coming towards him. It was a repeat of last Tuesday night, but this time there was no crowbar to save him from a kicking. He drew in his body against the boot which was about to strike him, but the pain of the first kick to his side was intense. Kordic had drawn back his leg for a second time when Mike heard the sound of a police siren coming towards them. The kick he expected did not come. Instead, a voice he did not recognise hissed, 'Come on. The cops are on to us.' Mike opened his eyes and felt the sting

144

of blood flowing from his eyebrow. At the head of the lane a man in a baseball cap stood with his arms outstretched and his hands upturned in a pleading gesture. Was this Rick Jennings, the other man in the photograph? Kordic turned and began to run from the alley, but the police car flew past the end of the street, taking with it Mike's despairing hopes. Mike saw Kordic stop and walk back towards him.

'You don't want to kill him,' Jennings said anxiously.

'Fuck off. He's had this comin' to him.'

'Come on. Remember what the boss said. We're late already.'

Bruno grunted and took another pace towards Mike who rolled over in a desperate attempt to give himself some protection. Instead of the pain of a boot thudding into him, he felt the pressure of Kordic's foot bearing down on his side, followed by the unlikely sound of a zip being released. He felt a warm stream flowing on to his head and down his face. The salty taste and smell of urine came to him as he squirmed under the flow but was too weak to break free. The stream moved down his shirt and on to his pants before coming back up to his face and stopping.

'That'll 'ave t'do,' Bruno said. He took his foot from Mike's side and zipped himself up before walking back down the lane to join the other man.

Cautiously Mike raised himself to a sitting position and ducked his head between his knees as a wave of nausea broke over him. He remained in this position until the discomfort from the cobbles pressing into his backside suggested he might now manage to stand. Uncertainly he achieved this and walked slowly to his car, unlocked the door and edged painfully into the driving seat where he sat staring blankly at the dark road running down to the lights of Nicholson Street. There was no trace of Bruno or his accomplice. The only signs of life were some intermittent cars on the main street and a tram thundering along its track. What should he do now? Should he drive himself to casualty and get himself checked out? In the state he was in, they would think he was some kind of derelict. He'd been shamed enough for one night. Should he go to the police? What could they do? Best to drive home and clean himself up. But he wasn't in a state to drive yet. Mike snuggled back into the seat and dropped into a fragmentary half sleep.

Later he stirred enough to glance at his watch – 9.30. Probably he could make it home now.

10

The shrill insistence of his phone woke Mike from a troubled sleep. 'Yeah,' he said groggily.

'Mike, it's Mary.'

'Yeah,' he repeated, more awake now and conscious of a dull ache in his head.

'Shane hasn't come home.'

Mike glanced at the clock radio beside the bed. It was showing 5.46.

'Who is it?' Lissa asked sleepily.

He put his hand on her shoulder to silence her. 'When did you last see him?' he asked.

'Did you call him last night?'

'No.'

'But you saw him yesterday afternoon at the gym,' Mary insisted.

'What's going on?' Lissa asked.

'Just a tick,' he said to Mary and took the phone from his ear. 'It's Mary. Shane went out last night and hasn't come home.'

He returned to the phone.

'Maybe he's had a night out with his mates and is sleeping it off somewhere. I wouldn't get too worried just yet.'

'Shane said you came into the gym yesterday and made a silly fuss. He made a joke of it, but I could tell he was really pissed off with you and I didn't blame him. What did you say to him?'

'Only the usual about not hurting you. You can't go on like

this, Mary. Lissa told you the same.' He felt Lissa squirm in the bed beside him.

'I'll do what I damn well want without your interference,' Mary snapped back. 'Are you sure you didn't call him?'

'Of course I'm sure. Why do you keep asking?'

'Somebody did and Shane got really annoyed. He said something like, "I've told you already, you've got it all wrong." After he hung up he told me he had to go and sort something out. He didn't say what it was but, when he was leaving, he said to me, "That brother of yours is a pest." Mike, I'm worried. Did you meet him again last night?'

Mike thought of the beating Bruno had given him. Was Shane supposed to be there as well, or was it Shane the two of them were going to meet?

'No, I was being mugged by one of his mates.' Anger welled up inside him. 'Did Shane organise that?'

'Are you OK? What happened?'

Already ashamed of sounding off, Mike said, 'I'm OK. You shouldn't worry too much about Shane.'

'Do you think he might have been hurt? I should check the hospitals.'

'You could do that, but see if he turns up at work first. I'll call you later.'

As he put down the phone, Lissa exploded. 'Don't use me to prop up your arguments with Mary. You never learn. I shouldn't have said a word to you about her. I know you've had a bang on the head, but really!'

'Sorry.'

'Don't sorry me. What's the story with Shane?' After Mike had told her what Mary had said, toning down her complaints about his interference, Lissa exploded again. 'You didn't tell me you'd been to see Shane.'

148

'There wasn't time. We were at the concert, then a quick meal with the kids and I was off again.'

'How's your head?' Lissa leaned over him. 'The cut on your eye doesn't seem too bad, although there's some nice colour in the bruise on your forehead.'

He sank back on to his pillow and tentatively fingered the swelling near his eyebrow with its thin scab of dried blood. 'Yeah, not too bad. If I take my time this morning I'll be fine.'

'You should go to the police. You know who did this to you and you know why. You shouldn't let him get away a second time.'

Mike started to shake his head but stopped quickly when it began to throb. 'No. I have no proof, no witnesses, and you can bet his mate will give him an alibi.'

'At least you should take the day off and have yourself checked by the doctor.'

'No, I'll be right. Just take it slowly.'

Lissa shrugged. 'Suit yourself. I'm wide awake now so I may as well get up.'

When she had gone for her shower Mike lay back and took stock. Apart from his head, he had escaped relatively unharmed. He was stiff from his fall, there were the bruises and he had taken some skin off his knuckles when trying to save himself, but the real damage was to his pride. Now he could see that he'd allowed his lucky hit on Bruno and the way it was received by the men at the site to delude him into thinking he had what it took to be a street-fighter. The truth was he was bloody lucky to have got off so lightly last night. How did they know he would be at the Lord Nelson? Had he been followed like Alan had feared? Where was Shane in all this?

All these questions made his head hurt again, but what hurt most of all was the memory of Kordic pissing on him. The shame of it pierced him. No one must know of that. As soon as he got home he had stripped off and, despite his thumping head and other aches, insisted on immediately washing all his clothes. Lissa had been worried about him and bemused by what she saw as his strange priorities, but he ignored her and for once she didn't pester him to explain. Shane had warned him to watch out for Kordic – not in so many words but his meaning was clear. They all had told him to go carefully – Bob Kennedy, Alan Reardon and finally Shane – but he paid no attention. Where was Shane now?

Suddenly another possibility suggested itself. He'd assumed the secretive Alan Reardon had wanted to alert him to what Alan saw as Vern's treachery so that Mike could keep an eye on Vern for him. But what if his real aim was to lure him to the pub for Bruno to deal with him? Vern had suggested Alan might be in league with Bruno. Was he shown the photograph of Vern to drive a wedge between the two of them? And was it treachery that had taken Vern to Flinders or had he been invited there by Angelo to discuss the takeover Vern had predicted might save the firm? Despite Alan's refusal to say, they surely were at Rossi's place at Flinders. Mike's head continued to throb.

He walked slowly into the bathroom. The shower made a big difference – he was almost human again. He needed to be. Today he was having lunch with Carla. He had almost forgotten her. He wiped the mist from the bathroom mirror and examined his face. It was a shame he wouldn't be looking his best when they met. He wondered whether he could camouflage the bruise somehow but decided against it. She would have to take him as she found him.

When he walked into the kitchen, Lissa greeted him with mock astonishment. 'My, you are dressed up – your best shirt and that tie I gave you for Christmas. Are you going for a job interview you haven't told me about?'

'Just a lunch I have to attend.'

He paused, but when he could see Lissa was about to ask for more detail, he added, 'An industry lunch where I'm representing the company. It'll be boring, but I need to look my best.'

Lissa raised an eyebrow and said, 'That shiner won't help your image.'

'Have you been in another fight?' Christos asked with an unaccustomed note of awe in his voice.

Mike turned to see his children at the breakfast table – three sets of curious eyes. 'No, just a silly accident. I should have been more careful. That was a great concert yesterday, Jac.'

—

Vern McKenzie knew it was time to act. He had checked the computer for the latest statement of the credit card issued to Mike and confirmed the two debits were recorded. Taking the printout with him he hovered at Ben's door until the MD looked up and saw him.

'I hear some guys from the commission are coming to see you,' Vern said.

'Yeah. The man who rang said they were investigators but wouldn't say what they wanted. It can't be a follow-up to the accident last week, can it? That's WorkSafe.'

'I think it might have something to do with this.' Vern walked to Ben's desk and put the sheets in front of him.

'What the hell are these?'

'They show two debits on the credit card issued to Mike Georgiou. Five hundred dollars each, for which there is no supporting paperwork. Last week I suggested he needed to get closer to the new assistant secretary at the union who, rumour has it, is not above putting the hard word on an employer. It looks like Mike walked straight in – the bloody fool.'

Ben jumped up, his face livid. 'That dunce has dropped us in it again! He must go.'

'Whoa, Ben.'

Vern shook his head and spoke in a slow, calming voice. 'Let's not get ahead of ourselves. We don't yet know why the commission guys are coming. I thought I should warn you, just in case. If my fears are justified we should be surprised when these debits show up. If we tell the commission straight off they might think we put Mike up to it and are trying to get out from under.'

Ben sat down again. 'I'm still going to suspend him. I don't want him here for a moment longer.'

'At least wait until the commission men have come and gone.'

'Yeah, OK.'

'Who will you replace him with? It's not as if we've got a reserve list of project managers waiting to take over.'

Ben sat back in his chair and looked up at him with that supercilious smile Vern so detested. 'While we think about that, I'll do the job myself. To tide us over. We need to tighten up at the CityView site.'

'But what about here?'

'You can cover for me. You did last week. You can do it for a bit longer. But, remember, keep me informed of everything that goes on and leave me to deal with Jim. I don't want him bothered, so leave him alone and come to me for anything you need or are worried about.'

—

Late in the morning Mike received a call from Ben Findlay's PA, Janine, delivering a summons to head office. She did not say why and, when he asked, was unconvincing in her claim not to know. As he came up the stairs he saw Freda, who gave him the kind of sympathetic smile he thought she might reserve for the condemned. Had Ben decided to follow through on his threat to replace him, even though the CityView project was again humming along? Janine was less friendly.

'You're to go straight in,' she said sternly.

There were three men sitting at the glass-topped circular table Ben had installed in Jim's office when he moved in. Each of them looked up at him as he entered, but all remained sitting, the two strangers with impassive faces, Ben ruddier and more awkward than Mike was used to seeing him.

'Sit here,' Ben said, indicating the vacant chair next to him. 'These gentlemen are from the commission. They are investigating a report that you have attempted to bribe a union official. Is there anything you wish to say?' He sounded like a judge delivering sentence.

'What?'

'This is a very serious charge.'

'I'm gobsmacked. Where did this come from?'

'I urge you to cooperate fully with the enquiry and be totally frank as to your actions and motives.' Ben seemed already convinced of his guilt. 'I have assured these gentlemen that such activity is totally contrary to company policy and procedures and that we, ourselves, would deal harshly with any member of staff found to have engaged in such behaviour.'

Ben turned to the two men, who had still to be introduced, and gave his attempt at an ingratiating smile. 'Janine will show you to the room where you can interview Mr Georgiou.'

'Thank you,' the elder of the two men said and stood up. He had the no-nonsense bearing and slightly crumpled appearance of an ex-copper who had interviewed suspects a million times before. His colleague, more like a young lawyer or accountant who had not made it at one of the major practices, nodded as if he felt the need to show solidarity with his boss and also rose to his feet, followed by Mike and finally Ben.

'Janine,' Ben called. 'Take these gentlemen to the conference room.' He turned to usher them to the door. 'Would you like coffee?' he asked.

'No, thank you.'

The room to which Janine led them was the same one in which Mike and Vern had met with the union people last week. The commission men sat on one side of the table and indicated that Mike should sit opposite them.

'As you heard, we are Building Commission investigators,' the elder man said and pushed a business card across the table. His colleague took a similar card from his pocket and slid that towards Mike. Now he knew the senior man was Clive Johnston and his offsider was Brett Funston. Funston took a pad from his briefcase and began to write on it.

'The commission has received a report that you have been engaged in attempting to bribe a union official. This is a preliminary interview as part of our investigation of this matter. You are free to leave at any time you wish, but we would be obliged if you would agree to answer a few questions and make available to us some material we would like to review.'

'Of course. You heard what I said in the MD's office.'

He stopped as the words Ben had used in his office, now repeated by Johnston, suddenly resonated in his head, ' ... *attempting* to bribe a union official.' Was the whistleblower who dobbed him in to the commission the union official he was alleged to have attempted to bribe? Was this Alan Reardon? He felt his head begin to throb again.

'This has come as a shock to me.'

'Has it?' Johnston said with a light in his eye that Mike did not like.

'Who am I supposed to have tried to bribe?'

'I thought you might tell us that.'

'I can't think. I haven't had much union contact. The union

delegate on the site has only just arrived. The previous one moved to another site.'

'Mr Georgiou,' Johnston said with a bored intake of breath. 'Unless we obtain an admission, this investigation is likely to drag on and none of us, you particularly I would say, really want that. It will go much better for you if you are able to give us any information that might assist us in bringing our investigation to a swift conclusion. You understand me?'

'I do. I wish I could help.'

'There are no other union officials with whom you have been dealing?' The question came from Funston, who had a precise and rather high-pitched voice.

'Union negotiations are usually led by one of our directors, Vern McKenzie. I sat in this room last Wednesday with Vern, the state secretary of the union, his deputy and the man who was the union delegate to our site at that time.'

'What was discussed at the meeting?' Johnston had taken over again.

'If it is in any way relevant to your enquiries, I think it best you ask Mr McKenzie.' Mike noted the quick glance his words brought from his inquisitors.

'And you're sure that is the extent of your recent contact with union officials?'

'I have had a couple of conversations with the deputy secretary, Alan Reardon.'

Mike could see Johnston's interest quicken. 'And what did you discuss?'

Conscious of the promise Alan had insisted on extracting from him, Mike tried to bluff his way through. 'We had an industrial accident on site last Monday involving a damaged sling from a crane. He wanted to know what progress WorkSafe had made in their investigation.'

'Are you sure that was all you discussed?'

Mike nodded without speaking. Johnston sat back, his face a portrait of disbelief, and his colleague took over again. 'We would like to examine your phone logs – your mobile, office and home phones – e-mails and any accounts you operate for the company.'

'You're welcome to all of these. While I initiate orders for the company and authorise payments, I do not operate any accounts.'

'Thank you. That will be all for now. We will want to speak again,' Johnston said and rose to his feet.

As Mike stood uncertainly watching the investigators return to Ben's office he saw Freda Bradshaw waving to him.

'Michael,' she called. 'Michael, Vern would like a word.'

Mike was hardly inside the door of Vern's office when he came from behind his desk like a charging bull.

'What the hell have you been up to?' he shouted. Mike was conscious of Freda closing the door behind him as though cutting off his escape. 'When I suggested you try to get close to Reardon, I didn't mean you should bribe him. I told you to be careful. I also told you he was likely trying it on with Rubicon for a kickback to keep him quiet. When the bastard put the hard word on you, why did you agree, you stupid fool?'

'You've got it all wrong. I haven't paid him anything.'

Vern turned back to take some sheets from his desk. 'So how do you explain these?' He waved the sheets in Mike's face.

'What are they?' Mike asked, taking a step back to avoid the sheets flicking him.

'These are your credit card records that I called up when I heard the commission guys were calling – your credit card Ben insisted I make available to you as project manager. You've almost never used it until last week. The two debits for five hundred dollars each, what were they for? You haven't put in any paperwork.'

Mike gaped at him.

'Think carefully what you say. Those guys from the commission will soon be asking you the same question.'

'Vern, this is a stitch up. Someone is stitching me up.'

'Why should anyone do that?'

All the jumbled thoughts about Vern and Alan that had entered Mike's mind in the past few days swirled together blocking him from replying. Vern scoffed. 'You've played right into Ben's hands, given him a great opportunity to get rid of you. Now, I suppose, you'll want me to find a way out for you. You certainly aren't capable of looking after yourself.'

He turned away from Mike as if dismissing him. 'I can't keep this from the commission guys, and finding an alternative explanation is going to take some doing.'

There was a soft tap on the door and Freda put her head into the room. 'The managing director wishes to speak with Michael,' she said.

'A moment,' Vern replied and she closed the door behind her. 'I won't be able to save you from Ben straight off. I'm sure he'll use this as his excuse to boot you out. But, trust me, I reckon I'll be able to fix it so you get back, if not soon, then eventually. Go now and, remember, not a word to anyone about what I've just said, and I mean anyone.'

Another demand to remain silent.

As Mike walked past Freda she whispered, 'You're looking very smart today, Michael.'

He nodded and touched his eyebrow. Perhaps the damage to his face wasn't that obvious. Usually Freda didn't miss a thing.

Ben was standing by his glass table when Mike entered his office. 'I'll make this brief,' he said. 'This latest escapade of yours leaves me with no choice.'

'I've done nothing wrong,' Mike interjected.

It was as though he had not spoken. 'You will continue to make yourself available to the investigators from the commission, but otherwise you are to stand down and not appear at CityView or any other Findlay site. I will take over your role forthwith. You are suspended.'

The embarrassment Ben had shown when the men from the commission were present had gone and the disdainful smile was back in full width. He was enjoying this.

'You still think I ran you down last week.'

'Did you?'

'Of course not.'

'I see you've been in another fight. Who was the victim this time?'

'You can't do this.'

'I just have. Now get out.'

—

Vern sat at his desk with his chair swivelled to allow him the view of rooftops he sometimes called on for solace or inspiration. Today, though, he was guardedly content. As he sat contemplating the events of the morning, he told himself things were working out very nicely. No, that was too comfortable a thought. It was more like he had been dealt good cards and taken some early tricks but needed to be vigilant and skilful in the way he played the remainder of his hand. With this in mind Vern called George Fowler.

'G'day, George, it's Vern here. How are you?'

'You don't make social calls, Vern. What is it?'

'I gather the young fools, Alan Reardon and Mike Georgiou, have some explaining to do to the commission.'

'How do you know that, Vern?'

'Two of their investigators have just been to have a preliminary chat with Mike. Someone has told them he bribed a union official.'

'We'll have to see what they say. There are two commission investigators due to arrive here in about half an hour. They didn't say what they wanted but asked me to make sure Reardon would be available. I s'pose it's the same ones who've been to you.'

'Perhaps we need to compare notes afterwards, George. I also think it's time you and I had a quiet chat about another matter.'

'You want a favour?'

'You owe me one.'

'Another one? Yeah, I s'pose I do,' George conceded.

'Usual place, tonight about seven. OK?'

'I'll see you then, Vern. You can tell me what's really going on at Findlay's.'

''Bye.'

Vern put down his phone and sat back in his chair. It was good that he could now give Sarac news of the strife he had created for Mike and for Reardon. Ivan hadn't called him yet – he'd had a day or two to set up the meeting

It wasn't until later in the day that Vern had the call he was awaiting.

'Sarac here,' Ivan said in a voice that lacked its previous smarmy warmth. Obviously he was not happy with the way things had turned out last Sunday. Good.

'I said Georgiou shouldn't be harmed.'

'Just a touch up. Couldn't have been Bruno. How are you going with Georgiou and Reardon?

'The commission investigators were here this morning to interview Mike and he has been stood down by my MD. They are about to visit the BCU head office'

'Good.' There was a silence before Ivan added, 'Next Sunday at Flinders. Lunch again.'

'Your boss will be present for sure?'

'We're not going down to enjoy the view.'

'I'll be there.'

Vern rung off without any form of farewell. Hopefully he would play better golf this Saturday than he had before his first visit to Flinders. Paul Jones would be after his money again, but the stakes on Sunday would be much higher.

———

It was one of those days on which early fog had cleared to a fine day and when Mike sat in his car outside head office the heat was oppressive. He wound down the window but there was no breeze to cool him. He did not start the engine but sat thinking about the meetings he had just been through. Only then did it occur to him to wonder how Vern had known Alan Reardon was involved. The commission people had been careful not to tell him which union official he was supposed to have attempted to bribe. Did Vern know because he had set the whole thing up? Surely it would need inside information to access his credit card, although he hadn't been very secure with it, leaving it in his desk drawer. He wouldn't be able to check whether it was still there – Ben had made it clear the CityView site was off limits and one of the first things Ben would have done was to make sure his suspension was well known. He needed to check whether Alan had been contacted by the commission. How should he play it with Alan, though? Mike took out his phone and placed the call.

'Hi, Alan. Mike Georgiou here.'

'G'day, Mike. How's it going?'

Was it his imagination or did Alan sound cautious?

'Been a bit busy since we parted last night. First of all, I was beaten up by Bruno on my way back to the car.'

'Shit!' If Alan was faking surprise he was good at it. 'I'm sorry. Were you badly hurt?'

'I got off better than I feared when he started on me. A passing police car and his mate telling him they were late getting to somewhere else they had to be saved me.' Mike thought again of the urine spray and cringed. 'What I wonder is how did he know I'd be there?'

'Perhaps they were following you. I did warn you. You hadn't seen any sign of him or one of the others earlier in the day?'

'Or perhaps they were tipped off.'

'You're not suggesting …'

'I've just been interviewed by two investigators from the commission who say I've been accused of attempting to bribe a union official.'

'You? I thought … I didn't think they'd involve you.'

'You knew about this?'

'I was expecting something like it, but not involving you.'

'There's a lot you need to explain.' Mike glanced at his watch. 'God, I've got to go. I'll call you after lunch.' He cut the call and started his engine. He had only fifteen minutes to make it to his lunch with Carla. He'd lost track of the time.

11

Mike parked under the casino and went up the escalator to find himself midway along the corridor he had walked with Lissa and his father last Friday. It was here the surroundings became more opulent, where his bad mood had begun to lift, and his father's confidence had begun to fade, just as Mike's did now. With his cut eyebrow and shiner he looked like the uncouth chippie he really was. His best suit and fashionable tie made him a joke.

Entering the restaurant he was again captured by the music: this time a superbly voiced trumpet solo. He did not recognise the player or the tune, and would very much like to know who and what they were.

'Mr. Georgiou?' Mike was surprised to hear the waiter ask. 'This way, please.'

He led Mike across the restaurant, where a number of couples and two larger groups were already at lunch, and brought him to the door through which Mancini and his party had disappeared last Friday. He opened the door with a flourish and gestured for Mike to mount the short stairway.

Carla stood waiting for him at the head of the stairs. She wore a white silk dress with a white jacket embossed with small pink and gold flowers. The mandarin collar of the jacket framed a pearl necklace that matched her pearl earrings. She looked cool and elegant; Mike felt sweaty and awkward.

'Michael,' she said with a restrained but welcoming smile. 'I'm so pleased you were able to join me at such short notice.' She held out her right hand and, when he took it, brought her other hand to enclose his in a form of embrace. 'You've been hurt,' she exclaimed, releasing his hand and examining his face with concern.

'Careless of me. I should know by now how dangerous a building site can be.' He tried for a reassuring smile. 'Fortunately no great damage done. It looks worse than it is.' He hoped this wasn't really true.

'Come and sit,' Carla said, indicating a square wooden table set with two places. She made it sound like he needed to be nursed. 'I hope you don't mind being cloistered in here with me. When I sit in the main room, too often I find others intruding on me and my guests. I don't run the restaurant on a day-to-day basis, too busy for that, and Guido does a superb job for me, but a lot of people still want to speak with me if they see me sitting out there.'

He glanced around the room. Platters of food and a bottle of wine in a cooler sat on the top of a dresser, which ran down one side of the room. At the end two other tables, matching the one at which they were sitting, had been pushed against the wall. There were no windows but the soft lighting, the deceptively simple abstract paintings and the roses in a tall, silver vase echoed the elegance of the main restaurant. One thing was missing. 'I do like the music you play downstairs.'

'You do?' Carla mixed surprise and delight in the two words. She rose from the table with the effortless grace that had entranced him last Friday and walked to the dresser. She opened one of the drawers to reveal a console, and after a moment the trumpeter he had heard came to join them. The quality of the reproduction and the acoustic of the room were even better than below.

'Who is he?'

'You enjoy jazz?

'Miles Davis is my favourite trumpeter. That's the era I prefer, but this is great,' Mike said.

164

'Kit Ronson. You probably won't have heard of him. Much of the music he plays is his own. Not all of his work is as good as this – he's just getting started, but I think he will eventually outdo James Morrison. I'm trying to promote him.'

'He's local?'

'Oh yes. I'll let you know when he's next performing at the Paris. You go to the Paris Cat?'

'Not lately,' Mike confessed. 'Jazz clubs don't fit in well with family life – at least not mine.'

Carla nodded understandingly. 'You have children?'

'Yes, a boy and two girls.'

'Ah, fortunate for you. I'm afraid I've left it to my sisters to provide my father with the grandchildren he so dotes on. Still, as you heard the other night, I'm looking after some of the business side for him.' She pulled a wry face. 'Here we are chatting away and I haven't offered you a drink. I hope you like white wine. I prefer it at lunch and I have to confess I want to try out a particular wine on you.' She brought the bottle in its cooler to the table and poured a glass for each of them.

'I'm no wine connoisseur.'

'All the better. They can be so stuffy and hidebound. The commercial reality is that it's what appeals to the public that matters, not what the connoisseurs say. She sipped her wine and looked over her glass at him. 'What do you think?'

Mike did his best to appear experienced as he took a sip and swirled it around his mouth before swallowing. 'Very good. But remember what I said.'

'It's from a start-up winery, which I've recently bought into in the Yarra Valley – Casablanca. The vigneron is Chilean and is adapting his traditional methods for Australian conditions. I think it shows great promise.'

Mike began to wonder when Carla would speak about their

fathers. It was supposed to be the reason for having lunch together. Not that he minded. She was every bit as charming as she looked and they seemed to be getting on really well. This enclosed room with Carla was a haven from the real world with all its problems and uncertainties. Why would he want to hurry back?

As if reading his mind Carla said, 'I must not delay you.' He was about to disagree but thought of the complicated explanation he must give if he went down that path, so merely shook his head politely. 'Come, I have arranged for a simple lunch: some antipasto.'

One of the platters on the dresser contained a variety of meats – ham, pepperoni, prosciutto and roast beef. Another had mushrooms, artichoke hearts, roasted red capsicums and pickled chilli peppers, while a third held taleggio, mozzarella and gorgonzola cheese with olives and stuffed pimento. After Mike had served himself, Carla would not let him return to the table. 'That's not a proper meal for a builder. Please take more and don't forget the herb bread. We pride ourselves on that.'

When they were again settled at the table, Carla smiled and said, 'I expect you find it strange that, having done no more than nod to you the first time we met, I should invite you to lunch with me in our private room.'

'The invitation did surprise me, but I can understand, with your involvement in Rubicon, you might not want to be seen lunching with a project manager from Findlay's.'

Carla looked away from him. 'I'm not involved with Rubicon.'

While Mike was surprised by what she said, he was even more surprised by the intensity of the regret in her voice.

'But the article in the *New Idea* with the shots of you and your husband in your Flinders house made a lot of the two of you working together.'

The sadness on Carla's face was lightened by an impish smile.

166

'Michael, I wouldn't have guessed you would be a reader of *New Idea*.' Lissa would have made the same joke but with an edge to it.

'Oh, I have to keep up with *New Idea*. How else can I stay in touch with the latest news on Kate and Will?'

The smile disappeared and she sighed. 'That article must have appeared over six months ago – in much happier times.'

Unsure how to respond, Mike said, 'You have a great house at Flinders.'

Carla nodded. 'Yes, that was one of my projects. I found the site and chose the architect. He did a great job. Perhaps one weekend you might like to stay with us, although Angelo often uses it these days to entertain his business associates – all male affairs, to which I'm not invited. He's got another session there next Sunday. I haven't been there for weeks, and heaven knows when I could invite you. I'm sorry.'

Mike was even more at a loss as to what he should say. He would have liked to take Carla by the hand and comfort her, but … 'No need to be sorry,' he tried in a sympathetic tone.

It was Carla who reached over to squeeze his hand. 'Thank you.' She took her hand away and lifted it to touch her face. 'I didn't invite you here to burden you with my troubles, but it is so good to talk.' She gave another deep sigh. 'I had such high hopes for the Riverside project. Angelo is a capable and experienced builder, but he lacked the ambition and the support he needed to make Rubicon a great company. I saw the potential of the site and convinced Angelo we could use it to lift Rubicon to the highest rung of developers. I knew my father had the contacts and the experience to secure the funding and help smooth our way with government and the bureaucracy.'

She looked around as though reappraising the room.

'This is where we entertained prospective investors and put our case to them. In fact it's where we met with anyone we needed to influence. Angelo had nothing appropriate at Rubicon. He still doesn't and continues to use this room.

'Working together as closely as the three of us did, there was always going to be a problem. My father has such a strong personality he finds it almost impossible to be involved in anything without starting to dominate. You would have seen that last Friday. I've learned to cope with him over the years. Before my involvement, Angelo had run Rubicon entirely on his own and couldn't abide what he saw as my father's interference. I had to be the peacemaker between them.

'That *New Idea* article you saw was written after we had finished the first two stages, which were hugely successful. Then, six months ago, when the prestige market went into a downturn, my father began to worry.'

'The money men are always the most nervous,' Mike said. 'It's the same for all building companies.'

'But he kept at Angelo until they had a flaring row and he taunted Angelo, telling him he couldn't survive without his funding. Angelo was furious. Somehow he managed to find alternative backers – he's never told me who they are – and took great pleasure in throwing Dad out. I've never held a formal position in Rubicon, but Angelo and I talked about and worked through all the issues. Now though, he's very secretive and tells me almost nothing. Although he says he has everything under control and is forging ahead, I can see he's worried. My father has prospered in some very tough businesses in very tough times and I'm sure he could help Angelo, if only they could find a way to work with one another.'

Carla broke off and Mike thought she was about to cry, but she swallowed hard, gently brushed her lips with her napkin and continued in a voice, which carried an edge of frustration.

'When you saw us last Friday, I was trying to bring the two

of them together again. It was a disaster. Both my father and my husband are too proud and too pig-headed to reach an accommodation. I despair of them. The way it's going, Angelo and I have little to keep us together.'

Mike leant forward so their heads were close together. 'Yeah, I can see how tough it is for you.' This time he did take her hand. 'I wish there was something I could do to help.'

'You have. You've listened.'

She took her hand away after giving his a gentle squeeze, lifted her head and squared her shoulders.

'Enough of this. Would you like coffee? I certainly need some.'

'A short black, please.'

Carla went to the doorway through which he had entered and pushed a button on the wall. Almost immediately a young woman, dressed in the black uniform of the waiting staff, came up the stairs.

'Gina, may I have a short black for my guest and a latte for me, please.'

When Gina had gone, Carla returned to the table and said, 'Now I must tell you why I invited you today. You know, of course, our fathers have been friends for many years?'

Despite the rapport Mike had established with Carla, the memory of how his father had looked and sounded when he spoke of his links with Mario Mancini, led him to be cautious. 'I didn't know, but on Saturday my father told me about their time together back in the old days.'

'You're lucky. My father refuses to talk about those times. I think he's not proud of the man he once was. What did your father say?'

'I don't think either of them were model citizens, but that was a long time ago.'

'Did he give you any details?'

The return of Gina with their coffee gave Mike time to think about how much he should tell Carla. 'They knew one another at the Wholesale Fruit and Vegetable Market.'

'But why won't your father talk with mine now? What happened?'

Mike was puzzled. Mancini had said something similar on Friday night. 'They haven't been in contact for many years.'

'So your father hasn't told you?'

'Told me what?'

Carla sat back and sighed. 'When your father said you were involved in the business I assumed you knew all about our proposition.'

'What proposition?'

'Riverside wasn't my only development project.' Mike noted how Carla now spoke as if she had been in full control of Riverside. 'For some years I've been working on the development of a joint commercial, retail and domestic complex to be built on a large chunk of the Bay Street precinct in Port Melbourne.'

'Including my father's shop?'

Carla nodded. 'Over a number of years we have quietly bought up the properties we need and hold them as a land bank, ripe for development. The key property we still lack is owned by your father. While we have tried to keep our interest secret, there's been some inevitable leakage and I'd be surprised if your father didn't know the powerful position he holds. We also know from our enquiries that he is not nearly as active in his business as he once was and his shops are not running well. I suppose you know, although perhaps he is holding out on you about that as well. This would be a great opportunity for him to get out at a large premium to the building's commercial value. For months now we have been trying to talk with him, but we can't make first base. He refuses to have anything to do with us. I can't imagine why.'

'I think I can.'

'You do?' Carla gave him an imploring smile. 'Please tell me.'

'You should ask your father.'

'He doesn't know.'

'He knows. He just prefers not to tell you.'

Carla nodded. 'I see. Both our fathers are keeping secrets from us. I've told you your father's secret. I think you owe it to me to tell me my father's secret.'

Mike shook his head, but when Carla continued to stare pleadingly at him, he weakened. 'OK but I'd much rather your father did this.'

He took Carla through an account of her father's early career, softening his crimes as far as he reasonably could, and giving her an expurgated description of how his father had arranged to protect himself. Carla listened carefully, her eyes seeming to grow larger as he went through the story. When he finished, she said. 'That explains a lot.' She wasn't going to let him off lightly, though. 'Did he actually kill someone?'

'I didn't say that.'

'No, you were careful not to. Too careful for my comfort.'

'He said he did, but Dad wasn't sure whether he had, or was trying to impress. Having a recording of him boasting of it would certainly have given my father a strong hold over him, although Dad is now ashamed he used it to give himself security rather than tell the police at the time.'

Carla lifted her chin and seemed to stare at something over Mike's head, her voice gaining a reflective tone. 'It also explains why my father was so reluctant to pressure him. I've never known him to hold back in a situation like this before. Do you think your father would deal with me, or has he got it in for the whole family?'

'Come on. He hasn't got it in for anyone.'

Carla reached out as though she intended to touch him again but did not go through with it. 'I'm sorry. You're right. Would you be willing to speak with your father and see exactly where we stand? Assure him my father need not be involved at all. This is my project, not his.'

'I'm certainly going to speak with him. He tells people I'm involved in the business and says nothing to me about a heap of important issues. This is probably the biggest, but it isn't the only one.'

—

Mike sat in his car in the casino car park. Which problem did he think about first? He had many to choose from. Had Alan or Vern set him up for the attempted bribery charge, or was it both, working together with Ivan Sarac? In their different ways, both had tried to reassure him, or was that just a ploy? And both knew more about the set-up than they were willing to tell him. Just like his father was unwilling to tell him about the problems in his business and the offer from Mancini. He had promised Carla to speak with his father. Mike thought again of the look she had given him when they parted, saying how good it had been for her to be able to share her problems with someone she trusted, and how she hoped they would meet again, soon. He could still feel the touch of her lips where she had lifted herself to kiss his cheek. He wasn't the only one looking for someone he could trust. Should he tell Lissa about his father's situation? No, that would involve telling her about his lunch with Carla. He also had to tell her about the bribery charge and his suspension. How would she take that news? And where was Shane? He needed to ring Mary.

Settling for the easiest option he called his sister.

'No, still no sign of him.'

'If he did go on a bender last night, he's probably only just coming to now. I'm sure he'll be in touch soon.'

'You're just like the rest of them!' Mike could hear the catch in her voice. 'The police aren't interested. All they want to tell me is how many people go missing each day and how all but a very few eventually turn up safe. They're not even trying to look for him. I've checked with the hospitals and been to a few of his favourite pubs but they haven't seen him. I went to Doherty's Gym. They remembered the argument you had with him all right – you made a real fool of yourself. Maybe Shane's decided he doesn't want anything more to do with a woman who has a brother like you.'

'I was trying to help you.'

'Great job you've done there.'

'He hasn't been in touch with anyone at Rubicon?'

Mike thought of Sarac but didn't suggest his name to Mary.

'I checked at Riverside. The man I spoke to there was worse than the police. "No, haven't seen him since last week," he said. "Sometimes other things take him away and we just have to put up with it." When I asked him to explain what he meant he hung up on me. Isn't there something you can do?'

'You seem to have done everything already. We're just going to have to wait.'

'You sure there's not something you're not telling me.'

'Of course I'm sure.'

'Thanks for your support,' Mary snapped and rang off.

His second call was to Alan Reardon. 'Sorry to have to cut you off earlier, but we need to talk.'

'Yeah, the commission people have been to see me now.'

'What did they say?'

'How about the Lord Nelson again tonight?'

'No. The Gainsville Cafe at the back of Southgate. I'll see you there in half an hour. There's a lot more going on than you've been willing to tell me.'

Mike passed the time waiting for Alan Reardon by watching the trickle of tourists pass the window of the cafe on their way to the lift which took them to the Skydeck in the Eureka Tower. He remembered the Gainsville Cafe from when Lissa and the children had press-ganged him into going with them to see the view from the tower. He had enough difficulty coping with the heights of building sites without going to the ultimate, glass-walled horror of the Skydeck. Reluctant to allow his children to know of his fear, he went with them but insisted on a coffee beforehand, delaying the inevitable.

How should he play it with Alan Reardon? The commission people had certainly said 'attempted bribery of a union official', so why were they seeing Alan? Was he giving them more evidence to frame him? But, if Alan was working with Angelo Rossi, why would he show him the photograph of Vern?

Alan was almost ten minutes late when he came through the door, wearing a deep frown. 'I don't like meeting in such a public place.'

'The sign outside says they make Melbourne's best coffee, it's not nearly as public as along the river and a lot safer than your choice last night.'

'I watched to see if you were being followed but I didn't spot anyone.'

'I wondered what delayed you,' Mike said. 'You are very careful, aren't you?'

'If the commission is on to you for bribing me, you shouldn't be calling me on your mobile.'

'A bit late for that now, isn't it?'

Alan shrugged. 'If this place has the best coffee in Melbourne, we'd better get some.' When they returned to the table, Alan's mood had improved. 'I'm sorry about last night. I had no idea it would turn out like it did.'

174

'But you knew something was on?'

'I certainly didn't expect you to be attacked, although I did warn you.' Alan leant back to appraise Mike's face. 'Are you sure you're OK? Quite a shiner you have there.'

When Mike continued to look at him enquiringly, he said, 'I was expecting there would be an attempt to set me up for a charge of taking bribes, but I didn't know how or when it might happen.'

'You were expecting it? You'd better explain.'

'I was expecting it because that was how I got into trouble last time.'

'Last time?'

'Yeah. Back in Perth. It didn't happen a lot, but enough. If a union official was being a nuisance then he might find a payment in his bank account, or maybe more than one, he couldn't explain. If he backed off – no problem, the money stayed and more came his way, provided he behaved. If he continued to be a pest, though, the authorities were tipped off about him taking bribes. That's what happened to me. That's why I'm here. I was naive then, but I learned. When Sarac's boys couldn't scare me off, I guessed they might be up for the same scam, so I got in first and went to the commission. I've got no time for the commission – I'm glad the Federal Government has decided to close it down – but I had to involve them if I was going to protect myself.'

'But you told me Sarac began to behave himself when you kept the pressure on.'

'Yeah, he did. I didn't expect it to last, though. The pressures on Riverside are too severe.'

'How do you know all this?'

Alan gazed, unblinking, at Mike before taking a sip of his coffee. 'Tell me what the guys from the commission said to you, Mike.'

'They haven't said much yet. They asked me which union

officials I'd been dealing with and I told them you and I had been discussing the WorkSafe investigation into last week's sling failure.' When Reardon gave an appreciative nod Mike flared. 'Can you tell me how someone's managed to hit the credit card I have from the firm for two whacks of five hundred dollars I can't explain or provide paper work for?'

'The commission got on to that quickly.'

'They haven't seen it yet. Vern showed me the card record he'd already called up.'

'Ah, Vern. Of course. I should have realised. I told you he's working with Sarac.'

'Yes, you did. Why did you show me those photographs? A bit of a risk for someone who's so careful.'

'You're still having trouble believing Vern is working with Sarac. What chance would I have had of persuading you without those shots?' When Mike didn't reply, Alan said, 'By the way, I let the commission boys know as soon as I found two unexplained amounts of five hundred dollars in my account, but I didn't suggest it was you who had put them there. I thought it would have been Sarac. They must be after you as well. Apart from getting up Bruno's nose, what have you done?'

'I have no idea.'

'You need to give them time for this investigation to be carried through and widen as I get more material.'

'Thanks very much.'

'Look, I'm playing for high stakes here. I had to spin the commission a story I was bothered about endemic corruption here in Melbourne before they'd take me seriously. The cosy deal McKenzie did with George Fowler was a gift.'

'You told them Vern was bribing George?'

'Perhaps he is. They're certainly close.'

176

'But when the commission guys came to Findlay's, why did they home in on me and not on Vern?'

'Because whoever tipped off the commission-is after both of us.'

Mike had felt his confidence in Alan grow as their conversation went on. He did seem genuinely committed to uncover all the problems at Rubicon and now, potentially, at Findlay's. His story hung together well, except for one thing. 'You've said a lot about Sarac and his hoods. What about Angelo Rossi?'

'I reckon he'd like to be shot of Sarac now.'

Mike thought of Carla. She had spoken of her father having prospered in some very tough businesses in very tough times and being able to help Angelo.

'Surely if Angelo wanted to get rid of Sarac he would. He has the right connections for dealing with anyone like Sarac.'

'You mean his father-in-law?' Alan asked.

'For a start,' Mike replied

'The Saracs of this world are like lice. Once you let them get a hold they're very hard to get rid of.'

'But that's what you're working on?' Mike said.

'That and other things.' Alan Reardon stood up. 'Other things I need to follow up now. Keep in touch.'

12

Lissa accepted the news of Mike's standing down surprisingly calmly, assuring him it was a dreadful mistake that would be rectified when the full investigation was complete. Mike was relieved she took it so well but disappointed she was not more outraged such a charge had been made against him.

'While you're at home, you can take over some of my jobs and I can work on getting this catering business of mine up and running,' she told him cheerfully. 'We might need it soon to support us. I went to see my friend Claire about publicity. She said she'd be happy to help and told me I should get a website. You can take the children to school for a start.'

Having returned from that duty and found Lissa already gone, he made himself a coffee and sat considering what he should do next. It was a good opportunity to visit his father.

He parked his car in Graham Street and walked around the corner into Bay Street, noticing the number of new, high-rise developments running down to the beach. The section that housed Georgiou's looked tired and defeated. Perhaps his father was the only one who had not accepted the inevitability of the change sweeping up the street towards him. When he entered the shop, Gail was the only person visible, the shop empty of customers.

'Out the back,' she said smiling at Mike.

His father was surprised to see Mike coming through the plastic strips and gazed at him anxiously. 'You have news of Shane?'

'No. He's still missing, I'm afraid. I thought we might have a coffee at … What's the name of the place?'

'They call it "Seven a.m." these days.'

'Yeah, that's it. There's something I want to discuss with you.'

As soon as they were settled Mike began. 'Dad, I have a problem at work. I've been accused of bribing a union official and have been stood down while the investigation goes ahead.'

Demetri's face flushed and his voice rose, drawing the attention of the couple sitting at the next table. 'How could anyone accuse you of such a thing? Nonsense.' This was more the kind of family support Mike was looking for.

'I think I've been set up, but I'm not sure who has done it. There are several possibilities.'

'These are the men causing trouble for you at the site?'

'Probably.'

'Never give in to them. If you allow bad men to prosper you will regret it.' Mike wondered whether his father was again thinking of Mancini. Not a good start.

'What will happen?' Demetri asked.

'The commission's investigators are on the job now. I don't know what they will do with me.'

Again Demetri became strident. 'You must fight such dishonesty.' He sat back to sip his coffee, and his face displayed a sequence of emotions: first his brow was wrinkled in thought, then his eyes were lit as if by a bright idea, and finally he said in a gentle voice, 'If, God forbid, things go badly for you, you could come into the business. There is always a place for you.'

'Ah, the business I'm so involved in. Why haven't you told me about the offer from Mancini?'

'Him! What have I just been telling you? A man who stopped at nothing to make his money and now pretends to be an honest businessman. I told you about him. Now he wants to stamp on our family name, wipe out our history. He has no respect and I will not speak to him.'

'How long do you think the family business can survive?'

'What do you mean?'

'You want me involved but you tell me nothing. I have to find out for myself the shops are losing custom and you no longer have the energy to drive the business forward but cling on like a ghost from the past in the shop where it all began. You won't save the family name that way. You'll see it decay and die.'

Demetri glared at him. 'If you know so much, tell me what I should do.'

'For a start you should give Peter Roberts his head, let him take over the running of the shops.'

'So it is Peter who has been talking with you.'

'Actually I've been talking with Carla Mancini. She told me about her plans, not her father's plans, her plans for the development of Bay Street. She also told me your business is not going well. Why should I have to find these things from someone I have only just met?'

It was rubbish he was speaking, but arguments with his father often brought out this histrionic strain in him.

'What are you doing with this woman? She is the daughter of her father; she will use you for her own ends. I know the family.'

Mike thought, when it came to histrionics, his father could still give as well as he got. 'What is it you want? Is there nothing Carla can do to persuade you?'

'Is is not her, it is you. What can you do to ensure the Georgiou name, the name of your grandfather and father, remains in Bay Street? Have you been so ensnared by this woman you come here, not as a Georgiou, but as a Mancini stooge?'

Mike was saved the need to reply when his phone sounded. 'Mary?'

'The police have come. A body has been found in the Yarra down near the Westgate Bridge. Some people on a ferry saw it.

The police don't know if it's Shane but want me to go with them to see. Can you come with me?'

—

It took very little time for Mike to reach the flat where Mary and Shane lived. He had expected to see a patrol car parked in the street but there was none. Mary, pale and hollow-eyed, answered the doorbell and introduced him to two plain clothes policemen: Detective Sergeant Phil Ryan, a man of Mike's age with close-clipped, curly red hair and intense blue eyes, and Detective Senior Constable Matt Clarke, a younger man, whose plump cheeks and shaven head made Mike think of Humpty Dumpty.

'Thank you for getting here so quickly,' the sergeant said and immediately led them down the stairs to an undistinguished blue Ford Falcon. He held open the rear passenger door for Mary while Clarke went straight to the driver's seat, leaving Mike to clamber in beside his sister.

They had gone only a short distance when Ryan turned to look back at Mike and said, 'I believe you were in touch with Mr Francis last Monday afternoon at Doherty's Gym.'

'Yes.'

'Working out with him?'

'No. I went to chat with Shane about a family matter.'

Mike felt Mary move next to him and resisted the urge to glance at her. What had she already told the policemen? He certainly wasn't going to speak about Shane's mistreatment of her. 'Have you found his car yet?'

Ryan gave a rueful grin. 'Yeah, in the car park at the Riverside site. No one noticed it until late this morning. Mostly it's for management and supervisory staff but he had parking rights or took them, anyway, and it wasn't unusual for him to leave it there overnight.'

Mike nodded understandingly. These would be the nights Shane went to the pub directly from work or the gym and was too drunk to drive home, the nights Mary was at risk.

The car braked sharply, and Clarke swore before saying, 'Pity we're not in the traffic branch.'

Sergeant Ryan turned back to look out of the windscreen and the rest of their short trip to Kavanagh Street was spent in silence. The grey panelled building was set back from the road in a paved courtyard, which carried the sign,

CORONIAL SERVICES CENTRE OF VICTORIA,
STATE CORONER'S OFFICE

It was dwarfed by the high-rise apartments across the street but retained a certain dignity. When the car continued through the barrier to the car park at the back of the block, Mike saw another low building, this time faced with blue panels, in front of which was a sign with the single word:

IDENTIFICATION

As they walked towards the glass door of the building, Mary took Mike's hand. She hadn't done that since her early days at school, when he had become her reluctant companion, responsible for seeing she made it safely to and from the school. There were two busy roads that had to be crossed and she was required to hold his hand during those crossings – an intimacy neither of them enjoyed.

It was clear they were expected. Sergeant Ryan nodded to the man at the reception desk and ushered them into an austere room just off the foyer, where they stood awkwardly for a few moments before a man dressed in the loose gown of a medical orderly wheeled in a tubular framed trolley with a white sheet hiding the body that lay upon it. He stopped beside Mike and Mary and with practiced solemnity folded back the sheet to reveal Shane's head and shoulders. Mary gave a strangled sob and looked away as she gripped Mike's hand with greater intensity. It was apparent the mortuary people had worked on Shane to enhance his appearance but they could not hide the scars of the severe beating he had suffered or repair the texture his skin had lost during his time in the river.

'Is this man Shane Francis?' the orderly asked Mary.

When she nodded, he looked into her eyes sympathetically and said 'Yes?' as if apologising for pressing her to voice her identification of Shane.

'Yes,' she said and turned away, brushing her free hand across her eyes, as he replaced the sheet.

The sergeant led them back into the foyer and said to Mary, 'I'm sorry we had to put you through this.'

'Was he murdered?'

'He had been attacked. The intention may not have been to kill him. We're still not sure how he died but will know more when the pathologist has finished his examination. Rest assured we will pursue whoever it was that attacked him.' He looked across to Clarke and nodded to him. 'Senior Constable Clarke has some forms we would like you to sign and then he will drive you home. We will be in touch with you again tomorrow.' He turned to Mike and said, 'Thank you for accompanying your sister Mr Georgiou.'

'Did he go in from the Westgate?' Mike asked.

'It could have been anywhere along the river. Forensics will give us a better idea.' The sergeant began to turn away, but stopped. 'Nasty whack you have there. How did that happen?'

'I was mugged.'

'You reported it?'

'No, I didn't bother.'

'When did this happen?'

'On Monday night outside the Lord Nelson in Fitzroy.'

'Not good.'

Mike wasn't sure whether Ryan meant the mugging or his failure to report it.

'Goodbye,' he said.

Lissa had taken special care over the coffee and baked a few pastries she thought might tempt Mary to eat without appearing to make their morning tea into some kind of celebration, but they were an awkward foursome who sat across from one another in Mike and Lissa's family room. Mary had refused their offer of a bed the night before, insisting on returning to her flat, but as she sat slumped in their armchair, her unkempt hair and red-rimmed eyes made it clear she had slept little, if at all. She had already rebuffed Mike's attempts to console her.

'You never liked Shane,' she said accusingly, 'so don't try to pretend with me now.'

'You're right. Shane was no friend of mine, but I am concerned for you. It's horrible that he's died the way he has, and you shouldn't have to bear it on your own. I want to help you if I can.'

'That's what families are for,' Lissa interjected lamely. She looked across to Demetri for support but he merely nodded and said nothing.

This was so different from what she had envisaged yesterday when she returned from her session with Claire, enthused by her ideas for setting up and publicising her catering business. 'Lissa Georgiou – Gourmet Catering' had a nice ring to it and the designs Claire had sketched for her business cards and flyers looked great. Claire insisted she needed a website and offered to prepare one for her. Perhaps best of all, she suggested that in lieu of paying her fees, Lissa could cater for several client lunches Claire was planning – she had her first booking!

She had thought she could tell Mike and Mary when they

returned from identifying Shane. Mary was keen to help and planned to leave her job as a dentist's receptionist and become fully involved when the business was securely established. It would be good for her to hear some good news and be distracted from her grief over Shane. It took only the sight of the pair of them as they came through the door to know her news would have to wait. When Demetri came in later, the gloom intensified as he sat mutely, shooting dark looks at Mike. Lissa wondered if the two of them had fallen out again over Mike's refusal to come into the business.

After they had gone, Mike's reaction was so disappointing; he showed no enthusiasm at her news and remaining preoccupied with his own thoughts. The problems at Findlay's, his suspension in particular, were weighing heavily on him. Surely, though, he could see how important her embryonic business was to her? She had spent a sleepless night but not from mourning Shane – after all, if the circumstances had not been so horrible, she would have been pleased Mary was free of him. No, she had been thinking of ways she could enhance the lunches she had been contracted to provide, making them more distinctive and appealing. Claire had suggested some of the guests might be interested in using her as well.

'I just wish I knew where Shane was going when he was killed,' Mary said. 'It was a funny time of night for him to get the call, though they did expect him to be on call and work odd hours at times.'

'Do you know what he did?' Mike asked.

'I think he was like a special assistant to one of the managers at Riverside, and last Friday you saw Angelo Rossi, the boss of Rubicon, knew him well.'

'Was the manager called Ivan Sarac?'

'Yeah, I think he might be the one. Why do you ask?'

Mike sighed and Lissa, who had been watching Mike's face

and wondering where he was going with his questions, could see his unease.

'His name has come up recently. Apparently there have been some dodgy things going on at the Riverside site that Sarac has been involved in. He has a few heavies who he uses as his enforcers.'

'There you go again,' Mary flared. 'Always trying to do Shane down, even now he's dead.'

'No. I'm just trying to tell you Shane has been around some pretty violent types. It was one of them who beat me up the other night.'

'I didn't think you knew who it was,' Lissa interjected.

'I just didn't want to talk about it,' Mike replied.

'You can say that again.'

She had never seen him in the state he was in when he arrived home from the mugging. Still groggy from the bang on the head, he had refused her offer to patch him up as best she could and insisted on washing all his clothes before he did anything else. Why would he do that? It wasn't as if they were covered in blood – or not that she could see. Getting him some treatment was much more important than washing some smelly clothes. And he wouldn't go to the police. There was more to all this than he was telling her.

Mike looked up again at Mary. 'Perhaps I shouldn't have said anything but I wondered if Shane had some kind of falling out with Sarac or one of his men and had been killed in a fight or something like that. I know how violent at least one of them can be.'

'What I want to know … ,' Mary said with her eyes directly on Mike, 'what I want to know is why the last thing Shane said to me before he went out was that you were a pest. What had you done and why did that mean he needed to go to the site? I've asked you before. Are you sure it wasn't you he was going to see?'

'I was a pest to Bruno Kordic. That's why he mugged me on Monday. I hit him with a crowbar last week when he was trying to steal electrical fittings from the CityView site and he wanted revenge. I was lucky to get off as lightly as I did. I'm not saying Shane was involved in any of that, but he might have known about it.'

Mary was breathing deeply as though her hostility to Mike had physically exhausted her and she continued to stare at him with dark eyes but said nothing. The silence was broken by the sound of Mike's phone.

'Hello,' he said uncertainly and followed this with, 'Oh, hi. That's very kind of you. Yes, it has been a shock. We're sitting here with Mary trying to come to grips with it.' There was a longer silence during which the frown on Mike's face deepened, until he said. 'I have spoken with him. It's a bit complicated.' He glanced at the others, shaking his head as though apologising for having to deal with a caller who would not be put off.

'I had better go. I'll call you later.'

After he had finished the call Mike said, 'Sorry.

'Who was it?' Lissa asked.

Mike swallowed before saying, 'It was Carla Mancini.'

'The gorgeous woman we met last Friday?' Lissa said. 'What did she want?'

When Mike did not answer her question immediately, Demetri sat up and heatedly waved his hands. 'She tries to turn my son against me. She is her father's daughter.'

'What?' Lissa said.

It was Mike, not Demetri, who responded to her. 'Carla Mancini has plans to develop the Bay Street precinct which includes Dad's shop, but he won't have anything to do with the Mancini family. Remember last Friday, her father complaining Dad wouldn't speak with him? That's what that was about.'

'I still don't see why Carla is ringing you.'

'I told you,' Demetri interjected. 'She is trying to seduce him.'

'Dad! Stop that! She got in touch earlier in the week and asked me if I could smooth the way between her and Dad.'

'Got in touch?'

Now Mike was not meeting Lissa's eyes. 'She invited me to meet with her at Café Filipo.' He turned to face his father again. 'Yeah. That's why you became anxious when you found out we were going to Café Filipo. You thought there was a chance you might bump into Mancini.'

'I knew it was his restaurant. I did not want to be there. I've told you I want nothing to do with him.'

Lissa was in no mood to be deflected. 'I hope she gave you something to eat,' she said tartly.

'We had some antipasto.'

'You went there for lunch?' This was becoming like the drawn-out interrogations she sometimes needed to conduct with the children when they were reluctantly owning up to some naughtiness.

'Yes. On Tuesday,' Mike replied.

Now she could understand. Tuesday was the day after he had been mugged, the day he wore his good suit and smart tie, the day he said he had an industry lunch. Perhaps Mike could sense the calculations going on in her mind. 'She asked me to keep it to myself.'

'And of course you did. I imagine she's pretty hard to say no to, pretty hard to resist.'

'Come off it. You're as bad as Dad.'

'Is she trying to seduce you? Even more interesting, has she succeeded?' Lissa was unsure whether she should be amused by Mike's discomfort or treat it as something more serious.

'She rang to offer her condolences on Shane.'

At this Mary sat up and pushed the hair from her eyes. 'We

should do something about a death notice. They wouldn't give us a time when we could collect Shane, though.'

There was a silence, each one busy with their thoughts. Lissa hadn't seen Mike like this before. No wonder she found him preoccupied last night. Apart from all his problems at work, he had the difficulty with his father and the lovely Carla on his mind. Had she seduced him? As far as she knew he had never been interested in anyone else. The occasional bit of flirting at a party when he'd had a bit much to drink. She was more prone to that particular foible than he was. That bitch, Celia, had been very obvious at one stage but he hadn't shown the slightest interest. Carla was gorgeous, but out of Mike's league, she would have thought. Since he'd been promoted to project manager at CityView, he had been taking himself more seriously, though. Perhaps he thought he could now play in a bigger league.

Mike's phone sounded again. Was she ringing back already? No, he had a very different tone to his voice.

'Yes, I can be there at eleven. Just a minute while I get a pen.'

He went to the kitchen bench on which was a pad and pen, and made a note. He closed his phone.

'That was the Building Commission. The investigators want to interview me at their headquarters in St Kilda Road. I'd better smarten myself up and think about how I handle them.'

After Mike left, Lissa and Mary cleared the table. When they were together in the kitchen, Mary said. 'You don't need to worry about Mike.'

'Yeah?'

'She's not his type – too smooth, too controlled. You've been the only one for him for so long he couldn't break free, even if he wanted to.'

'Thanks very much. You make it sound like he's rusted on to me. Let's hope she isn't the WD-40 in our marriage.'

190

13

Mike was able to squeeze his VW into a two-hour spot in the centre lane of St Kilda Road, just across from the building which housed the commission. He was amused to find the US Consul General was also a tenant. He had heard the commission accused of many things, but never as a front for the CIA. He was made to wait for ten minutes in the commission's upstairs foyer and wondered whether this was a deliberate ploy to unsettle him. Several other people arrived and were quickly ushered away – perhaps they were complainants or whistleblowers, rather than being under investigation.

Eventually he was shown to a small room already occupied by the men he had met a couple of days before. This time they did stand when he entered the room but did not greet him with a handshake.

'Morning, Mr Georgiou,' the senior one, Clive Johnston, said. 'Please sit here.'

Neither of them was wearing a jacket; Johnston's collar slightly dog-eared held a tie that had seen long service, while the French cuffs on Funston's precisely ironed, white shirt were secured with jade cufflinks. Neither of them suggested that Mike remove his jacket. Funston again had a pad at the ready and pushed a small recorder to the centre of the table.

'We will be recording this interview and you will be given a copy,' he said and went on to recite into the recorder a preamble stating the time, date, participants and purpose of the interview.

There was a short silence while Johnston examined Mike as

if looking for any changes which might have occurred in him since they last met. At least his bruising had lost some of its colour and size.

'Mr. Georgiou, thank you for helping us with our enquiries into the claim you attempted to bribe a union official. You are not obliged to answer any questions or make any statements and, if we do reach the conclusion that you have committed a crime, then the replies you give to our questions at this interview may be used in evidence against you.' He paused but, when Mike made no response, went on. 'We have now had the chance to view a number of documents, which we will show you during the course of this interview, and we have spoken with a number of people. You may remember, when we last met I suggested you would help yourself by giving us any information that might assist us to bring this enquiry to a rapid conclusion. It would appear you chose not to accept my advice. Nevertheless, I repeat it and tell you it is a matter of record that, when an individual is guilty of an indictable offence, an early admission is greatly to that individual's subsequent benefit.'

He waited for Mike to reply and, when he did not, nodded to Funston who opened a folder and withdrew some sheets which he pushed across the table for Mike to examine.

'On Tuesday you told us there were no accounts within the company that you operate directly. You omitted to mention the credit card issued to you for dealing with minor purchases and approved entertaining. These are the current records of expenditure against this card. Have you seen them before?'

'Yes, they have been shown to me.'

'How do you account for the two recent five hundred dollar debits?'

'I cannot. I believe my card has been used fraudulently without my knowledge. Do you know where those payments went?'

'You said you had been in touch with the deputy secretary of the union, Alan Reardon, on several occasions.'

'Yes.'

'Would you think carefully and recall for us each occasion on which you spoke with Mr Reardon in the past fortnight?'

Mike did not answer immediately but then listed his meetings with Alan on the afternoon of the accident, the following morning and on the Wednesday at head office. 'I called him on a couple of occasions after that and he called me once.' Mike noticed that Johnston, who had been sitting with his habitual, slightly bored expression, took greater interest when he reached this point.

'He called you?' Johnston repeated in a questioning voice.

'Yes, he called me last Monday afternoon, but there was a lot of background noise and he had difficulty hearing me, so we cut the call and I rang him after I reached a quieter location.'

Funston pushed another batch of papers across to him. 'There is no instance of him calling you at any time on your records or his.'

'That's wrong. He called me to invite me to meet with him on Monday evening.'

'Why would he want to meet with you?' Johnston had taken over again and was sitting up quite straight.

'He had concerns over a number of industrial issues at the Riverside site which he feared might spill over to our CityView site.'

'What were these?'

'Best you ask him.'

'Don't tell me you can't remember,' Johnston said.

'They are sensitive issues, which he told me about only after I promised to keep them to myself.'

'Where did you meet?'

Mike hesitated but, when Funston began to open another

folder, he said, 'At the Lord Nelson Hotel in Fitzroy.' Funston closed the folder.

'Bit out of the way for you,' Johnston said.

'I told you Alan Reardon was concerned about keeping our discussion confidential, so he chose a place where he said it would be unlikely we would be seen.' When Funston began to fiddle with the folder again, Johnston shot him a dark look which stopped him dead. 'But we were expected,' Mike continued, pleased to see both men's interest quicken. 'Two thugs by the names of Bruno Kordic and Rick Jennings were waiting for me when I left the pub and Kordic beat me up.'

'Why would they do that?' Funston asked as he ran his fingers down the side of the file once more. Mike guessed Funston, being the one who did all the hack work compiling the evidence, enjoyed tossing incriminating documents in front of suspects and felt miffed when Mike had pre-empted him.

'I was beaten up by Bruno because he wanted revenge on me for injuring him when we prevented him stealing material from the CityView site last week.'

Funston was unimpressed. 'You reported the theft to the police?'

'No.'

'But the beating, surely?'

'No.'

Funston sat back, a cynical smile stretching his pale cheeks, and looked across at Johnston. 'You tell a good story, Mr Georgiou,' Johnston said in a tone that made it clear Mike had impressed him even less than he had Funston. 'The trouble is you have little in the way of facts to back up your story and we have evidence your story is false. Mr Reardon did not call you. He tells us it was you who brought him to the Lord Nelson and the phone records support his version of events.'

'So Alan did set me up,' Mike said more to himself than the commission men. That explained the business about the phone records: Alan must have called him from another phone and had him ring back so the idea to meet at the Lord Nelson would appear to have come from him.

Johnston gave a short cough. 'Mr Georgiou, we will be submitting our report to the commission in the next few days and our recommendation will be that the files be handed to the police for their action. Is there anything else you wish to put to us before we conclude this interview?'

When Mike shook his head, Funston leaned forward to recite the formal end-piece for the recording and switched off the recorder.

Johnston sat back and put his hands behind his head. 'I think we've made it clear we do not accept your story you've been set up but, assuming for the moment you are telling the truth, why would anyone want to set you up like this?'

'Understanding that will be key to my defence.'

—

After Mike returned to his car he sat trying to allow his anger to settle before driving away. He'd been a fool to swallow Reardon's story the other day and the bastard must be laughing at how easily he'd been able to con him. It still didn't explain how they had set up the debits on his credit card. At every turn it seemed more likely Vern had gone over to the Rubicon camp. He had no proof without the photographs, so there was no point in accusing Vern or telling anyone else. Not yet. He started the car and, still angry, was driving around the lake towards home when his phone rang. His first reaction was to ignore it but, when the caller persisted, he relented and pulled to the side of the road.

'Michael?' The music was unmistakable.

'Hello, Carla.'

'I hope I haven't rung at a bad time again. It was just my phone has been off for most of the morning and I thought you may have tried to ring me but been unable to get through and reluctant to leave a message.'

'No, I've been tied up until very recently myself.'

'I need to talk with you. It's about Shane. I'm at home again now. Is there any chance you could drop in to see me?'

'Where's home?'

'We have a unit in one of the completed Riverside towers – the first – number 261. Have you had lunch? I'm just about to make myself a sandwich.'

—

Mike found a vacant spot in the small visitor car park only twenty metres from the entrance to the tower. He thought such luck only occurred in the movies. He entered the glass-walled foyer with its gleaming marble floor and indoor garden of potted annuals, shrubs and even several small trees. At the security door he punched in the number 261. Almost instantly he heard Carla's muffled voice. 'Come on up, Michael.'

The spacious lift took him rapidly and silently to the twenty-sixth floor. There were only two units at this level and Carla stood in the open doorway of one of them. She was more casually dressed than he had seen her before, wearing a white cotton blouse above a blue miniskirt, her bare legs in navy slip-ons. 'Michael! I'm so relieved to see you.' She made it sound like his appearance at her door was a surprise, and grasped him by the elbows as she raised herself to kiss his cheek, lingering longer than she had when farewelling him the other day. 'Are you all right?'

It wasn't just the style of her clothing that had changed. She had lost some of her cool elegance and her voice carried an edge of anxiety.

'Come in,' she said and turned back into an entry lobby with an archway on either side. She chose the one on the right and led him into a spacious, open plan living and dining area, which was backed by a gleaming kitchen, separated from the remainder of the space by a marble bench. At the far end he could see an off-white, modular longue suite, arranged to enjoy the view of Port Melbourne and Williamstown through the full-length, glass wall of the room. Presumably there were several equally sumptuous bedrooms and bathrooms on the other side of the entry. Mike could now appreciate what a major task it would be to redesign the latest Riverside tower for a lower-budget market similar to CityView. There would need to be major changes to the internal layout as well as the finishes and fittings. From somewhere within the apartment he could hear a trumpeter who sounded like the man Carla had played to him on Tuesday. Today he was playing in a slower, more romantic tempo, almost ballad-like.

'It's such a lovely day I thought we should eat on the balcony,' Carla said.

Mike turned to find her standing in a wide doorway, which led on to a balcony large enough for a slatted, timber table and chairs as well as several canvas sunlounges.

'Often the breeze can be a problem, but today we have mild sun and nothing to disturb us.'

Despite his unease with the height, he came to stand beside her. 'You certainly have a great view of the CBD from here.' The city buildings appeared as a vertical sculpture embedded in the background blur of the western suburbs – far superior to the sight from CityView.

'I like the view of the marina you get from up here,' she said as she walked to the frosted glass panes of the low wall and leant over to look below. Mike felt tension grip his thighs and stomach but took a seat at the end of the table.

'Mike, what is the matter?'

'You said you needed to talk with me about Shane.'

Carla came to sit beside him and said, 'I want to say again how sorry I am about Shane. Terrible for all of you, but particularly Mary. How is she?'

Mike thought of his recent confrontation with Mary. 'Shocked of course. It's terrible for him to die the way he did, but I must admit I never cared for Shane, and he treated Mary very badly. In the long run she'll be better off without him.'

'Angelo was very upset when he heard the news.' Carla paused as though expecting Mike to respond but, when he remained quiet, she said, 'He was very surprised when he saw the two of you together last Friday. He didn't know you were related.'

'We weren't,' Mike snapped.

'OK, he was surprised you were together at a family party,' Carla replied gently. 'You thought Angelo was kidding you when he said Findlay's was a rival to Rubicon.'

Again she paused and this time he did respond. 'Yeah, I did.'

'Angelo doesn't know I've been speaking with you.'

'Is that ...'

'We need a drink. I'm sure you're thirsty.' Carla hastened away, leaving Mike to puzzle over their edgy conversation. After a surprisingly long delay, she reappeared with two glasses of white wine. 'Same winery but a different wine. See what you think of this one.'

Mike sipped the wine and said, 'Yes, I like this one as well. But you were saying ...'

'Do you know a man by the name of Ivan Sarac?'

'I've heard of him,' Mike said noncommittally. 'He works at Rubicon, doesn't he?'

Carla eyed him carefully. 'He came into Rubicon after ... I've never met him.' She lifted her glass and took a mouthful of wine. 'All I know about him is what my staff at Café Filipo say about him. He goes there with Angelo and sometimes he uses the private room for his own meetings. They say he's an arrogant man who treats them like dirt and has his own people to guard him. They don't know what he's frightened of. Angelo should never have let him into Rubicon. I don't know ...'

'Carla, what has this to do with Shane?'

'It so hard to find ... Let me bring the lunch. It won't take me long to prepare. 'Just a minute.'

Carla rose hastily and went inside, leaving Mike to piece together the apparently unrelated strands of their conversation. She was away even longer than the first time, giving him ample time to decide what he needed to do. Eventually she returned with two white plates, each holding a mixture of sandwiches made from crusty wholemeal bread and what looked like some of the antipasto he had enjoyed on Tuesday. She placed the plate with the largest share of the sandwiches in front of him, while the modest one she retained for herself.

'Here we are. Sorry to take so long,' she said with an apologetic smile.

'Carla, I think I can make this easier for you. Let me tell you what I know and how I see things.'

She gave him a sharp glance before settling to listen.

'The sales of luxury units at Riverside have continued to be poor, leading to a cash flow problem that is probably worrying the new investors just as it worried your father. Construction on the latest tower has been slowed and its design altered to go for the middle rather than the top end of the market. This does make CityView a direct competitor with Riverside. Ivan Sarac doesn't mind breaching the law and the union has been involved in attempting to protect their members from Sarac putting off workers without their proper entitlements and cutting corners on a number of work practices. Sarac has several men who do his dirty work for him. When he came to Rubicon he recruited Shane as his man on the Riverside site. Another of them, Bruno Kordic, was involved in trying to sabotage the CityView project. We caught him at it the other night but he escaped. I can now understand why Shane was so awkward when Angelo saw him with me. Is this what you wanted to tell me or is there more?'

Carla nodded slowly as Mike made each of his points. She leant forward.

'It was Sarac who rang Angelo to tell him Shane was dead. I was not in the room but could tell Angelo was furious about something. After he finished the call I went to Angelo and we talked. He told me more about Riverside than he has for months. Angelo feels responsible for Shane's death.'

'He had him killed because of his link with me?'

'No. No. Angelo wishes he had never allowed Sarac into Rubicon but says it's too late to get rid of him and his men now. Angelo loathes them all. He couldn't resist stirring up trouble by telling them he'd seen the two of you together at Café Filipo and was surprised at how seriously they took it. Sarac and Bruno, the other one you mentioned, were very suspicious of Shane. They're an untrustworthy bunch and don't even trust each other. Something happened to make their suspicions boil over and that's why Shane was killed. Sarac didn't admit anything but he did say he knew Shane was a traitor and they were well rid of him. Angelo feels guilty he started them down this path.'

'Will Angelo go to the police?'

'Oh, Mike, you don't know what you ask. These men are ruthless. I only told you because I'm fearful for you.' She reached out to take his hand. 'Sarac is a vicious man who will stop at nothing to get his way. I'd be distraught if you came to harm because of these men. I'm so powerless.' She lifted her hand to her eye and he thought she was about to cry, but instead she placed a gentle finger on his damaged eyebrow and said, 'You told me you'd been in an accident Was it one of Sarac's men who attacked you?'

'It was my own fault. I had an earlier run-in with Bruno when he came off worse than me and I became cocky. I won't make that mistake again. Besides, they've come up with a different way to put me out of action.'

'What?'

'Do you know Alan Reardon, the deputy secretary of the BCU?'

'No. Why do you ask?'

'I've just come from a grilling at the Building Commission where I've been accused of attempting to bribe Reardon. He's set me up very neatly.'

Carla, in the process of lifting a sandwich to her lips, stopped her hand. 'Why should he do such a thing?'

'I guess Sarac has paid him off.' It was now clear to Mike that, if he was going to clear himself he would need to expose much of what was going on at Rubicon and Findlay's. 'When Angelo was talking with you last night, did he say anything about Vern McKenzie?'

'No. Who is he?'

'Vern's currently my boss. I wondered whether he might be targeted as well.' Mike sat back and squared his shoulders. 'Thank you. I can understand it wasn't easy for you to tell me what you have.'

'Oh, Mike. I wish I could be more help to you. Please eat up. You've hardly touched those sandwiches.'

'Neither have you. We've both been a bit preoccupied. Let's talk about something else.'

Carla rose to her feet and raised her arms above her head to stretch her body in a feline gesture Mike found intensely alluring.

'The breeze is getting up now. Let's go into the living room for coffee and some special cakes I hope will tempt you more than my sandwiches have done.' She led him inside and, with a wave of her hand, indicated he should sit on the spongey cushions of the settee while she went to the kitchen to brew the coffee. Mike had not been able to hear the trumpeter on the balcony, but now the warm sounds of his dreamy tune flowed over him and he felt happier than he had been for days. The talk with Carla had not solved any of his problems, but her concern for him was something to savour.

Carla returned with their coffee and a plate containing pieces of katafi and baklava, which she placed on a low table in front of them, and sat close beside him on the settee, her skirt riding up so that he found it difficult not to keep glancing at the length of smooth thigh snuggled beside him.

'Now,' she said, 'tell me what your father said when you told him about our conversation.'

Mike took a sip of coffee before replying. 'Our chat didn't go too well. He wants nothing to do with your father. I don't believe it's so much dislike for him as it is Dad's shame he held back the evidence of his guilt and used it to protect himself. It's shame rather than hatred.'

'But that's my father,' Carla said a little impatiently. 'Why won't he deal with me?'

Mike chuckled. 'I have to tell you Dad has admired you from afar. When he saw those shots of you in *New Idea*, he said you looked like that old screen star Sophia Loren. For him there can be no greater beauty.'

Carla smiled and took a deep breath, emphasising some of the reasons Demetri had been struck by her similarity to the film star. 'I hadn't realised how many of you Georgiou family take such an interest in *New Idea*. So, if I invited him for a private lunch at Café Filipo, would he not be pleased to accept? We can talk there.'

'Do you get your way with all men by inviting them for a private lunch at Café Filipo?'

'You sound a little miffed. If that is my method, it doesn't seem to have worked with you.'

'I don't know. Dad accused me of having been seduced by you.'

'Have you?'

Carla turned towards him, her blouse twisting to reveal the curve of her breasts and the lace at the edge of her ivory bra. When Mike put his hand on her shoulder and turned his head so their faces were close to touching, Carla looked earnestly into his eyes before suddenly pulling away.

'No, of course you haven't. It is you who has seduced me.' She smiled sadly at him. 'You are such an attractive man, Michael – so strong and yet so gentle. There must have been many women who have told you this.' Carla stood up and looked down on him. 'I began to believe something special was growing between us. I began to believe I could look to you, not just to offer me comfort, but to support me with your father. But why should you? Your loyalty is to your father not to me, the daughter of the man he is ashamed to have known and the wife of the man whose company has put you in such danger.' She shook her head and pursed her lips as though annoyed with herself. 'I shouldn't have declared myself to you like this. Forgive me.' She paused before adding, 'But that's the effect you have on me.'

Carla walked into the kitchen, further distancing herself from him. Mike's thoughts were in turmoil: the undeniable glow of contentment from her words, the throbbing pulse of arousal, the jagged disappointment of her withdrawal. To his surprise Mike found he must have taken a piece of katafi from the plate and bitten into it – the overly sweet cocoon had a slightly flabby texture, not nearly as good as those Lissa baked, triggering a prickle of guilt, which he pushed away. He stood up and came to Carla.

'I haven't given up on trying to persuade Dad. I do want to help you however I can, more now than ever.'

Carla turned to face him. 'You are a kind man.' She made no move to come to him. 'Perhaps you should go before I embarrass you any further.'

'No. Don't be silly.'

'Still, I think it best you go,' she said in a wan voice and turned to lead him to the door. 'I hope I haven't frightened you away and we can meet again. I so value your company.'

She gave Mike an enigmatic smile before adding, 'You can assure your father I haven't succeeded in seducing you.'

—

When Mike reached home Mary had gone and Lissa was busy in the kitchen. 'How did it go?' she asked. For a second Mike thought she was asking about his lunch with Carla but then recovered and said, 'I've been set up by the union guy, Alan Reardon. The commission investigators are convinced I tried to bribe him and will be sending the file to the police after they complete their report.'

'But Vern said you'd be OK.'

'I'm learning not to trust anything said to me by anyone. Reardon has played me for a sucker and the longer this goes on the more I think Vern's working for Rubicon and against Findlay's. I'm pretty sure he helped set me up.'

'Vern? That's terrible. You haven't said anything about Vern turning traitor. How long have you suspected him?'

'Just a few days. I didn't want to believe it.'

'You should have said.' Lissa's wide eyes made her words sound like an accusation 'You're keeping a lot to yourself and not telling me what's going on. It's as if you're drifting away and I don't know where you are.' Mike knew she meant Carla. When he did not respond she shook her head and said, 'They certainly grilled you for a long time.'

'Carla called me on my way home. I went to see her.'

'Another lunch at Café Filipo?' Lissa said with mock astonishment. 'Just as well you had your suit on to front the commission.'

'We had a sandwich in her apartment. She wanted to tell me she thinks Shane might have been killed because the thugs he hung out with suspected he was spying on them for me.'

'Really?'

'She didn't put it so directly, but that's what she meant. She was worried something might happen to me, too.'

'What gave her that idea?'

'It's a complicated story.'

'Here we go again. You'd better tell me all about it.'

After Mike had taken Lissa through the details of Angelo Rossi's baiting of Shane and the phone call he had received from Sarac, Lissa said, 'You should tell this to the police.'

'Yeah, I know. But if I just appear out of the blue with this story, the first thing they'll want to know is where I got it from. I can't say it was Carla who told me.'

'Why not?'

'First, I'd be breaking her trust, when the only reason she told me was her concern for my safety.' When Lissa began to object, Mike continued over the top of her. 'And if I don't worry about that, it won't work anyway. Rossi will deny everything and Carla will have to back him. That's what you'd do, isn't it?'

Mike had not intended to signal doubt over Lissa's loyalty but he could see that was how she interpreted him. She stared hard at him before saying, 'Did she tell you anything else I should know?'

'She's still keen that I should persuade Dad to sell to her.'

'Did she offer you any inducements?' Lissa asked.

'What do you think?' Mike answered testily.

'I think it's time to pick up the kids from school. We mustn't forget them.'

Lissa complained about him holding things back but she continued to send him coded messages. Would they ever get back to speaking directly again?

14

Next morning Mike was in no mood for chatter, so the drive to school with the children was a silent one until they turned into the tree-lined street which led to the red-brick school buildings.

'Are you sad about Shane dying?' Leila asked.

'No, he didn't like Shane,' Christos answered before him. 'It's just he doesn't like doing the mother thing now he doesn't have a job and Mum is busy with her plans to cook meals for other people.'

'I don't like it when you and Mum don't talk,' Jacinta said, always concerned she not be overlooked.'

'Better than when they have fights,' Christos replied.

'Hey, hold on,' Mike interjected. 'We don't have fights.'

'Well, arguments, then,' Christos conceded. 'You don't hit her like Shane hit Mary,' he added in a voice that told Mike his son was rather proud of knowing this.

'Look, I'm having to deal with a heap of problems at work at the moment.'

'But you're not at work,' Jacinta objected.

'That's because of the problems I've got. I'm not on holidays.'

'No, you're Mum's driver,' Christos said with a cheeky grin.

'Here we are,' Mike announced with relief. 'Everybody out.'

—

When he reached home, Lissa was waiting. 'Detective Sergeant Phil Ryan called. He'd like you to go into the homicide squad office for an interview.'

'Did he say when he wanted me?'

'He's picking you up. I told him you were taking the kids to school and he said he'd drop by in half an hour. He rang just after you left, so he should be here soon.'

When Mike answered the door he found not only Detective Sergeant Ryan, but his mate, Detective Senior Constable Clarke, as well. Behind them in the street Mike could see the same blue Ford Falcon.

'Good morning, 'Mr Georgiou.' Ryan's voice completely lacked any warmth. 'Do you mind if we come in for a moment?'

Mike led them into the house and introduced them to Lissa before Ryan spoke again.

'Our investigations so far have raised a number of questions and we think you might have some of the answers.'

Mike couldn't believe his good fortune. Here was his opportunity to pass on what Carla had told him. 'Sure. Let's sit over here.' He gestured to the chairs in the family room.

'Better at the office,' Ryan replied and then had second thoughts. 'But there are one or two things we'll do here first.'

'You'd better sit down,' Mike said.'

The sergeant remained standing beside the bench dividing the kitchen from the family room.

'The other day you mentioned you had been mugged last Monday night.'

'Yeah, that's right.'

'Could you look out for us the clothes you were wearing?'

'Whatever for?'

'We have various lines of enquiry running in this case. By having a look at your clothes we may be able to eliminate one of them.'

'I don't understand.'

'We'll explain more fully later. Could we see the clothes, please?'

Ryan's request had become an order.

'As I recall I was wearing a shirt, jumper, jeans and sneakers, apart from socks and jocks, of course. Do you want all of them?'

'Thank you.'

The senior constable followed Mike to the bedroom, leaving the sergeant to wander into the kitchen and begin chatting with Lissa.

As Mike took each item of clothing from the cupboard, Clarke asked 'Sure these are the ones?' He had conjured several plastic bags from somewhere. 'They've all been washed.' He sounded disappointed.

'What did you expect?' Mike demanded, releasing some of his growing anxiety. 'I was mugged in a filthy alley.' He looked down at his feet. 'You'll be pleased to know I haven't washed my sneakers; I'm still wearing them.' The senior constable looked straight into Mike's eyes and held the stare for a moment before saying, 'Better take them off, then.'

When they returned to the family room, Ryan was engaged with Lissa.

'Yes, I'm sure it was very upsetting,' he was saying. He broke off, glanced at the bags of clothes held by Clarke, looked up at him and received a confirmatory nod. 'Right. We'll be on our way.'

The policemen led Mike to their car where Ryan held open the rear door for him. The pleasure Mike felt when they first arrived had disappeared, replaced by anxious uncertainty. In a few minutes his self-image had gone from being a valuable ally of the police to what he often heard described as 'a person of interest taken in for questioning'. At least the sergeant did not put his hand as protection over Mike's head in the way the police were seen to do in news clips of them loading an arrested man into a car. As before, Clarke drove and Ryan sat beside him. 'Where are we going?' Mike asked.

'Our office in St Kilda Road,' was the terse reply.

They travelled in silence and, although the trip was a short one, it gave time for Mike to collect his thoughts. Mary would have told them about the phone call Shane received on the night he was killed and how he called Mike a pest before he went out. It would be natural for them to jump to the conclusion he was going to meet Mike – Mary had done the same. He would have to deal with that issue before he told them about Rossi and Sarac. Feeling reassured, Mike sat back and recalled the tall police building that looked as though it had been rendered with wet sand and often appeared in news reports of high profile crimes. He did not see the familiar facade of the building, however, as Clarke drove them into an underground car park from which they travelled by lift to an anonymous corridor where he was led into a small windowless room containing a deal table and four wooden chairs. Ryan left him there with the comment that he would be back shortly. After ten minutes Mike began to wonder whether this was some kind of softening-up technique akin to the delay he had suffered at the commission. There was no hidden camera; it was prominently mounted in a corner of the room opposite where he was sitting.

Eventually the door opened and a thickset man of medium height with a square face and bald head entered the room. He was dressed almost entirely in grey: a grey single-breasted suit, a grey and white striped shirt and a grey tie. Behind him came Sergeant Ryan. The two of them sat across the table from Mike and the man in grey said, 'Mr Georgiou, I'm Detective Senior Sergeant Max Robbins of the homicide squad. Thank you for coming in this morning.'

Mike had thought Robbins might thank him for helping them with their enquiries, but he did not look like a man who went in for clichés. The senior sergeant nodded to Ryan who leant forward to the console which sat on the end of the table beside the wall and flicked a switch, before saying, 'Mr Georgiou, this interview is being video-recorded and you will be given a copy.'

He then made a preliminary statement, eerily similar to the one the commission man had made yesterday. Mike reflected ruefully that the police went one better than the commission: he would have a DVD of this one.

The first questions Ryan asked established for the record Mike's full name, address, occupation and employer. The next question was unexpected.

'How well did you know Shane Francis?'

'Not very well at all. After he linked up with my sister, he came to the occasional family lunch, but that was about it.'

This was far too curt an answer for Ryan who sought much greater detail, including many questions Mike considered irrelevant, such as when they had first met, how often they had met and whether they had met other than on family occasions. When Mike said there were none, Robbins intervened. 'You're both in the building game. I would have thought you would have bumped into one another from time to time. Most recently you've been on adjacent sites.'

Mike was becoming irritated by the policemen's persistent interest in what he saw as trivia. Why didn't they come to the point? He smiled and said, 'Building sites don't welcome drop-ins.'

'A common interest though. Something to talk about when you did meet.'

'I guess neither of us liked to bring work home.'

'What did you think of him?' Ryan asked sharply.

'I didn't like him.'

'No. Why was that?'

Mike did not answer immediately, wondering whether Mary had told them about Shane hitting her. She had done her best to camouflage the marks from her most recent beating, and they had faded, but the police would probably have noticed.

'He was a loudmouth who was too sure of himself.'

'A loudmouth? But you didn't talk much. Anything else?'

Ryan's tone was challenging and Mike decided he should not hold back. 'Shane hit my sister on a number of occasions.'

'Have you ever taken this up with him?'

'Yeah, last Monday at Doherty's Gym. I should have done it a lot sooner, but Mary didn't want me to get involved.'

'Did your sister ask you to go?'

'No, she was in denial. I believe that's common.' He appealed to the police with his eyes; they would have much more experience of domestic violence than he had.

Robbins continued to examine him as though observing an interesting specimen, before saying, 'So you did meet him outside the family?'

'Just that once. I thought you were asking whether we had met socially.'

'Best if you answer the questions and leave the thinking to us,' the senior sergeant replied gently.

'What did you say to him?' Ryan asked.

'He tried to pretend it hadn't happened and I was imagining it. That made me angry. I don't remember the exact words I used.'

'You don't remember any of your words?' Mike noticed Ryan calibrated the level of his doubt by the pitch of his voice. This time it rose into the range of outright disbelief.

'No.'

'We have spoken to witnesses of the confrontation between you and Shane. They say you threatened to kill him. They also say he was the one who calmed things down and got you out of the gym.'

'Shane was like that. He could be a brute but he liked to wrap it up as though he was on good terms with everyone.'

'You threatened to kill him.'

'I might have said something like that, but I didn't mean it literally. Haven't you ever said anything like that when you were angry?'

Robbins nodded and Mike thought the senior man was showing some sympathy for him, until he realised the nod was a signal to Ryan that Robbins was taking over the questioning. He took Mike back through the material already covered, pushing him to recall more detail of his conversation with Shane. Eventually, he said. 'It must have been galling for you to go to Doherty's to sort out the man who was beating up your sister and have him patronise you.'

When Mike made no reply, Robbins nodded again and Ryan continued.

'Where did you go after you left Doherty's? Tell us about the rest of your evening.'

'I went home. Then I went with my family to a concert our younger daughter was in. Later I drove to the Lord Nelson Hotel in Fitzroy to meet a union official, Alan Reardon.'

'What time was that?'

'I arrived there just before eight. We spoke for about half an hour. Returning to my car I was mugged by a man called Bruno Kordic.'

'Unusual to be mugged by someone you know?'

'I don't know him,' Mike snapped back. 'I know his name.'

'Why did he mug you?'

'He was taking revenge for some damage I did to him the previous week.'

'So you can handle yourself – no stranger to fights.'

'Kordic was involved in an attempted robbery on the CityView site where I'm project manager. When we caught him at it, he went for me, but I got in a lucky blow with a crowbar and he got away without seriously harming me.' Mike no longer carried any illusions about his abilities as a street-fighter – the other night had taught him that. And there was certainly nothing to be gained by pretending to these two cops.

'The robbery was reported to police?'

'We prevented anything being taken and my boss, Vern McKenzie, decided nothing was to be gained by reporting a failed robbery.

'And the mugging? Did you keep that secret, too?' Ryan asked.

'I felt the same. The only other witness was one of Kordic's mates, Rick Jennings, and all he would do would be to give Kordic an alibi.'

For an instant Mike thought that Ryan was about to smile but, if he was, he changed his mind and his face remained set.

Robbins stirred himself to say, 'You told us you didn't know Kordic but you do know his name and the name of his mates, it seems. How come?'

Mike noticed that Ryan shot a dark glance at the senior man. Perhaps Ryan had been about to ask the same question. This was the chance Mike had been looking for to start talking about Sarac's gang.

'Alan Reardon told me about them when we met at the Lord Nelson. He's been involved at the Riverside site, which has switched the design of its latest tower to compete directly with our CityView project. Reardon told me there have been a number of problems at Riverview where a man called Ivan Sarac has been involved. Sarac has a gang of heavies he uses to threaten people who get in his way. Reardon showed me some photographs he had of the gang and I recognised Kordic. He told me the names of the others as well. One …'

'So when did you leave the scene?' Ryan asked impatiently.

'I remember looking at my watch. It was about nine-thirty.'

'It took an hour to mug you?' Ryan's voice reached the height of the red zone on his disbelief scale.

'I had a bang on the head. After they left me it took me a while to feel up to driving.'

'And when you did reach home, what did you do?'

'You know what I did,' Mike answered angrily. The drip, drip of this man's questions, most of which he knew the answers to already, was getting to him. 'I washed the filth of the alley off my clothes.'

'Are you normally that neat and tidy?'

Mike struggled with the conflict between making clear the reasons for his strange behaviour and facing the shame of what had happened to him. He could see both of them watching him closely. They hadn't yet got to the phone call and Shane calling him a pest, but Mike could see they had accumulated much more circumstantial evidence than he had appreciated which pointed to him as Shane's killer. Mike took a deep breath and said, 'After he had me down in the lane, Kordic pissed all over me. I don't know if you've ever had something like that happen to you, but I found it completely humiliating. I wanted to get rid of it as soon as I possibly could.' He lowered his eyes and added, 'My wife normally does most of the washing.'

'It took you a long time to come up with that,' the sergeant said drily. 'Show me your hands.' Mike gaped at the unexpected question but then held out his hands in a gesture that the camera might register as supplication. 'No, turn them over.'

His knuckles still showed the scabs from the damage he had done when clawing the pitchers in the lane on Monday. 'Got those in the mugging on Monday?'

'Yes.'

'Funny that. Your hands look more like you were handing out punishment, not taking it, wouldn't you say?'

'I scraped them on the stones in the lane trying to save myself as I was knocked to the ground.'

'It's been a bad couple of weeks for you,' Ryan said. 'I'm told you've been stood down from work because you're accused of bribing this Alan Reardon you met on Monday night and your boss has the idea you might have run him down after the two of you had an argument about your lack of performance. Still, some of the men at your site speak well of you.' When Mike's face softened in response to this single ray of light, Ryan nodded. 'They say you're quite a scrapper.'

When Mike made no response, Robbins took over the questioning as he had done before, going back over the details of the mugging and Mike's response to it. This time Mike did speak of his suspicion that Reardon was in league with Sarac and started to tell them about the bribery allegations, but Robbins cut him off, returning to more questions about his mugging and his movements afterwards. Mike could feel himself beginning to fray under their unremitting questioning and they hadn't yet raised Shane calling him a pest after the phone call.

'Look I can see where you're going with this,' he said, 'But you're wrong, totally wrong.'

'So tell us what's right,' Ryan snarled at him. 'Tell us why the last thing Shane Francis said to your sister before he went out to his death was that you were a pest. Tell us that.' At last they had got to it.

'He also said to whoever called him that they had "got it all wrong",' Mike replied. 'I'll tell you what happened. Shane was part of Ivan Sarac's gang of thugs I told you about earlier. Shane was Sarac's man on site at Riverside. Last week Angelo Rossi, the head of Rubicon, saw Shane and me together at a family dinner. Rossi told Sarac and Kordic. They were suspicious Shane had told me what they were up to. On Monday

Sarac rang Shane, demanding he come and explain himself. That's why Shane said, "You've got it wrong," and that's why he told Mary I was a pest. But before Kordic dealt with Shane he came to the Lord Nelson, having been tipped off by Alan Reardon that I would be there. Kordic took it out on both of us the same night, going further with Shane than he did with me. Maybe I was lucky not to be killed and maybe Shane was unlucky; I don't know.'

'You don't know anything,' Ryan spat back at him. 'You made that up as you went along. I could see the wheels spinning in your head. Suddenly you know a lot about what Shane Francis did on the Riverside site and who he worked for, although back at the start of this interview you said you knew nothing about him.'

'I said Shane and I didn't talk about work. My information came from Alan Reardon.'

Ryan scoffed. 'Alan Reardon, the man you say tipped Kordic off that you were going to be at the Lord Nelson and is trying to frame you for bribery? You ask me to believe he told you that the guys he's working with killed Shane Francis?'

'No not that. He told me Shane was one of the gang – showed me photographs of them together.'

'So how do you know they killed Shane?'

Mike hesitated before saying lamely, 'You should talk with Angelo Rossi.'

Again Ryan scoffed. 'You'll have to do better than that. You …'

'Mr Georgiou,' the senior sergeant said with an authority that silenced Ryan. 'You have the bones of a theory there. There are a lot of loose ends dangling from it that would need to be tied up before anyone is likely to believe you. Worse still, you lack evidence for most of your claims and we have statements from witnesses that rebut those claims.'

Mike had been right when he guessed that they had been

talking with Sarac and his gang, who were sure to give one another the alibis they needed.

'I'll put it to you this way, Mr Georgiou. We have considerable evidence that points to you as the killer of Shane Francis and we are confident we will find more. We have more work to do and we will want to speak with you again. However, over the weekend, I want you to think about this.

'Perhaps you didn't intend to kill Shane Francis. Perhaps you were goaded into wanting to give him a taste of his own medicine, the medicine he gave your sister. But sometimes your temper gets the better of you and this time you went too far. Or perhaps in the process he fell, was killed and you panicked. An early plea of manslaughter, triggered but not excused by the victim's treatment of your sister, is the best course of action for you. You should take legal advice before we meet again.'

15

The overnight rain had cleared, but heavy cloud remained and a chill south wind clawed at the small group of spectators watching Christos' soccer match. Mike wished he had worn more than a padded bomber jacket and woollen scarf as his defence against the cold. Disconsolately he watched the ball wander up and down the muddy pitch surrounded by a swarm of players, none of whom seemed capable of driving it into open ground. Not that he paid a lot of attention; his thoughts, like the soccer ball, were wedged amid his problems without any idea of how he might find space to deal with them. When one of the other spectators, perhaps as little interested in the game as Mike, said, 'Nice car!' he turned to see what had caused the admiring comment and was surprised to find Mario Mancini stepping from a large, silver Mercedes sedan. Mancini did not hesitate but strode directly towards him. The black ankle-length overcoat, maroon woollen scarf and nautical cap gave him a presence among the spectators as imposing as his car parked among the other vehicles. He removed a leather glove.

'Good afternoon, Mike,' he said, taking Mike's hand in a firm grasp. 'Must be great to come along and support your lad. Never had that privilege myself.'

Recovering from his surprise, Mike said, 'How did you know to find me here?'

'I thought we should have a chat,' Mancini said and stepped away from the crowd, drawing Mike with him. He didn't say how he knew where to find Mike. 'You told Carla that Demetri

219

is feeling guilty about having used his recording of me as insurance, rather than giving it to the police.'

'I can understand why that would worry you.'

'You understand nothing,' Mancini declared. He lifted his chin and said in a challenging voice, 'Have you listened to the recording of my so-called "confession"?'

'No, I haven't.'

'I thought as much,' he replied disdainfully. 'You should. When I first heard it, all those years ago, I found it damning. But I was young and inexperienced. For a long time now, I've been vastly more experienced and able to afford the best legal advice. Without any corroborating evidence – and there is none – it would be dismissed in court as the very thing it is – the posturing of a young hood.'

'Then why come here today?'

'It's time Demetri heard the truth. But he won't listen to me, so you must tell him.'

'But ...'

Mike got no further before Mancini spoke over the top of him. 'It served me well in those days for it to be thought I murdered Drago Fontini and what I said to Demetri was the bravado of youth. Fontini led a gang that fought with mine for control of the market. He looked and sounded like someone to fear, but at heart he was a coward. When his gang was there to protect him he was cruel and fearless. Without them he was nothing. Yes, I started the fight the night I found him alone, but very soon Fontini turned tail and ran. In his rush to escape he tripped and fell, hitting his head against the edge of a row of bricks lining the alley. It was a freak accident.'

The further Mancini went with his story the more he seemed to retreat into memory and, when he was done, he looked around as though puzzled to find himself where he was. It was the first time Mike had seen him appear anything but completely assured. Mancini pushed his hands into the pockets of his coat and said, 'Demetri need not be ashamed. The world's better off with Fontini dead, and the police of the time knew it. That's why they spent so little effort trying to find out what really happened. There was no murder – not even manslaughter.'

'And you want me to tell all this to my father. You think it will help persuade him to sell to you?'

'Nothing to do with it.'

Mancini smiled and opened his arms in an unconvincing gesture of self-deprecation. 'I would be silly to pretend I've led a blameless life – far from it. If I go back far enough, I can say the same thing about Demetri. But he left the old ways behind and became an honest man with an honest career. It took me longer to realise he'd made a wise choice but, when I did, I quickly prospered. Demetri and I have followed very similar paths through our lives. It is just that mine has led to greater heights than his.' Mike could not understand how Carla could be the daughter of such an arrogant man. 'We were friends once and should be friends now.'

'You like to be well regarded.'

Mancini gave Mike a sharp glance.

'My daughter cannot understand why I'm so reluctant to put any pressure on Demetri for him to sell to her. I don't want it to come to that.' He let his implied threat hang in the air for a moment before adding, 'If we talked things through I'm sure we could find a mutually satisfying outcome. But, as he won't speak with me, it's up to you. Don't be coerced by Carla into trying to force Demetri to do something he'll regret. Find out what he really wants.'

Irritated at being talked down to, Mike said, 'I know what that is; he wants me to take over the shops from him.'

'No. That's a means to an end. Find out what he really wants to achieve by having you take over and see if there are better ways of meeting his wishes.'

The game had reached half-time and the teams were gathered in two small clumps, shivering in the wind while the coaches harangued them. Mike noticed Christos looking towards them and waved to him. Christos acknowledged the wave with a small one of his own and quickly turned back. Mike realised he had no idea what had happened on the field in the first half. It had not looked as though any goal would come from the pack engulfing the ball but, such was his preoccupation, he couldn't be sure it hadn't.

When the game restarted, Mancini said, 'Walk with me,' and strolled towards the far end of the pitch, well away from the other spectators. He stopped to watch the game, standing beside Mike, and after a while began to speak again.

'I know you and Carla have become close and I'm sure she will have unburdened herself to you. She will have told you how Riverside was her idea, how she first persuaded Angelo, and later me, to pursue the project, and how badly I have behaved, resulting in her exclusion from the project and the fracturing of her relationship with Angelo despite the efforts she has made to bring the three of us together again. You will have been very sympathetic – comforting a beautiful woman has great appeal for any man.'

Mike had no doubt Mancini's teasing tone was intended to plant the idea Carla often used such a ploy. Perhaps he saw their relationship as some kind of threat – maybe a threat to Carla's marriage. But Mike had to admit Mancini was accurate in his portrayal of what she had told him. There were shouts from the field and from the supporters as a goal was scored.

'Your son has just put the ball in the net,' Mancini said and slapped his gloved hands together. Mike could see Christos high-fiving his teammates, and belatedly joined in the applause.

After the restart, Mancini said, 'Let me tell you about my

daughter. She has many talents and I have looked to her as the only one in my family with the ability to follow me into my businesses. I'm deeply disappointed she refuses to come into my transport company. I've begged her many times, but it's a complex undertaking and she would need to spend time learning the business through postings in various parts of the company before she could take over at the top. This she refuses to do.' Mancini gave Mike an ironic grin. 'Jim Findlay obviously had the same problem with his son. The difference between us is that I stood firm and all of you at Findlay's now know I was right.

'Carla has great ambition. Ambition is a fine thing, but must at times be tempered by commercial reality. Carla has been slow to learn this. Take Café Filipo. I established it as a profitable but unremarkable trattoria. When Carla came into it she immediately set out to make it a distinctive restaurant of the highest quality. Were it not for my patience and my deep pockets, it would have gone out of business in the first year.'

Mike hunched his shoulders and swung his arms against the cold, showing his impatience with this long-winded man, but Mancini went on. 'When Carla married Angelo Rossi, he was the owner of a successful, medium-sized building company – Rubicon. Angelo is a very good builder but has none of Carla's driving ambition. Although she held no position in her husband's company she was determined Rubicon should become a major developer. Angelo preferred to run the firm in his own way at his own pace but Carla prevailed, as she does with most men. She was the first to see the potential of the Riverside site for a vast and prestigious development and carried Angelo along with her ideas. When she came to me for support I was happy to work with her and Angelo on the project. I do have sway with a number of influential people; have twisted some arms and called in some favours. I also put in a significant amount of my own funds. The first stages were highly successful, although it was apparent Angelo deeply regretted no longer holding unquestioned control. I don't blame him. I would have hated to have my father-in-law and my wife taking the lead in any of my companies.

'I was the first to see the coming downturn in the property market and the need to recast our plans. Again Carla was unwilling to curb her ambition in the face of commercial reality and we argued. Angelo may be a very capable builder, but he's out of his depth in the other aspects of such a large and complex project. He could only complain that we were the ones who had created the problems. Carla lost her temper ...'

Mancini paused to give Mike an appraising glance. 'Her delightful serenity can crack if the pressure becomes too great. She ordered Angelo to stop complaining and pointed out he now depended on me for the viability of Rubicon. She thought I would rescue Rubicon as I had done for some of her earlier ventures, but this was on a much larger scale. When I refused to put in more funds, Angelo decided to show the Mancini family he could get along without them.

'Carla continues trying to reassert her influence, but her efforts are futile. In the end it's always the men with the money who rule. Angelo has lost control of his company.'

'You mean Sarac ?'

'Sarac?' Mancini scoffed. 'A low-grade thug who likes to put on airs. Incompetent, too. Look how ineffective he and his gang were in trying to disrupt CityView. They had to go elsewhere to set you up.'

'Who do you mean?'

Mancini turned to look directly into Mike's eyes. 'Why is Vern McKenzie working with them?'

'Is he?'

'You know he is. What I need to understand is why.'

'Vern has a high opinion of Angelo Rossi. I think he may have gone to him when he realised CityView and Riverside were coming into competition with one another.'

Mike could hear the lameness of his reply but, sure as hell, was not going to say anything to Mancini about his fear of Vern's treachery.

'Come off it,' Mancini said. 'Why did he set you up with this bribery scam?'

'How do you know about that?'

'I know a lot about you and your problems.'

Mike's voice rose as his irritation with Mancini's all-knowing arrogance spilled out.

'If you know so much about me, you should know it was the union official, Alan Reardon, who set me up, not Vern.'

Mancini was unfazed. 'No, you're wrong. Reardon needed to protect himself, but it was McKenzie who set you up.'

'Why are you so interested in my problems?'

'I'm not. But I am interested in McKenzie, the loyal deputy to Jim Findlay who must be bitter that Findlay was stupid enough to bring his son in over the top of him. Is he taking his revenge?'

'He's not selling him out.'

'Ah, so you do know more. What is he doing?'

'I told you. He's looking for cooperation, not confrontation with Rubicon.'

Mancini touched Mike on the arm. 'Look, I'm sorry if I've offended you. I know you're under great pressure at the moment.'

'Oh, yeah.'

'You should take some comfort from the line the police have taken with you over the killing of Shane Francis.'

'What?'

'When a murder is involved the police dig much further and much deeper than for lesser crimes.'

'I've seen that,' Mike said.

'Yes, but take heart from the way they're trying to frighten you into a confession. It means they haven't enough to charge you. It also means they'll keep digging despite the impression you were given.'

'How do you know this?'

'I can understand why you're reluctant to tell me all you know and I admit I'm not primarily concerned for you, but our interests are aligned. I'm sure McKenzie is the key to unravelling this whole can of worms, including the strife you're in.'

Mancini delved below his overcoat and produced a card, which he handed to Mike.

'Now I've taken you into my confidence call me if there's anything you think might help me or any way I can help you.'

'You've told me nothing. A bit here and a bit there to show how clever you are, but you haven't levelled with me. Why should I have anything to do with you?'

'If I told you any more I'd be putting you in more danger than you are already. You should help me where you can because it's in your interest to have me succeed.'

'What the hell's going on?'

'Ah, the game is over and your son has had a win. We should go to congratulate him.'

Mancini turned and began to walk back to where Christos' jubilant team was being congratulated by their supporters. 'One last word of advice.' He paused and turned to look directly at Mike beside him. 'Be patient – something you must find difficult in your situation.'

'Hey, Dad, did you see it?' A beaming Christos was still ten metres away but he had no patience, either.

'Yeah. Great,' Mike said uncertainly. Did Christos mean the goal or the win?

226

'I liked the way you waited your chance and measured it off before you buried it in the net,' Mancini said with an enthusiasm which brought Christos' faltering smile back to full width.

'This is Mr Mancini. My son, Christos.'

Mancini extended his hand to Christos as he had earlier to Mike. 'It's a pleasure to meet a fellow footballer.' He paused and affected a modesty which Mike felt was quite out of character. 'Not of your class, I'm afraid. I was too big and awkward, but I made a formidable goalie. Many years ago I played for Brunswick Juventus.'

'My grandfather played for South Melbourne Hellas.'

'Very good he was, too. I was in the 1958 Juventus side that won the premiership, but then, along came Hellas with your father in their team and we found it hard to get a look in. We did sometimes, though. We had to be patient. Like you were today. I've been saying the same thing to your father. You have to wait patiently until you see your chance and then you don't hold back – you strike.'

He gave what amounted to a small bow and left them staring as he walked to the silver Mercedes and was driven away.

Christos maintained a constant stream of excited chatter about the game on the way home. Demetri came towards them as they reached their front gate.

'Grandpa! I scored a goal and we won,' Christos shouted.

'Well done, my boy. Great news. Let's go inside and you can tell me all about it.'

Mary's car pulled up beside them and the four went into the house together. Almost immediately the family divided into groups. Leila and Jacinta set the table and served the drinks their mother had poured. Mary and Lissa went to the kitchen to put the finishing touches to the meal and to talk about Lissa's next commission – lunch for eight people in the office of a local solicitor.

Demetri and Christos settled on the couch for a detailed description of his triumph. Mike, as he had been at the game itself, became an uninvolved spectator, lost in his own thoughts. Mancini had annoyed and intrigued him. He was certainly a showman – the arrogant way he presented himself, the pleasure he took in letting Mike know he had a well-placed source in the police force, his oblique endorsement of Alan Reardon and his references to Jim and Ben Findlay.

Mancini's supposed concern for his father was probably a pretext to gain Mike's attention before asking about Vern. Trying to find out what Vern was doing was his real interest; that and his attempt to undermine Carla in Mike's eyes with his sly digs at the way she manipulated men. Was he just a father, unhappy about his married daughter showing interest in another man? Mike needed some time by himself to sort through what Mancini had said and, more importantly, what he had hinted at but left unsaid.

Demetri broke into Mike's thoughts as if he had been listening to them. 'Mancini! What was he doing there this afternoon?' he demanded. 'Up to no good, I'll bet.'

Taken aback by his grandfather's vehemence, Christos looked across to his father for support.

'He gave Chris the same advice you're always giving him,' Mike said.

'What would he know?'

'Grandpa, he told us he won a premiership with Juventus before Hellas became the top team when you were there.'

'He was never a good footballer. He scraped into the Juventus team a few times when their regular goalie was injured, but he didn't have the skill or the commitment to be a good player – too busy running his gang.'

'Dinner everyone,' Lissa called and Mike was the first to move, eager to break away from his father.

While Demetri spent the meal quizzing the children about their activities, Mike took the opportunity to scrutinise Mary who sat opposite him at the end of the table away from their father. She still looked strained, but some colour had returned to her face or perhaps been put there for the occasion. Conscious of Mike's eye upon her, she gave him a tentative smile; the most pleasant she had been to him in days.

When the meal was over, Lissa announced she had rented a DVD of *Harry Potter and the Deathly Hallows* that Christos could set up on the TV upstairs while the adults had coffee. As soon as the children left the room, Mary came over to Mike.

'I never thought you did it,' she said. 'I just couldn't understand why he mentioned you before he went out. The police have got it all wrong.'

'Lissa told you?'

'What is this?' Demetri asked querulously.

'The police have got it into their heads – some of them anyway – that I was the one who killed Shane. One of the reasons your old mate Mario Mancini came this afternoon was to tell me not to lose my nerve under the pressure from the police. He seems to have someone in the force who keeps him very well informed of what's going on in the homicide squad.'

'He probably always has had,' Demetri lamented.

'He also wanted to tell me the man he was supposed to have killed – Drago Fontini, was that his name? – died accidently when he tried to run away from a fight with Mancini. You don't have to be ashamed about having sat on the tape.'

'And you believe him?'

Demetri's voice made it clear he certainly didn't.

'As it happens, I do.'

'But what can you do to clear your name?' Mary asked.

'I reckon Mancini agrees with me that Shane was killed

because the thugs he hung out with …' Mike saw the look Mary shot him. 'Sorry, Mary.'

'No. I know more about what Shane was doing now. When the police started asking me some questions I didn't understand, they had to tell me. What were you about to say?'

'I was going to say some of the guys Shane was working with are hard cases. One of them mugged me on the night Shane was killed. I reckon they found out about Shane and me knowing one another and thought he was telling me what they were up to. That's why they beat me up and killed him.'

'Yeah,' Mary said. 'That would explain what he said, and the police told me they think it was a fight that went wrong for Shane. He was badly beaten and unconscious but still alive when they dumped him in the river.'

'There's a lot going on Mancini wouldn't tell me about although, being the kind of man he is, he couldn't resist dropping some hints. I reckon all of it is somehow linked together. I'll have to work it out for myself.'

'So many problems,' Demetri said mournfully.

'Cheer up, Dad. We'll be OK.'

'Sorry. I'm feeling tired. It was a busy day at the shop.'

'I'll drive you home,' Mary volunteered.

'No,' Mike interjected. 'It's just around the corner. I'll walk with you, Dad.'

As soon as they were in the street Mike said, 'For years now, you've made it clear you dearly want me to come into the business with you, but what do you want to achieve by having me there?'

'Have you come to your senses? You've seen what troubles your job brings you?'

'No, Dad, I still feel the same, but this isn't about me. It's about you. I've never asked you before. What would having me come into the business achieve for you?'

'You will follow me. The name will continue.' Demetri gave an irritated shake of his head. 'I've told you this many times before. Weren't you listening? My father promised his father and I promised him the Georgiou name would be maintained in Bay Street. We kept our promises and now it is up to you to do the same.'

'Yes, you're right,' Mike replied, surprising his father. 'I haven't been listening.'

'So you will come?'

'No. I've told you that many times as well. But we'll talk again when I've cleared away some of the problems I have at present.'

After he had seen his father into his house and left him rather mystified but happier than before, Mike took a much longer route to return home. The sky remained overcast and the wind biting, but he did not notice, lost in thought. He needed to convince the police he had not killed Shane and his best chance of doing that was to have Angelo Rossi tell the police what he had told Carla. That wasn't going to happen while Rossi remained beholden to whoever it was now running Rubicon - not Sarac but the crime boss who had put money into Rubicon and was now after Findlay's. The meeting at Flinders tomorrow was a chance to see who was involved. It would be difficult to get close without being discovered but Reardon had done it. Reardon had used him. He would use Reardon.

Lissa confronted him as soon as he got home.

'Where have you been?'

'I went for a walk to clear my head.'

'In this weather? You've been complaining about the cold all day. You haven't been making a quick call on Carla, have you?'

Before Mike could reply Mary said, 'Did it work? Are you any clearer on what you should do to get the police off your back?'

'Yes it did. I'm a lot clearer.'

Mike took his phone from his pocket, made a call and waited for a short time before saying, 'Alan, it's Mike Georgiou.'

'Hi Mike,' Alan Reardon replied and paused before asking, 'How are you?'

'Your boss visited me this afternoon.'

'George came to see you?'

'No the one who's sending you to Flinders tomorrow.'

'I don't know what you're talking about.'

'That's a pity. I was going to bum a lift with you. I'll just have to go by myself. Barging in might get me a quicker result than skulking round outside. '

'Mike, please don't do that.'

'You have a choice.'

'Where do you live?'

'14 Martin Street, South Melbourne. What time?'

'I want to arrive down there well before anyone else. I'll pick you up at 8.30. You can explain what's brought this on.'

'And you can explain what you've really been up to and what you hope to achieve at Flinders.'

Mike finished the call. Lissa and Mary gazed enquiringly at him.

'As you heard, I'm going to Flinders tomorrow. I'm going with the union guy, Alan Reardon, to Carla and Angelo Rossi's house we saw in *New Idea*.'

He looked directly at Lissa.

'Carla won't be there, but I'm confident others including Vern McKenzie will. Don't ask me what I'll achieve because I don't know. But at least I won't be mooning around here wondering what to do.'

16

Mike was watching through the bedroom window when the late-model, white Hyundai 120 drew up outside.

'I'm off,' he called to Lissa.

'You be careful. You've been beaten up too often lately,' she said, her attempt at a grin twisting further when she added, 'And give my regards to Carla if she happens to turn up.'

When Mike came through the front door Alan had reached the gate. 'G'day,' he said, frowning. 'You sure you know what you're doing?'

Mike opened the rear door of the car to toss his small back-pack on to the seat. 'I have no idea what you're doing. That's why I want to come with you.' Alan shrugged and took his place behind the wheel while Mike eased himself into the passenger seat. 'New car?'

'It's rented for the day. It has the advantage of being anonymous.'

'God, you are careful.'

Alan started the car and they moved off. 'I thought by now you'd learned how dangerous it can be if you're not careful with this lot.'

They drove in silence through the Sunday-quiet streets until they joined the freeway, when Alan sat back and said, 'How did you know I'd be going down today and why are you tagging along?'

'Before I tell you anything, I want you to tell me why you hung me out to dry with the commission.'

Alan did not reply, concentrating on passing a slow-moving

233

truck. Eventually he said, 'I told you I'd tipped off the commission that I expected an attempt to set me up with a bribe but I didn't know when or how. I thought the commission would have trouble tracing the source – shifting money in ways hard to trace is routine for the man I'm after. Instead, you were made the fall guy – something I wasn't expecting. When you told me Bruno and Rick had been at the Lord Nelson I knew our meeting there'd come out and I had to avoid it looking like I'd asked you for the bribe. I certainly didn't want to tell the commission about the photos I showed you, so I told them you asked to meet with me and wanted to know how you could improve relations with the union. The only call I made to you wasn't from my usual phone – I have another I use for any calls I want to keep quiet – so it was easy to make it appear you'd set up our meeting. Sorry.'

'Who is calling the shots at Rubicon?' Mike asked. 'I know Sarac's just the middle-man, the fixer.'

'Hold on. You said you'd tell me why you wanted to go to Flinders with me if I explained how I dropped you in it with the commission.'

'OK. I'm trying to work out what's really going on in Rubicon to help me convince the police it wasn't me who murdered Shane Francis.'

'You?' Alan turned his head sharply to glance at Mike. 'Why do the police suspect you?'

'I told you when Shane got drunk he beat up my sister. He did it again last weekend and I had a go at him on the Monday, telling him it had to stop. When he pretended it hadn't happened and gave me his sleazy smile, I did my block and told him if he did it again I'd kill him. Several people heard the bit about killing him. Later that night someone phoned him and he told my sister I was a pest before he went out and got himself killed. The police put this together with the fact I was in some kind of fight the same night and I'm their man.'

'Yeah, that was the night we were at the Lord Nelson. I can give you an alibi.'

'Thanks, but it won't work. You didn't see me get mugged and there was time after you left for me to call Shane, have a fight and kill him.'

'What a bugger.' Alan sounded genuinely sympathetic. 'But I don't see how coming with me today will help you.'

Mike had regained some of the trust he'd lost in Alan but not enough to tell him anything more. Not yet, anyway. 'Maybe if you tell me what you're up to and why.'

'I don't know for sure, but I reckon your pal Vern McKenzie will be going down there again today to meet with the guys from Rubicon. He's proven himself to them by setting you up. He probably thought he'd get me as well. What I don't know is why he wants to get in with these thugs.'

Mike pursed his lips, coming to a decision. 'He did have ideas of having Findlay's merge with Rubicon. He thought Angelo Rossi was running Rubicon, but he isn't any longer, is he? Who is?'

'How long have you known what McKenzie was up to?'

'He sounded me out around ten days ago, but I wasn't keen on the idea. I reckon that's why he wants me out of the way.'

Alan turned his head to grin at Mike. 'So, you've come to your senses. What convinced you McKenzie is no friend of yours?'

'I've been coming to it for a while. Listening to your boss, Mancini, yesterday afternoon, I finally decided you were both right about Vern.'

'He's not my boss,' Alan declared.

'Don't kid me. How else would he know some of the things I told you the other day? I bet he tipped you off more was going on in Rubicon than the fiddles Sarac was into at Riverside.'

'If you're right about McKenzie, then the man who really interests me will likely be there today, as well.'

'Does he have a name?'

'Jerry Kane is a reclusive type who keeps himself well hidden but, among other things, runs one of the biggest drug syndicates in the country. From time to time the police arrest some of his people and close down one arm of his empire but they've never been able to get him.'

Mike guessed Kane must be the supplier of the funds Angelo Rossi used to get Mancini out of Rubicon but didn't want to reveal all that Carla had told him.

'What's he got to do with Rubicon?' he asked.

'When I started looking into what was going on at Riverside I thought Mancini was behind it all. Despite his current, airbrushed community standing, he has a track record that would say he'd be just the type to go in for the scams and the coercion I was uncovering. But then I found he's out of it now.'

'He told you?'

Alan stared straight ahead down the road. 'The word is that Rossi got fed up with his father-in-law looking over his shoulder, got rid of him and found another backer. No one seems to know who that backer is and the only company info I've been able to see is shrouded in the kind of financial smoke screen these guys are so good at putting up. I think it could be Kane. He needs to do a lot of money laundering and Rubicon would have seemed like a good place.'

'How did you get on to him?'

'Obviously what was going on at Riverside had to have a purpose and it didn't take long for me to realise the downturn in property sales was causing cash flow problems for Rubicon. Cash flow is vital to money laundering as water is for growing crops. That's why Sarac was moved in and the scams began.'

236

Mike shook his head. It must have been Mancini who put Alan on to Kane.

'Vern thought cash flow might be a problem at Rubicon. He saw the steady cash flow from our other projects as one of the advantages to Rubicon if we merged.'

'Well, there you are.'

Mike decided to have one last try. 'Mancini *has* briefed you fully. He wouldn't tell me any of this.'

'Jerry Kane isn't the only one taking a lot of trouble to keep a low profile in this business. You obviously know Mancini. How did that come about?'

Mike explained how Mancini and his father had known one another years ago, but omitted any mention of the recording Demetri had made. 'Mancini's daughter wants to buy Dad's shop as part of a large development she has planned for that section of Bay Street. When he wouldn't sell, they asked me to persuade him.'

'So you've met the lovely Carla. They say she's a real stunner.'

'Yes, she is attractive,' Mike said in a voice he strove to make neutral. 'A capable business woman, I'd say from what I've seen of her. It's her father I've heard most from, though,' he lied. Anxious to move on from the topic of Carla, Mike grinned and said, 'You say you're not working for Mancini. So who are you working for?'

Alan gripped the wheel fiercely and shook his head. 'Christ! You management types can only think in terms of bosses and underlings. I'm my own boss in this. I want to stop crims getting into the industry. Believe me, I've seen what they can do once they get a toe-hold. That's why this is much bigger than Riverside.'

They drove in silence until Mike judged Alan had calmed down. 'You obviously had a hard time in the west. Tell me about it.'

Alan shot Mike a questioning glance but, reassured his interest was genuine, began to speak of his experiences, at first hesitantly and then with greater freedom. After he had finished they were silent again and Mike reflected on what he had heard. The further Alan had gone the better Mike could understand why he was so focused on trying to root out criminals from the building industry, why he was so cautious in all that he did and why he saw himself as a loner pursuing his own crusade and working for no one. He most likely was working *with*, even using, Mancini but certainly not working *for* him. Mike wondered whether Mancini appreciated this. He still had no clear idea why Mancini was so interested in 'unravelling this whole can of worms', as he had put it to Mike. He no longer had any financial interest in Rubicon. It seemed unlikely he wanted to free Angelo Rossi from the control of Jerry Kane and his men although that would suit Mike very well. More likely he wanted to enable Carla to regain her influence over Riverside.

Alan interrupted his reverie by asking how he had come to work at Findlay's. Mike was pleased to find his account of starting as a chippie apprentice and rising through the company provoked admiring comments, although Alan did say he thought Jim Findlay's interest in developing his staff was unusual for a boss. Mike had come on this trip determined not to put his trust in Alan, but the more they talked and the better he came to know him, the less likely it seemed he needed to be so cautious. Once this business was over they might even become friends. Perhaps Vern and George Fowler had started in a similar way.

As they approached Flinders, Alan asked the question that could well have been on his mind since early in their drive. 'You said your aim today was to help clear yourself from suspicion of killing Shane. Let's say we somehow succeed in nailing Kane and McKenzie. How does that help you?'

'I need Angelo Rossi not to fear what Kane or Sarac might do to him.'

'I still don't get it.'

'As I'm sure you know, Angelo loathes them all. He saw me and Shane at a family dinner in Café Italia a couple of weeks ago. Angelo couldn't resist trying to stir up trouble within Sarac's gang by telling them he'd seen us together. Something happened to make them even more suspicious of Shane and the night he was killed Sarac rang Angelo to tell him Shane was dead. He told Angelo Shane was a traitor and they were well rid of him. Angelo feels guilty he started them down this path but won't go to the police.'

'How do you know this?'

'I know.'

'Did Mancini tell you?'

'No.'

'No?' Mike could see Alan turning over the possibilities. 'No, of course he wouldn't. Angelo wouldn't tell Mancini. That's it. Carla told you.'

Alan gave a large grin that displayed both self-satisfaction and irony. 'Angelo told his wife and she told you. No wonder you looked so coy when I mentioned her earlier. You sly bastard. From what I've heard, half the men in Melbourne lust after her. How did you make it with her?'

'It's nothing like that.'

Alan continued to grin but did not pursue Mike further. They drove through Flinders and towards Cape Schanck. Some kilometres on Alan turned the car into a clearing among the trees growing beside the road and brought it to a stop.

'I didn't realise we were having a picnic,' Mike said.

'Better than that, we're going on a hike.'

Alan took a backpack from the boot and led the way down a

sandy track towards the sea. The track wound through banksias with yellow bottlebrush flowers, sheoaks and eucalypts, the bush made even denser by the vines which clung to the trunks and branches. A strong breeze tossed the tops of the trees. It was still cold but the cloud cover was not nearly as dense as it had been yesterday – an increasing number of blue patches broke up the white and grey. As they neared the coast, the breeze began to snatch at them and Mike was glad he had worn his hooded anorak. Alan did not seem to feel the cold and was comfortable in jeans and T-shirt topped by a green woollen sweater. A break in the trees at the end of the path let them look down on the surf breaking across the rocks at the base of the cliff on which they were standing.

'Where do we go from here?' Mike asked.

'Now we have to bush-bash along the cliff-top.'

'Isn't there an easier way?'

'You could climb down the cliff and swim around if you like. The Rossi property is wedged between two arms of the national park – that's what makes it such a secure place for the meetings they have down here. If you don't go in the front gate, you have to come through the bush. Only people as silly as you and I do that, so they think they're secure and don't worry too much about checking for interlopers. Come on.'

They pressed on through bushes barring their way and stumbled in holes left by burrowing animals and nesting birds. Their route took them around a succession of small coves nibbling into the cliff face and offered spectacular views of rocks and sea. Their trek was enhanced by a sense of isolation with the rhythmic boom of the surf, the sigh of the wind in the trees and the cries of the keening seabirds as a mournful chorale. He hoped it was not an omen. Despite his light frame, Alan coped better than Mike with the difficulties of their walk.

'How about a break?' he pleaded.

'If you like,' Alan allowed. 'But it's only about another ten minutes.'

Mike nodded his reluctant acceptance and they continued until confronted by a barbed-wire fence running from the clifftop back up the hill. A sign prominently displayed on the section of fence they faced told them all they needed to know:

PRIVATE PROPERTY: KEEP OUT

'At least it doesn't say, "Trespassers will be shot",' Mike said. Alan, ever cautious, held up his hand to silence him and stood for a minute or so looking and listening.

Satisfied, he held the strands of the fence apart and nodded for Mike to squeeze through. After they reversed roles and both were on the other side, Alan said, 'There's about another forty metres of trees and bush before an open paddock. We need to go further up the hill so we're closer to the house. There's a clump of bushes up there where we can get a good view without being seen.'

He led Mike along the fence before turning left and carefully picking his way to the side of the paddock that ran back down the hill. Through the bushes Mike glimpsed a swimming pool and the tiled patio of a glass fronted building set into the hill, clearly recognisable as the house featured in *New Idea*. Alan took a small pair of binoculars from his pack and swept down the paddock, which sloped to a break in the cliffs – where a creek flowed on to a small, sandy beach – and then up the heavily wooded other side to the house itself. He handed the glasses to Mike, who repeated his survey. When he sighted on the house, he noticed a movement: it was Angelo Rossi, with a mug in his hand, walking to the window and gazing out to the cove beyond the beach.

'There's Rossi,' he said.

'Yeah. He comes down the day before. I can't help thinking he likes to get away from all the others.' Alan gave Mike a sidelong glance and added, 'Even away from Carla.'

He pointed to the trees further up the hill from where they were standing. 'There's a spot higher up where we can see the others arrive. Let's go there now.'

They reached a place where a gap in the covering hedge of trees allowed them a view of the carport above the house. Alan reached into his pack and drew out a camera with a telephoto lens and slung it around his neck.

'I've got some back-up for you,' Mike said and took his own camera from his pack.

'Nice,' Alan said. 'Looks like a good quality video-camera.'

'Moment of weakness when the kids started arriving and I wanted to record their every move.'

—

Vern McKenzie sat in exactly the same seat at the Flinders Village Cafe as he had the previous week, another cup of sweet, black tea in front of him. He felt more settled than last week, knowing better what to expect. He also knew that, having set up Mike and Reardon, he could not turn back and no longer needed to contemplate that option. Yesterday he had played good golf and, together with Paul Jones, had won their match – a promising omen for today. Although it was cold, it was dry and clear – something else to be pleased about. He finished his drink, climbed into his car and soon reached the unimpressive carport. Unaware of the two cameras recording his arrival, he glanced at the cars he had seen parked there the previous Sunday. Shane Francis would be missing this time. Why was he killed? Had it anything to do with his dealings with Rubicon, or something quite different? His absence would leave room in the SUV for Sarac's boss, although Vern suspected he would prefer to come separately. In which case he had yet to arrive.

When Rick admitted Vern to the house, he found Sarac and Rossi sitting at the small table beside the bar each with a stubbie in front of them. There was no sign of Bruno. 'Come over here and sit with me, Vern. I've got your Glenkinchie,' Sarac said, pointing to a glass which sat beside the stubbies. Rossi nodded to Vern but said nothing.

Vern remained at the base of the steps, enjoying the view, before he took a seat at the small table opposite Sarac and beside Angelo. 'Where's the boss?'

'Not far away,' Sarac said.

Rick, still by the front door, opened it to admit Bruno, who nodded to Sarac. 'Good. Bruno, come over and we can get all the checking out of the way at the start.'

He turned back to Vern. 'The boss is a careful man. If you don't mind standing again, Bruno can see you're not carrying anything we wouldn't like.'

Vern shook his head as if about to object but then stood and, with scowling face, allowed Bruno to check him over. That done, he sat down again and lingered over a mouthful of the whisky before saying, 'I'm sorry about Shane. What happened there?'

'Yeah, unfortunate,' Sarac replied.

His head swung around with an angry frown when Bruno gave a humourless laugh and said, 'Why don't you ask Georgiou what happened?'

Rossi shook his head and drew in an irritated breath.

Puzzled by their reaction, Vern said, 'Can't ask Mike anything at the moment. He's been suspended.'

'Yeah. Pity we can't say the same for Reardon. He's still round and about.'

'Just the commission taking it's time,' Vern replied. He was worried though. Had Reardon found a way to wriggle out, or was George making it difficult for the commission? He had been cagey the other night.

'Looks like we'll have to deal with that loner ourselves,' Bruno told him, receiving another frown from Sarac as he pulled out his phone and made a call.

'OK, we're all set,' he said and closed the phone.

—

After Mike and Alan had recorded Vern step from his car and watched him disappear inside the house, Alan said, 'Did you know McKenzie is back running head office while Ben Findlay does your job at CityView?'

'I didn't know that, but it doesn't surprise me.'

'Not a happy place, I'm told. You seem to have a loyal team behind you down there and Ben Findlay is not getting on well with them. Unfortunately for him, the union delegate George provided to replace poor little Ted Horton is turning out to be just as prickly as Ted. They say the way things are going you may well have a strike at CityView in the next week or so.'

'That bad?'

Mike had never given Ben much chance of succeeding as project manager at CityView, but he thought it would have taken longer than this for problems to surface.

They took shots of Bruno when he returned from checking the road by the front gate. 'You were right about their confidence,' Mike said. 'Careful attention to the top of the block and bugger all anywhere else.'

'Only Mr Kane to come,' Alan said and they resumed their wait.

After about ten minutes, a dark green Mercedes SUV emerged from the screen of trees and parked under the carport. The man who stepped from the passenger door looked to be in his middle to late fifties. Of medium height and bulk, he had straight, red hair, somewhat longer than was common these days. He wore a white rollneck jumper and navy corduroys.

'Ah, Jerry! Welcome to Flinders,' Alan said.

The driver, a short man in a blue bomber jacket, stood behind him as they waited to be let into the house.

'You said Kane was reclusive, but you recognised him,' Mike noted. 'Did Mancini show you a photograph or just give you his description?'

Alan sniffed and said, 'Time to go back down and hope we get something useful through the windows or, better still, they don't think it's too cold to sit outside.'

—

When Vern saw the red-haired man come down the steps he stood to greet him, but no one made any attempt to introduce them. 'G'day,' the man said, but did not offer his hand and stood at a distance, scrutinising Vern.

'You know I'm Vern McKenzie. Who are you?' When there was no reply, Vern tossed his head. 'I'm not here to play silly games. If we're going to work together I'll eventually need a lot more than your name, but that's a good place to start.'

The man nodded and gave a crooked grin while his eyes continued to study Vern. 'Didn't they say? Jerry Kane.'

Sarac pointed to the leather suite where they sat last time.

'Let's go up the other end,' he said. 'The rest of you can fire up the barbecue and get lunch started.'

When Angelo moved towards them Sarac waved a dismissive hand. 'You can show them where the stuff is, Ang. If we need you we'll give a shout.'

Bruno, Rick and the man who had driven Kane were already on their way to one of the glass doors leading to the terrace. Rossi scowled at Sarac and followed them. 'Bring your glass, Vern. Jerry enjoys a good whisky, too, so I'll bring the bottle.'

Once they were settled with Vern on the chair between the other two, Kane said. 'Ivan's given me the guts of what you're proposing. Take me through it in detail.'

Vern embarked on his account of the scheme he had put to Rossi and Sarac last Sunday. Kane frequently interrupted, intent on understanding every step in Vern's plan to bring Findlay's down. Twice Sarac broke in with a comment but, after the second occasion, when Kane had glared at him and drawn in a tight breath, he remained silent. When Vern became coy about detailing his links and influence with the union, Kane nodded and gave the same crooked grin he had used earlier.

'People to protect. Just like me.'

For once he allowed Vern to continue without insisting on an answer.

When Vern moved on to how Kane would take over and control Findlay's, he was not surprised Kane asked for greater detail about the company's finances and structure. As Vern went through these with him, he nodded in a manner that encouraged Vern to believe he was both understanding and buying the scheme. At the end of Vern's description, Kane, who had been leaning forward throughout, sat back and said, 'And what do you want out of this?'

'I want to be the well-paid MD of Findlay's, have Ben Findlay out of the firm and, by our success, show Jim Findlay how it could have been if he'd let me follow him instead of ignoring me and bringing his son into the firm.'

'I'll give you the first two. The third will be up to you, just like it was up to Rossi. Fail to deliver like he's failed and we won't leave you to hang around like we've done with him. You'll be out.'

'Talking of delivering, before I go any further, I want you to show me you can deliver on your side of the bargain.'

Kane's eyes remained steadily on Vern's as he lifted his glass to drink. He put the glass down carefully and was about to speak when there was a shout from outside.

'What the fuck is that?' he said.

—

From their position opposite the house Mike was able to film the threesome move to the near end of the room where he lost them in the reflections from the windows. Alan had stopped taking photographs and was busy setting up a small conical dish he had taken from his pack.

'I got this during the week – a parabolic ear they call it. Supposed to let you listen in, even through glass, and has a built in mini-recorder.'

He attached a set of headphones and pointed the dish at the house but was not pleased with the result. 'I can hear them – just – but it's too fuzzy to tell what they're saying most of the time.' When the men came from the house and went to the barbecue area at the other side of the pool, he pointed the dish at them. 'That's better. The one we haven't seen before is Billy. Bruno's giving him heaps – says he has a cosy job driving Kane around. Now if I could get the same quality from inside …'

He scrutinised the side of the house nearest to them and his face took on the concentrated expression of a man making calculations. 'If I come from the rear and then down the side I could put the dish in the bush on the corner. It would be close enough the glass shouldn't be a problem. They won't be able to see me if I stay next to the side wall.'

Before Mike could reply Alan stood and began walking back up the hill. Mike used the viewfinder of his camera to search for him and, after what seemed a long time but was probably only a few minutes, saw him emerge from the trees above the carport, slip down to the flat of the parking area and then emerge at the side wall of the house. Carefully he edged down the slope, delayed by the tendency of the feet attached to the dish to stick in the grass. Eventually he reached the corner and paused for a moment before taking a quick look at the pool and barbecue area through the foliage at the corner of the building. Satisfied he could not be seen, he pushed the dish under the small branches at the base of the bushes, positioned it to face the nearby windows and sat with his back against the side wall. With the headphones attached, he remained motionless for a short time before glancing over towards Mike and shaking his head. It seemed he was still not getting the clarity he needed. He dropped his head to fiddle with the control knobs for the unit.

Mike swivelled the camera to cover the barbecue area again and could see Bruno cutting up sausages while Rick fired up the barbecue. Angelo and Billy had turned away and were making their way back inside, perhaps to bring out the remainder of the meat. Mike stopped filming the barbecue area and swept the areas below the house. There was no question the view of cliffs, beach and cove was magnificent. Suddenly, a shout from the other end of the house brought Mike's attention back to Alan. Above him on the slope stood Billy, who must have gone through the house to the car park and circled around to the side. He began to run down the slope but slipped and pitched forward into the grass, giving Alan the chance to tear off the headphones and begin to run. He could not escape the way he had come as Billy, now on his feet again, blocked that route. The best alternative would be to head straight towards Mike who, without conscious thought, had begun to film the chase. Alan rejected this option, perhaps fearful it might result in Mike being discovered as well. He took a long loop around the end of the pool and down the hill towards the beach. Rick came from the barbecue area to chase him, but Alan was the faster runner and the gap between them widened as they careered down the slope. Mike hoped Alan would be sufficiently far ahead by the time they reached the bottom that he could lose Rick in the thick bush of the national park. Should he go to join him, should he disappear into the bush behind him, or should he remain to observe? The decision was made for him when Alan stumbled and fell. Quickly he regained his feet, but Rick was now only twenty metres away and Alan must have twisted his ankle or knee in the fall, because he could no longer outrun his pursuer and was soon brought to the ground. Mike continued to film as they wrestled, neither one able to overcome the other. Rick clearly lacked Bruno's brutal strength and Alan, despite being much lighter, had a wiriness and determination that Rick could not subdue.

When Bruno arrived, he stood above the two on the ground. The knife he had been using on the sausages was still in his hand. Alan levered himself up and over Rick and sat on his chest, his knees pinning Rick's sides. For a moment the writhing bodies remained still. Bruno took his chance and plunged the knife into Alan's back. Alan pitched forward and Bruno thrust the knife into him again and again before grasping him by the shoulder and pulling him off Rick and on to the grass where he lay lifeless. Slowly Rick climbed to his feet, looked down on Alan and said something to Bruno that caused him to brandish the knife at Rick as though he might be next. Rick spat into the grass, picked up his cap, which had been knocked from his head during the struggle, and turned to trudge slowly up the hill. When Mike turned his camera back to the house he could see Rossi, Sarac and Vern lined up watching through the windows. There was no sign of Kane or his driver.

— —

Sarac was the first on his feet when they heard the shout and moved swiftly to the window. 'Christ. That bugger Reardon's turned up.' Vern and Kane came to stand beside him while Rossi appeared from the other end of the house and stood apart from them as the four watched the chase.

Kane's driver came across the patio and in the door, carrying with him the receiving dish and headphones. 'Time to go,' he said, coming to stand beside his boss. When Kane did not reply but continued to stare at the figures down the hill, he turned and the five of them watched as Rick brought Reardon down.

'Got him,' Sarac said triumphantly.

They continued to watch the struggle until Bruno drove his knife into Reardon's back. Even from this distance, the ferocity of the attack was plain to see. Kane broke the shocked silence.

'You're right,' he told his driver and began to walk to the door. At the top of the steps he turned and fixed his gaze on Sarac.

'Ivan. Clean this up. No loose ends.'

He opened the door and was followed out by his driver.

Sarac walked over to stand directly in front of Vern.

'You're one of us now. You saw nothing. You weren't even here. Now go.'

He did not wait for Vern to respond but walked out on to the patio and began to make his way down the hill. From the other end of the room Vern heard Rossi say, 'We're all in the shit now. Go while you can.'

Angelo went to the bar, took another stubbie and carried it into the kitchen. Left on his own, Vern decided there was nothing to be gained by staying. He went to his car and drove away, puzzling over what he should do now. He had always known that achieving his aims might involve bending or even flouting the law, but concealing a murder was something else. Reardon couldn't have blundered in at a worse time: Jerry Kane was just on the point of committing himself. He needed to get back to Kane as soon as he could.

Sarac met Rick on his way down the hill. 'Is he stuffed?'

'Yeah, I reckon so. Careful with Bruno. Once, I could talk him down. The way he is now, though, he'll kill anyone who looks sideways at him.'

'You'd better come with me.'

———

Mike heard the cars departing. There was no question Alan was dead. The best thing he could do was to make his escape and get to the police as soon as he could. Yet he couldn't leave Alan lying there in the paddock. Mike gathered the two backpacks and walked slowly down the hill within the covering bush until he reached a point across from where Alan's body lay. Sarac, Rick and Bruno stood silently looking down on Alan like three crows beside some road-kill. Mike lined up each of them in his viewfinder as if sighting them with a rifle. He wouldn't be capable of that but he would have to make sure Alan was properly avenged. All these men, not just Bruno, but all of them, including Kane and Vern, must be punished for their part in bringing about Alan's death. He would stay until they moved him, as they surely must.

Sarac began to speak to the other two, using his hands as though reassuring and persuading them of something. Eventually Bruno tossed the knife on the grass beside Alan and sat down with his knees drawn up under his chin. Rick turned and walked back to the house. Sarac remained standing and at one point turned to stare straight at Mike. For a moment he thought he had been discovered, but Sarac checked his watch and gazed into the sky before turning back to look towards the house. Rick emerged carrying a set of keys. Mike continued to film these trivial events. It was something he could do.

When Rick reached the other two, there was another conversation, with Rick doing most of the talking. Sarac appeared to question him on a number of points before taking charge again. He took a handkerchief from his pocket and wrapped it around the handle of the knife before picking it up. He said something that brought a surly response from Bruno, who then bent to raise Alan from the ground and awkwardly lift his floppy body across one shoulder. With Rick leading the way, Bruno carrying Alan and Sarac coming behind with the knife, they made for the beach.

Mike went back to the boundary fence and forced his way through the bush beside it to the cliff above the beach, where he returned to the edge of the scrub. Below him on the small, sandy beach stood a corrugated iron shed previously hidden by the fold of the hill. There was no sign of the men. The alarm he had begun to feel ramped up when he heard a rasping screech, but it was merely the doors at the front of the shed being pushed open from inside. A medium-size cabin cruiser on a four-wheeled trailer slowly emerged from the shed and rolled down concrete tracks hidden under a thin layer of sand. Sarac sat under the canopy and Alan's body was slumped in the rear of the boat. Bruno and Rick waded out to release the boat from the trailer and clambered aboard. Sarac started the motor. Slowly they travelled along the narrow cove and out into the open sea.

Gloomily Mike sat to await their return. As the sun began to dip and the breeze freshened further, the cold became more intense. It would be even more uncomfortable in the chop of the sea. After half an hour Mike heard the sound of the motor and shortly the boat reappeared in the cove. There was no sign of Alan. Again Bruno and Rick were forced into the cold water to manoeuvre the boat on to the trailer, after which they started a motorised winch within the shed to haul the boat back inside. They closed the doors with the same shrieking noise and walked slowly back to the house, leaving Mike alone on the headland. There was nothing more to film.

Not long afterwards he heard the sound of the remaining two cars starting up and leaving the property. He thought about exploring the surrounds of the house – even breaking in to search the interior – but did not have the heart for it. What was the point? He began the difficult walk back to the car and had gone only a short way when he realised he didn't have its ignition keys. As he approached the road, he saw the car was no longer there. For a surreal moment he imagined Alan had somehow recovered, swum ashore and driven off. Then it dawned, Sarac wouldn't want the police to find Alan's car anywhere near Flinders. It was probably on its way to the long-term car park at Tullamarine.

17

Mike had passed through many emotions since finding the car gone on Sunday afternoon. There had been the initial fear they were waiting for him to return to the car. Too late, he ducked into the bushes beside the path but, finding he was alone, his fear turned to lonely despondency. He was cold, bereft and had no means of getting home. It was then he called Lissa. Despondency overtook lethargy as, tired and stiff, he sat waiting for her to pick him up. By the time she reached him it was dark and he was shivering with the cold. Once within the warmth of the car, he told her what had happened and was overcome by grief at Alan's death. The only other time he could remember breaking into such choking sobs had been when he gave the instruction for the hospital staff to turn off his mother's life support. Lissa wanted to take him to the police immediately, but he refused. He needed time to think how best to use the evidence he held. Arriving at a local police station on a Sunday night with an unlikely story and a video he had not yet viewed was not the way to do it.

When Lissa insisted it was wrong to delay and they began to argue he became angry, initially with her, but then with Alan. Why had this ultra-cautious man taken such a risk to place the receiving dish close to the windows? Why had he been so foolish? His anger moved on to Vern. If it had not been for his treachery, none of this would have happened. Vern and Jerry Kane, the men who drew Alan and Mike to Flinders, had driven away and he had nothing that could incriminate them in anything. When he started trying to explain to Lissa how he felt she must have realised he was in no state to make a coherent statement to the police and gave up trying to persuade him, agreeing they should go directly home. Exhaustion soon replaced anger and Mike fell asleep, waking again when they were half-way home. Physically refreshed but still deeply troubled, he could not settle. Debating within himself what he should do, he thought of Mario Mancini's edict that you have to wait patiently until you see your chance and then you don't hold back – you strike.

As the taxi pulled into the entry to the Crown Towers Hotel, Mike's heart began to pump. Immediately he stepped from the cab he saw Rick waiting for him. Earlier, he had couriered a data stick to Sarac with the message, 'No one but you and I need see this. I have a proposal for you. Mike Georgiou.' When Mike had added a postscript to his message, saying that if any harm came to him or to anyone close to him, the video and Mike's statement would go straight to the police, he thought how similar his father's message to Mario Mancini must have been – history repeating itself – although he wanted a lot more than self-protection. Sarac's response had been to call him and say he should come to the Crown Towers at three.

Rick nodded curtly and turned to lead him through the hotel foyer to the concourse beside the river. They went only a short distance before Rick halted and scanned the people coming towards them from each direction. Apparently satisfied he ducked into a narrow alleyway concealed by a box hedge and leading to what appeared to be an electrical services cabinet with two head-high grey doors. He opened the left hand door and gestured for Mike to enter. As Mike walked up the short staircase alone, Rick closed the door behind him – no going back now. Sarac was seated at the table where Mike had enjoyed his lunch with Carla less than a week ago. There was no food, no drink and no music this time. Sarac stood up.

'Before we start, I need to make sure you're not trying any fancy tricks. Put your arms up and let me check you over.'

After he had run his hands over Mike's body and assured himself that he was not carrying a wire, he gestured for Mike to sit beside him and said, 'So, what's this proposal of yours? What do you want?'

This was the first time Mike had been close to Sarac and heard him speak. He had the look and the sound of the enforcer Mike knew him to be, but there was something he had not expected: the menace was there but so was a surly weariness.

'Give me what I want and, before I hand the video to the police, I'll edit it so you and your boss don't appear.'

Sarac gazed at him for a moment before he replied and Mike thought some of the weariness on his face had been replaced by the watchful mask of a poker player.

'What do you want?'

'For a start, I want to know why you had Shane killed.'

'Shane deserved everything he got, the bastard.'

'But why?'

Sarac gave a scornful laugh. 'You know why. How else would you know to go to Flinders yesterday? After Angelo saw the two of you together at that cosy, family dinner, Shane tried to tell us he hated your guts and wasn't tipping you off, even though you knew when to stake out Bruno at the CityView site. You thought you were so smart, but we kept an eye on the two of you, and when Rick saw you and Shane coming out of Doherty's Gym so chummy together, we knew. What we didn't know was how much he'd told you. Bruno kept hitting him but he wouldn't cough up – the silly bugger. That's when Bruno lost it and beat him to a pulp. We wouldn't have been able to stop him even if we'd wanted – just like yesterday. A pity he didn't stay in the river where we chucked him. No chance Reardon will surface any time soon, though.'

'I want you to tell this to the police.'

Sarac laughed again, this time with what seemed like genuine amusement. He wiped his hand across his face and gave a low chuckle full of disbelief.

'To save me from a charge of dumping Reardon's body you want me to cough up to being involved when Shane copped it? Get real.'

'Why did you set me up for the bribery charge?'

'I didn't. That was McKenzie. He wanted you out of the way.'

'Out of the way? Why would he want that?'

'He reckoned you'd make it harder for him to do what he wanted at Findlay's. I don't know how he thought you'd do that but I do know you keep getting in the way.'

'He and Kane are working up something between them, aren't they?' Sarac glanced at him sharply when Mike mentioned Kane. 'Yeah, I know it's Jerry Kane. Tell me what it is they're up to.'

Sarac shook his head. 'If I were you I wouldn't let it get around you're trying to meddle in Jerry's affairs. Not good for your health.' He paused, reconsidering. 'Yeah, why not? You might be able to stop McKenzie, which could be a good thing, and you won't do any harm to Jerry – he's a lot too fly for the likes of you and McKenzie. What I know is McKenzie offered to white-ant Findlay's so that Jerry can buy in and take control, just like he controls Rubicon, using the money he launders from his other interests. That's why McKenzie wants to get rid of you. He reckons he can stuff up Findlay's easier if you're not around.'

Mike knew if he was going to stop Vern he needed more detail. 'And how is he going to stuff up Findlay's?'

'You expect me to know? You're the one who works there.'

Mike could hear the mockery in Sarac's voice – he was playing with him.

'So why tip me off about Vern? Do you want me to stop Vern?'

Sarac chuckled indulgently. 'Aren't you a clever boy to work that out? McKenzie says all he really wants is revenge on Jim Findlay for dumping him and putting his son into the firm, but I know what he's really after. Becoming MD at Findlay's is just the first step in his plan to move into Rubicon. That won't happen – I'm not that stupid. I almost feel a bit sorry for Vern. I know what it's like to work your butt off, doing all the nasty jobs for a boss who stays clear of trouble but gets all the benefits of the work you do, and who will ditch you whenever it suits him. Look how Jerry got out yesterday and left me to clean up the mess. Jerry will use McKenzie and when he's not useful any more, he'll spit him out. I know he'll do the same with me one day, and the more stuff-ups we have with Rubicon, the closer the day gets. If I had a good, safe alternative I'd get out now, before it's too late.'

'Here's your chance to get even. Come and talk to Jim Findlay. Tell him what you've just told me. Kane need never know.'

'Get even? I'm not a delicate flower like McKenzie who has to have his revenge when his boss dumps him. I know how the world works. Jerry will keep me on for as long as I'm useful to him. Past service counts for nothing. Only the weak, the ones who can't look after themselves, need to depend on their boss's loyalty. If I'm going to shop Jerry there has to be a lot more in it for me than you can offer. God, you're an amateur. Go and give your video to the police. I'll do a deal with them over Bruno, get a short sentence and be looked after by Jerry for keeping him out of it. I'll say he was long gone when the fight started. You've got all you're getting from me.'

—

Mike sat gloomily sipping his coffee. He had hoped to get so much more from confronting Sarac with the video. Sure, he now knew for certain Bruno had killed Shane and had a better idea of what Vern was doing, but he had no proof of anything beyond Bruno's murder of Alan. The promise he had made to avenge Alan by bringing down Jerry Kane and Vern McKenzie, which sounded so fine when he stood in the bushes at Flinders, he now saw as the vain posturing it had always been.

Reaching home last night, wrestling with the problem of how he should follow Mario Mancini's edict to wait patiently and then strike, it occurred to him he should call Mancini to tell him what had happened. After all, it was Mancini who had triggered Alan's pursuit of Kane that led to his death. He also wanted Mancini to know that if Mike had taken his advice and done nothing, there would be no evidence of the murder.

Mike's opinion of Mancini softened when he appeared shocked and distressed by the news, but when he recovered quickly and began to think aloud about how best to capitalise on the tragedy, Mike's distaste for him returned, even though this was the very issue Mike had been struggling with. He had to admit it was Mancini who suggested how he should use the video and it was Mancini who gave him the confidence this would lead to the unmasking of Kane.

Mike looked at his watch. Mancini should be here soon and would be disappointed, too. It occurred to him that, in a strange way, he seemed to be replaying the events of last Tuesday with different actors: Sarac replacing Carla in the private room at Café Filipo and Mancini replacing Alan here, at the Gainsville Cafe.

The glass door of the cafe swung open and Mancini strode through in the imperious manner Mike had seen at Café Filipo and at the soccer match. He looked across at Mike and beamed at him. That smile would soon disappear when Mike told him of his failure with Sarac.

'Well done, Mike. I didn't think you'd be able to draw him out as well as you did.'

'But …'

Mancini cut him off by tossing two data sticks on to the table in front of him. 'One for you. One for the cops.'

'What are these?'

'Your conversation with that arrogant fool, Sarac.'

'But how …'

'You really should thank your father, but we can't tell him, or anyone else, how we did this. He was the one who showed me so many years ago the value of secretly recording conversations. When I put in the private room with its own entrance, I took the opportunity to hide a few things. I'll leave you to figure out how I'm able to set up and retrieve the recordings. But, when you do, keep it to yourself. Not even Carla knows. Been very useful to me over the years with all the special dinners and private meetings that are held there.'

'Why didn't you tell me?'

'I thought you'd perform better if I didn't burden you with too much prior knowledge. I was confident Sarac would choose that room to meet with you. I also thought you wouldn't be able to shake him into helping us willingly, and I was right there, too. We needed more and now we've got it.'

Mancini continued to beam at him and Mike flushed with irritation at being patronised in this way: first Sarac and now Mancini, treating him as though he was a child among adults. And Mancini wasn't finished. 'When you take the video and the sound recording to the police, there'll be interest far wider than the homicide squad. Don't mention my name. I'm more than happy for you to take all the credit. I suggest you call Senior

Sergeant Robbins straight away and tell him you want to speak with him urgently.'

Mike could understand how Angelo Rossi would have become fed up with his father-in-law talking down to him.

'Hold on. What do you get out of this? You're a man who likes to be at the centre of things; not the kind who wants to stay out of the limelight. But in this you've been skulking in the shadows just like Kane.'

Mancini's eyes flared, but then his face softened. 'I understand. You've been through a lot. I've known Jerry Kane for more years than I like to remember. Back in those days, the days I've already told you I'm not proud of, he worked for me.'

'You taught him?'

'You might say that. But I became an honest man. He never did.'

'Was this before or after you moved into the trucking industry. Is that where he learned how to launder money?'

Mancini took a deep breath. 'You go too far. Be careful. I will not have Jerry Kane take my place at Rubicon.'

'Even though that may see Rubicon shut down and your son-in-law ruined?'

'He is already ruined. That happened as soon as he took Kane's money.'

It was the same room in which Senior Sergeant Robbins and Sergeant Ryan had questioned him on Friday. When Mike said he had a video and a voice recording for them, Ryan did not turn on their recording equipment, but went to find a laptop, which he placed at the end of the table so the screen was visible from both sides. Mike hesitated for a moment, but decided on the video first and pushed the data stick across the table for Ryan to load. The

262

two policemen sat back to watch the rather jerky and at times indistinct footage of the various people arriving.

'Where is this?' Robbins asked.

'The house of Angelo Rossi at Flinders,' Mike replied.

They appeared to have no need to ask the identity of the arrivals, except that Robbins did not know Vern. 'Vern McKenzie, a director of Findlay Construction,' Ryan told him. They began to lose interest at the lengthy coverage of the indistinct figures in the house and the clearer shots of the men around the barbecue. When Alan appeared, Ryan said, 'Who's this guy?'

'Alan Reardon, deputy state secretary of the Building and Construction Union,' Mike said.

Ryan glanced at Mike and appeared about to ask a follow-up question when the chase began and his attention became fixed on the computer screen. Mike still found the brutality of Bruno's attack on Alan sickening, even though he had now watched it four or five times. He found the coverage of the disposal of Alan's body somehow anticlimactic and wanted the video to end so he could discuss the implications with the police, but they were equally interested in the aftermath as they were in the attack itself. When the video did eventually end, Robbins looked across at Mike and said, 'Presumably you were hidden somewhere nearby?'

'Yeah, in thick bushes and trees which run down the side of the property.'

Ryan gave Mike a sceptical smile and said, 'You were with this man Reardon on some kind of secret surveillance caper? An unlikely pair – a union official and a project manager. How come?'

'I'll play you the voice recording.'

This time the policemen showed no sign of boredom. When it was finished Ryan gave Mike another of his crooked grins.

'Looks like you're off the hook for the murder charge. We'll have to content ourselves with doing you for trying to withhold evidence. How did you record the conversation? Surely he checked you over before you started.'

'Before we go any further, I need to speak with the boss,' Robbins said. 'I reckon there'll be a few people want to talk with you about Jerry Kane.'

Mike had been to Jim Findlay's house on a number of occasions over the years, but had never felt this uneasy before. It had been late when he returned home from police headquarters and he had not slept well, so he was looking far from his best when he stood on Jim's front veranda. Judith Findlay let him in, her carefully presented appearance contrasting with his dishevelled state, reminding him of the contrast he had felt on the day he first had lunch with Carla. At least his shiner had pretty much disappeared.

'Do come in, Mike,' she said in a voice and with a look that told him she was curious as to why he had phoned her husband so early in the morning. She took him through to the back room where Jim, dressed much more casually in a grey tracksuit, stood waiting for him.

'G'day, Mike,' he said. 'Seems ages since I last saw you. Come and sit over here.'

He gave Mike his disarming, shaggy smile as they shook hands, but there was something in his eyes: he was anxious about something. It could be he was embarrassed to be receiving Mike when he had been suspended or thought Mike was here to complain about Ben's treatment of him. Jim carefully lowered himself on to a straight-backed chair and waved Mike into the padded chair opposite him.

'I didn't knock Ben off his bike,' Mike said.

'No, I know you didn't. I'm sorry.' Jim looked even more sheepish than before. How did he know? Had Ben changed his mind? Was that why he was apologising?

'I know it must be a bit awkward for you, letting me come here when I've been suspended.'

'No, that's OK, Mike. I think I might know why you're here. That's what's awkward for me.' So he did expect Mike to be complaining about Ben. 'Best, Mike, you say what you've come to say.'

'I've come to tell you Vern is trying to white-ant the company and he must be stopped.'

Mike prepared himself for the hostile rejection of his claim and was staggered to find Jim ruefully shaking his head.

'Yeah, I thought that was why you'd come. I'm told you've got a recording of this man, Sarac, telling you about it.'

Recovering from his surprise, Mike recalled that Mancini had his own source embedded in the police force. Now Jim. Mike looked at him steadily.

'Would you like to hear it?'

'Yes, I would. And if you don't mind I'd like Vern to hear it as well.'

This time Mike was not surprised. It was typical of Jim to give Vern the opportunity to explain himself. This was going to be even more awkward than he'd expected. Vern was sure to try to wriggle out of it.

'Darling,' Jim called, and Judith appeared immediately – she must have been outside waiting for the call. 'Would you ask Vern to join us, please? And I reckon we could do with a cuppa as well.'

'Tea or coffee, Mike?' she asked. 'I know what the others have.'

Vern entered the room and nodded to Mike.

'I'm sorry about this, Mike.'

It was the morning for everyone to apologise.

Mike addressed himself directly to Jim. 'Before I play you the recording, I need to give you a fair bit of background so you'll properly understand what led to the conversation.'

'I think I've pretty well got the background, thanks Mike. If I need to, I'll ask questions as we go along.'

Further surprised and nonplussed, Mike busied himself with setting up the laptop he had brought with him and loading the contents of the data stick. Before he could start playing the conversation, Judith returned with a tray containing three cups – she must have had their drinks already prepared. This whole thing had been set up well before he arrived.

Mike carefully watched the other two listeners as the recording played. Jim sat with his head bowed as though deep in thought and Mike was unable to gauge his reaction. Vern was more animated, gazing thoughtfully at Mike when Sarac was describing his suspicions of Shane and the beating before his death. His mood appeared to lighten when the conversation moved on to him and he even gave an amused grin when Sarac described how Vern aimed to oust him. Mike couldn't help admiring his coolness. When the recording finished Vern was the first to speak.

'I bet there was a lot of interest in the recording at police headquarters.'

'Yes, there was,' Mike replied. Was it going to be up to him to state the obvious –that Vern had been caught out?

'Did they tell you not to share it with anyone else?'

The gall of this man. Here he was trying to put Mike in the wrong, while Jim sat there like he was watching a show on TV.

'They said something like that, but I felt I owed it to Jim to let him know what you were up to as soon as I could.' Surely that would get this strange meeting back to the real agenda.

Vern nodded as if agreeing with him. 'Yeah, I'd do the same.

I just want to make the point that this conversation, just like your recording, has to remain between us. I want to tell you what I have been up to – Jim already knows. My long time golfing partner, Assistant Commissioner Paul Jones, and I have shared our problems and advised one another over many years. Quite recently he told me he had intelligence that Kane, well known to the police, had moved into the building industry but Paul didn't know any details. The police have been trying to nail Kane for a long time, but he covers his tracks very well and, without any evidence of wrongdoing, the police can't require a private firm to open its books to them. When I heard some of what was going on at Rubicon, I suspected Kane might be involved and when we began to have our problems, I thought he might be moving on us. So I came to Jim and told him I wanted to present myself as a target for Kane. It all moved much faster than I imagined it would. I hoped I would learn enough on Sunday to give the police some detail of what he was up to, but almost before we got started young Reardon burst on to the scene. I guess you were there, too.'

Mike nodded without speaking.

'It must have been horrible for you to film. It was shocking to watch even from the distance of the house. I told Paul Jones what had happened and assumed it put an end to the plan we had hatched for bringing Kane into the open. Paul suggested we do nothing for a day or two and see what Kane and his gang did. You changed all that and, from what I've been told, the police are now very optimistic they can roll up much of Kane's operation. I don't know what will happen at Rubicon and Riverside, but we can start to get back to normal.'

'Back to normal?' Mike spat the words at Vern. 'We've had two people murdered as a result of this business and you want us to forget about them and go back to normal. One thing I've learned is that normal isn't what I thought it was. My normal isn't there anymore to go back to.'

Jim reached out his hand to Mike in a gesture of entreaty. 'I hear what you say, Mike, and I've felt really bad about what we've put you through in the past couple of weeks. I'm also very sorry about Shane Francis. I had no idea he was a member of your family. I expect you were close.'

'Yes,' Vern said before Mike could respond. 'Did you talk with one another about what was going on at CityView and Riverside?'

'Of course we didn't. We detested one another. I'm really glad my sister is free of him, but not like this. No one should die that way.'

'No. Sorry,' Vern said. 'I'm still too wound up in what's happened. Someone in Findlay's has been talking with Sarac or one of his gang. I don't know who it is.'

'Thank you, Jim,' Mike said more calmly. 'I know none of this is down to you. But what about you, Vern? Why did you set up Alan and me on the bribery charge? I still have to deal with that.'

'No, the police will speak with the commission and put it to rest. I had to do something beyond talk to get onside with Sarac and Kane. Sorry.'

'I'm getting used to people using me.'

'Of course, you're reinstated immediately,' Jim said. 'No question. But why don't you take some time off? A break will do you good and set you up for when you're back at CityView.'

Mike was about to say he would prefer to get back to work when it occurred to him Ben probably didn't know what had been going on, either. Jim needed time to put him in the picture. It would be interesting to see what Ben's attitude to him would be now. Would he want to stay on, replacing Mike as project manager? That's what he said he wanted to do when they had that row. Was it only a fortnight ago? It seemed like months had passed.

18

Shane's funeral was a dispiriting affair. Mike, Lissa and Demetri attended, more to support Mary than honour Shane's memory. Shane's mother was there – a surprisingly small, mousy woman, Mary had never met, although Shane had mentioned she lived in Bendigo. He had never mentioned his father, and Mrs Francis came with her brother. A few of his mates turned up, but there was no sign of Sarac or any of his gang. There had been nothing on the news about the investigation into Shane's murder and not even a mention of Alan's disappearance. The police had told him it would be at least some days before they would be in a position to make any arrests and Mike found it hard to contain his impatience. Angelo Rossi was not there either, although Rubicon sent a man who told them he represented the company and bore commiserations from the owner and staff.

Lissa prepared food for a wake at their house but only Shane's mother and uncle came back with them and, after an awkward half hour of desultory conversation, they said they needed to be on the road to Bendigo before the peak traffic. When Lissa and Mary cleared away and were chatting in the kitchen, Mike saw his opportunity.

'Dad,' he said. 'I've been thinking about what we should do about the shops.'

Demetri eyed him suspiciously. 'What is this "we"? You keep telling me you're not involved.'

'Dad, I'm your son. I want to find a way you can be happy and I can be happy, too. You said you wanted me to honour the promise grandpa made to his father and you made to him – that the Georgiou name would be maintained in Bay Street. Is that what's most important to you?'

'What good is that if you will not continue in the shop?'

'I've seen the new development that's going on down towards the beach. Whatever you do, one day a development like that will roll along the street and engulf the shop. You know that.'

Demetri did not reply, his face still dark, but Mike took the almost imperceptible nod of his head as encouragement to continue. 'What if that development – which is likely to include shops, apartments and possibly even offices – what if it was called The Georgiou Centre?'

'That woman has been at you again.'

'No, I haven't spoken with Carla. I've already told you how Mancini and I worked together. He wanted to bring down Kane, I wanted to clear my name and, through Alan's tragic death, it's likely we've achieved both. He spoke to me about Bay Street and told me to ignore Carla.' Mike smiled at his father. 'Yeah, I thought that'd surprise you. What he actually said was that I should not be coerced by Carla into trying to force you into doing something you'd regret. He also said I should find out what you really want to achieve by having me take over the business. That's where I got the idea for the Georgiou Centre. Even if I was to take over the shop, one day – quite soon I'd say – I'd have to sell to a developer. Perhaps it would be the Mancini family or perhaps it would be someone else. The result will be the same – the name will go. But if we make a condition of sale that the development must enshrine the Georgiou name, we honour the memory of our family in that place for far longer than could be achieved any other way.'

'Did he put you up to this?'

Not long ago Mike would have let anger at his father's apparent mistrust of him show. Today he saw it for what it was – a reluctance to give up the position in which he had so entrenched himself. 'I've discussed this with no one. I don't even know whether the Mancinis will be willing. Perhaps they want to see a Mancini Centre on that spot. But surely it's worth a try.'

'And the shops?'

'Apart from maintaining the name you will make a lot of money from the sale of your building. The Mancinis will have to pay well over market value and they know that. Keep the other two shops but bring Peter Roberts into the business and let him run them for you. When it comes to the shops he's the true heir to you. Let him have his head. It's high time you were free to come to Christos' soccer games and the girls would like you to be at their events as well.'

Mike saw his father's interest grow as he spoke. Perhaps he might make a negotiator yet.

'You will speak to Mario?'

⸺

At last the TV news led with a report of the sensational disappearance of what the newsreader described as 'leading union official Alan Reardon' and the charging of Bruno Kordic with his murder. They had a short interview with a police inspector Mike did not recognise, who said several other men were helping police with their inquiries and he expected that further charges would be laid soon. Before moving on to the next item, George Fowler made a cameo appearance to tell the public what a fine union official Alan had been and how he had been pursuing illegal practices in the building industry before he was cut down. He didn't name Rubicon as being responsible for Alan's death, but when the reporter asked him if Rubicon was involved, George said it was one of the firms Alan had been investigating. He did not elaborate – he didn't need to.

⸺

Mary rang the next day to say that Sergeant Ryan had called to tell her Bruno Kordic had been charged with Shane's murder as well as Alan Reardon's. He told her further charges would follow involving other men who had been present when Shane was killed.

Mike had hardly finished his conversation with Mary when there was a ring on the front door. He opened it to find Vern McKenzie standing with one eye cocked at him. Mike stood squarely in the doorway.

'Didn't expect to see you, Vern,'

'A few things I have to tell you.'

'Who is it?' Lissa called from the kitchen.

'You'd better come in,' Mike said with a reluctance he made no effort to hide. 'You took a chance not calling me first.'

'Is Lissa home?'

'You just caught her. She's about to go off to prepare a client's lunch for a local accountant. She's in the catering game these days.'

'Hello, Vern,' Lissa said, the welcome in her voice quite different from her husband's. 'Would you like a cup of tea?'

'Thanks, Lissa. Black with sugar, please.'

'Come on through.'

Lissa ushered Vern into the family room with Mike trailing behind. As she entered the kitchen to put on the kettle, she tossed back over her shoulder, 'I hear you've been causing a lot of trouble for my husband. Not like you, Vern.'

Vern sat on the couch in the family room. 'Yeah, we've been going through a tough time. Still, I've got some good news for him.'

He lowered his voice and looked directly at Mike, who had come to sit opposite him. 'I thought you'd like to know, strictly between us, that Sarac has cut a deal with the police and is giving them plenty of material to use against Kane. It will be a while until they charge him – they're going through the books of Rubicon and several other companies in forensic detail.'

'What about Rubicon and what about Angelo Rossi?'

'After this it will be months before Rubicon can make any progress on the Riverside site. We'll be well finished before they can give us any competition.'

'I was more interested in whether Rossi would be charged.'

'From the contact I had with him during my two visits to Flinders, I began to feel sorry for the man. He'd got himself in far too deep with Sarac and Kane, and hated them as much as we do. I think the police will realise he's more a victim than a criminal, but they won't let him off scot free – they can't do that.'

'I remember you telling me what a smart guy he was. Have you changed your view, or was all that stuff over lunch a load of crap you were giving me to find out how loyal I was to Jim?'

'Actually, if Ben had stayed as MD, a takeover might have been the only way to save Findlay's.'

'What do you mean, "If he had stayed"?'

'That's the main reason I came to see you: Ben's resigned and is going back to Cunnards.'

Mike recalled Alan telling him about Ben's unpopularity and the likelihood of industrial action at CityView. He also remembered Sarac's description of how Vern was going to disrupt the project. 'Did you connive with George Fowler to make life impossible for Ben?'

'You really have a low opinion of me these days.'

'Did you?'

'Ben had a row with Jim. He was furious that neither Jim nor I told him what I was up to. At least that's the reason he gave for leaving. If you want my opinion, I reckon the time he spent trying to do your job finally convinced him to face up to what he's known for some time: he hasn't got what it takes to head up a building company.'

'You still haven't answered my question.'

'Here's a pot of tea,' Lissa said depositing a tray on the low table in front of the couch. 'I have to go now, so you will have to pour your own after it draws.'

She leant over to kiss Mike on the forehead.

'Don't let Vern out of here until you and he have sorted out your differences.'

She turned back to Vern.

'I should say the same to you. I'm sick of having a grumpy husband stuck here at home.'

She picked up her handbag from the kitchen bench and went down the passage to the front door.

'That wife of yours doesn't ever hold back, does she?' Vern said without smiling, although his tone suggested more admiration than offence.

'You still haven't answered my question.'

'If it's question time, I have one for you. Jim wants me to sit in for a couple of years as MD while we groom you to take over from me. It's time for generational change and you're the best prospect we have. Already you've shown you have what it takes to be a top builder like Jim was when he started the company. What you need to run the show is the knowledge and experience I can give you. Jim wanted to put this to you himself, but I told him it would be no good unless you and I could find a way to work together again. Lissa seems to have reached the same conclusion.'

'I didn't like Ben Findlay, I didn't respect his competence and we disagreed on many things, but none of that justifies setting him up for failure. I've always respected your capability and what you bring to the business, but what you've done in the past few weeks – doubting my loyalty to the firm, keeping me in the dark, trying to undermine me and Ben as well – that's destroyed the trust we once had. How can we work together if we don't trust each other?'

Vern leant forward to pour tea into their cups. He offered Mike the milk jug and stirred two heaped spoons of sugar into his tea. He took a mouthful of the tea and sat back savouring the flavour before replacing the cup on its saucer.

'Yeah, it's true: I did wonder whether you'd been sounding off to someone outside the firm about the problems we were having. That was why I gave you that spiel about looking for a takeover. I pretty soon knew the leaks weren't coming from you, but they were coming from somewhere, and the other day I found out who.'

'Surely not Ben?'

'Freda Bradshaw confessed.'

'Freda? I don't believe it.'

'There's a lot gone on in the past few weeks that you're having trouble believing. She told me there was this charming man who bumped into her car when she was in the supermarket, stayed around to make sure she had his insurance details and insisted on taking her out for dinner to make up for causing the scrape on her car. They got on well and went out together a couple of times. Freda found it easy to confide in her new friend and started telling him how unfairly the firm had treated her boss by bringing in the son of the owner over him and how the son was ruining the business. He was very attentive and rang to speak with her almost every day. It took until last week, but finally he overreached and she became suspicious. He didn't like it when she started questioning him and got nasty so she broke it off. Yesterday she told me.'

'Poor Freda.'

'Poor all of us.'

Vern sat up and leaned forward to stare at Mike over the tops of his glasses.

'Earlier on you made it sound like I was having fun setting you up and telling a couple of crooks how I was going to sabotage the company. I'm not proud of some of the things I did, but for me the end justified the means. I was prepared to do whatever it took to secure the future of the firm. To run a company like ours over a long stretch, you need to take risks. If the risks you take only have consequences for you, that's easy. But when you have to put others at risk, that's when it gets really hard. If you want to stay in a huff with me because I went out on a limb and took you out there with me, then you'd better find another job. On the other hand, if you want to learn how to keep our company afloat in good times and in bad, I'm willing to teach you all I know.' Mike went to respond but Vern continued. 'No, don't say anything right now. Think it over. Talk it over with Lissa. You're due back in a few days. Come and see me first thing with your answer.'

—

Lissa was in high spirits when she returned from her lunch. As she came down the passage from the front door, Mike could say no more than, 'Hi. How did it …' before she swept into the family room and spoke over the top of him.

'It went really well and several of the guests asked for my card.'

'Great.' Mike hesitated for a moment before adding. 'I know you won't like me saying this, but you've gone much better and much faster than I thought you'd be able to.'

Lissa sat beside him on the couch and gave him a thoughtful glance.

'That's OK. I didn't like it when I first told you my idea and you sounded so doubtful about it. I thought you had no confidence in me but, as we've talked further, I could see you were thinking about the problems I'd run into. That's the way you are; the way you've always been – don't let enthusiasm for what you're about to do blind you to the problems. I get pissed off with your attitude at times, but it's worked well for you so far and now I'm in business for myself, I need to be more like you.' She grinned at him before saying, 'Not too much like you, though. That'd be too boring.'

'Mary was going to help, wasn't she? How did she seem?'

'She was great, too. It would be good if we can build up the business so she can leave that dull job at the dentist's.'

Lissa turned to face Mike and took a deep breath. Perhaps it was the excitement of her success reflected in her colouring, but he was struck by how attractive she looked and the impish gleam in her eyes added to her allure.

'One of the guests was greatly taken by her and asked for her phone number.'

'That's a bit quick isn't it?'

'Argh, Mike, you're hopeless.' Lissa punched him in the arm with enough force to make him flinch – he still carried a few soft spots from his encounters. 'He wasn't suggesting he move in with her and I don't even know whether she gave him her number. It was good for her, though. She needed a boost after the past weeks. You get so protective over her that sometimes I think you'd prefer she went into a nunnery.'

'Sorry.'

'How did you get on with Vern?'

Mike took Lissa through his conversation with Vern and the ultimatum he had put to him.

'So what's the problem?'

'How can I work with someone who goes off on his own and doesn't tell me what he's up to, even though I'm directly affected by what he's doing?'

'Surely you can understand that sometimes he might find himself in a situation where he thinks it best not to tell you what he's doing? That's how you run your marriage.'

'Aw, come on, Lissa,'

'Did you tell me what you were doing when you went to the site that night, or when you went to the pub to meet Alan Reardon, or when you called on Shane at the gym? Did you give me the full story when Carla told you about the offer she had made to your dad? Do you always tell me what you're thinking? Do you *ever* tell me all you're thinking?'

Mike held his arms over his head as though warding off blows. 'OK. OK. You've made your point. I have been keeping a bit to myself and perhaps I should have told you more. But we still trust each other, don't we?'

Lissa glanced quickly at him and then turned her head away.

'There's another way of looking at it, you know,' she said. 'Vern put together an elaborate plot to save Findlay's from this guy, Jerry Kane, but that wasn't what saved the firm – you did! Even though, as you see it, Vern let you down badly, you were the one that came out on top – not Vern. Over the years that firm has been very good to you and now they've offered you the best opportunity you're ever likely to get. So take it. Learn all you can from Vern and now you have a better idea of what a wily man he is, keep a close eye on him. Do that and you'll come out on top again.'

'Yeah. If I'm honest, it's what I really want to do. Perhaps I am being too precious. Thanks.'

Mike leant across to kiss Lissa on the cheek, catching her unawares, so that they made awkward connection.'

'No time for this, lover-boy. One of us has to pick up the kids shortly.'

'There's something else I want to tell you.'

The note of anxiety in Mike's voice caused the smile to disappear from Lissa's face. 'Oh yeah? What's that?'

'I think I have a solution to Dad's problems.'

'Really?'

After Mike had taken Lissa through his proposal, she nodded and pursed her lips. 'What does your dad think?'

'He wants me to speak with Mario Mancini.'

'When are you going to do that?'

'Actually I think it would be better for me to speak with Carla.'

'Of course.' Lissa gave him a quizzical glance. 'Another lunch date, I suppose.'

'You want me to tell you everything I'm thinking about Carla? OK, here goes. I find her a very attractive woman. She is beautiful, elegant and I enjoy speaking with her. She is also ambitious and ruthless and has been using her charm on me to get what she wants from Dad. For a while I was under her spell, no question about that. Her father, a shrewd but arrogant man, was on to it straight away and I guess you had some idea of it as well. In the past few days I've woken up to a few things. One of them is that what we have, with its occasional rough spots, is so much more real and more important than any fantasy. I need to speak with Carla again because she's the one calling the shots on the development of Bay Street, not her father. I'm going to ring her now to set up a meeting at a place I will choose, where I will put my proposal to her. You have nothing to be concerned about.'

———

Mike decided it was not politic for him to use his old spot at the CityView site, so went to the Convention Centre car park and walked back down the river to Bistro Vite. Yesterday Carla had sounded a little distant and distracted when he rang to suggest they meet for coffee at the bistro.

'After last time, you feel more secure with me on the ground rather than up in the air,' she said.

Perhaps she meant it as a joke about his fear of heights but she sounded more depressed than amused. The lunchtime crowd had not yet arrived and there was no breeze, so he chose to sit on one of the wicker chairs outside, overlooking the marina. He turned away from the sight of the gently rocking cabin cruisers and gazed downstream past the Riverside towers to the Bolte Bridge. How long would it be before so many sights would immediately take him back to Alan's murder?

He saw Carla approaching along the path by the river. She wore jeans and a leather jacket over a white blouse, a subdued style that made no difference to the graceful elegance of her walk, the walk that had first captured him.

'Michael,' she said and he was surprised by her reserve. She took his hand as he stood to greet her and stretched up to brush her lips quickly past one cheek. Immediately they were seated, a waitress appeared. 'My, what good service,' Carla exclaimed. 'I will have a skinny latte, please.'

'Nothing to eat?' Mike asked, and when she shook her head, he looked up at the waitress. 'A long black, thank you.'

'My father has shown me the film you took and played me your conversation with Sarac. I'm so sorry for all you've been put through.'

'Not your fault. It's the death of Alan Reardon that troubles me most. Nothing happened to me that hasn't already been fixed or won't mend, and it was certainly worth it all in the end.'

Carla nodded. 'I couldn't be more pleased to see Kane and Sarac get what they deserve.'

It occurred to Mike that Mancini, through his police contacts, would certainly know about the deal Sarac had struck, but it appeared he had not told Carla. He also wondered if Mancini had explained to her how the recording of the conversation with Sarac had been made. Probably not.

'You must be sad that Rubicon has been caught up in all this.'

'I told you I'm not involved in Rubicon,' she stated with an annoyed toss of her head. 'I am sorry the Riverside project will be held up, but one day I hope my vision for it will be realised by someone, and it doesn't matter to me if that's not Rubicon.' She lifted her chin and smiled. 'After all, I have my other interests and I hope you have brought me good news about one of them.'

The waitress returned with their coffees, allowing Mike an opportunity to concentrate his thoughts and give Carla a concise account of his proposal. When he had finished she said, 'And this is what your father wants most of all? It's funny what major decisions can sometimes turn on. It was smart of you to see that, or did you have to persuade him?'

'I have to confess it was something your father said to me that started me along the track that led to this.'

'He's a shrewd man, my father, who gives good advice. The trick is not to let his overbearing manner prevent you from taking it.'

'I know what you mean,' Mike said before looking intently at Carla and asking, 'So you agree with my proposal? We haven't talked money yet, but the name is vital.'

'The name is fine. It's time to bring the lawyers in and for me to make you a formal offer. I'm sure the money will not be a problem, either. We both know how crucial your father's building is to my plans. As soon as I have title to the property I can begin to obtain planning permission. I've already had work done on the design. Maybe, within the year, we will be able to begin demolition prior to construction.'

The businesswoman who had been sitting before him as she spoke suddenly transformed herself with a coquettish smile. 'I'll need a good builder, of course. Would you like a job? We would make a good team.'

'I think Findlay's would be keen to do it – maybe as a joint venture if that appeals to you.'

The smile left Carla's face and her voice rose. 'You're not going back to Findlay's after the way they've treated you? Surely you couldn't work with Ben Findlay or Vern McKenzie.' She paused and her face softened into an appeal. 'I could make you a much better offer.'

'But you've already got Angelo.'

'Not anymore.'

'Surely he won't be out of it for long, if at all. He was coerced and had a minor role – the police know that.'

Carla shook her head dismissively.

'I'm not talking about Angelo's problems with the law. My father has already offered him a very good lawyer who believes, at worst, he can get him off with a minor penalty. Angelo has found his own lawyer, though; he doesn't want anything to do with our family. He blames me for his troubles and continues to complain Rubicon wouldn't have run into the problems it has if it were not for my determination we should press ahead.' She tilted her head and shrugged. 'He's right to an extent. It's a good example of what happens when I refuse to listen to my father, but it's not the main reason Rubicon is in trouble. That came when Angelo brought Kane in to the business.'

Carla sipped her coffee and took a deep breath.

'It's all over between Angelo and me. This business has been the final breach. The truth is we should never have married in the first place – we have so little in common. It was a mistake we soon realised but we kept working together on the Riverside project and treated one another with politeness, neither blaming the other. Angelo is a handsome man who can be most engaging and I was charmed by his passion for building. What I should have seen much earlier is that he is a one-dimensional man – a man with very limited interests outside building. He is bored by many of the things that excite me. We only stayed together out of convenience. Angelo wanted desperately for Rubicon to grow and to prosper, and my ideas were important in achieving that, but he was never comfortable having me or my father involved. Rubicon had been his creation and he didn't want to share it with anyone else – even his wife. If one of us had found an interest in someone else, we would have parted earlier. But we did not.'

Carla seemed to retreat within herself, becoming more down-cast the more she spoke. Mike had to restrain himself from reaching across the table and taking her hand. She took another mouthful of her coffee and sat up straight, as if summoning her resolve to go on.

'So many men are such stunted creatures. The first thing they think when they meet me is how they would like to take me to their beds. I see it in their eyes. Early on, I was flattered and will-ing to play up to my image but I soon tired of that. Many of them fluff their plumage and strut around like birds in a courtship dance, some become tongue-tied and awkward, trying to keep their urges hidden, and a few try to intimidate me, knowing I have no interest in them and pretending they don't mind. I soon learned I had a weapon I could use with men to get what I want but I despise those men who so easily succumb.'

Mike gave a rueful smile. 'Of course, I'm one of those you were able to entrance so easily.'

'What?' Carla looked at him sharply. 'Oh, yes, I see. I am very determined – as a woman I have to be. I will do whatever it takes to achieve my aims.'

For a moment Mike thought of Vern making the same

claim for himself. In all other respects he could see no similarity between Carla and Vern.

'I did start with you as I do with any man who finds me attractive,' she said. 'I saw you looking at me that night in Café Filipo and when I found who you were, began to plan how I could use you to advance my plans for Bay Street. But that changed. Even at our first lunch together, I saw you were different but I persisted. Then in my apartment I could not continue leading you on. That's why I broke away from you. I wanted you, but not like that – such affairs always end badly and I couldn't bear the thought of that. I'm sorry for burdening you with my confessions. I should have just shut up, but who else can I be open with like I am with you? Very few men treat me as a person with whom to share conversations, opinions, ideas or feelings. You're one of those few – a very special one. I began to realise that when we first talked about jazz and then you listened so attentively and sympathetically to me telling you my problems.'

Mike leant forward to look into Carla's downcast eyes.

'I was so thrilled to find someone who shares my love of jazz, someone who understands how I feel about music,' he said. 'Music finds its way into all parts of my life. I even believe I can tell the state of a building site by listening to its sound. On a good day there is an energy and a cohesion in the sound that, for me, is a form of music. Do you think that's silly?'

'No, of course not. I hear music in many places.'

284

ACKNOWLEDGEMENTS

While this story is set in Melbourne, I have appropriated a number of well-known locations and, in some cases, replaced the occupants with my fictional businesses and characters. There is no connection between my fictions and the actual occupants of the sites.

I am grateful to Mike King, Jenny Strangward and John Sewell for advice on building practices as I am to Paul Delianis and Nick Parissis for their tutoring on police procedure.

I also wish to thank my editor, Tony Berry, for the work he has done.

That leaves me to thank my stalwarts, Jo, Noelene and Bish, who read and comment on the drafts of all my stories. On this occasion Bish was concerned that the severity of his critique might endanger our friendship; on the contrary, it led to a substantial rewrite, which I believe improved the story significantly. In recognition of his contribution, I have dedicated the book to him.

B.S.

ABOUT THE AUTHOR

Brian Smith was born and grew up in Melbourne, where he now lives with his wife, Josephine. They have two daughters and three granddaughters.

Brian began his professional career as an engineer and finished it as vice-chancellor of the University of Western Sydney, having previously been the head of RMIT.

In retirement he has served on a number of committees, including chairing the board of UniSuper, the company that provides superannuation for the staff of all Australian universities.

Among a range of current activities, the two that most consume him are playing golf and writing stories. He has published two sets of short stories. *Facing the Music* is his fifth novel.

BY THE SAME AUTHOR

NOVELS
All in the Telling
The Art of Illusion
Escaping Freedom
Too Close to Home

SHORT STORIES
The Man Who Loved Books
Mixed Fortunes

New Releases ... also from Sid Harta Publishers

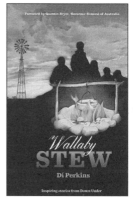

OTHER BEST SELLING SID HARTA TITLES CAN BE FOUND AT

http://sidharta.com.au   http://Anzac.sidharta.com

***

HAVE YOU WRITTEN A STORY?

http://publisher-guidelines.com

New Releases ... also from Sid Harta Publishers

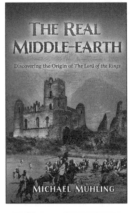

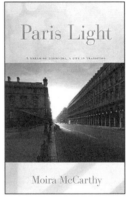

OTHER BEST SELLING SID HARTA TITLES CAN BE FOUND AT

http://sidharta.com.au   http://Anzac.sidharta.com
***
HAVE YOU WRITTEN A STORY?
http://publisher-guidelines.com

Best-selling titles by Kerry B. Collison

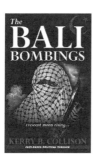    

Readers are invited to visit our publishing websites at:
http://sidharta.com.au
http://publisher-guidelines.com/

Kerry B. Collison's home pages:
http://www.authorsden.com/visit/author.asp?AuthorID=2239
http://www.expat.or.id/sponsors/collison.html
email: author@sidharta.com.au

Purchase Sid Harta titles online at:
http://sidharta.com.au

New Releases ... also from Sid Harta Publishers

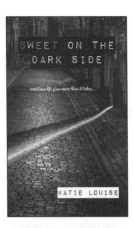

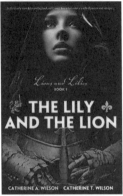

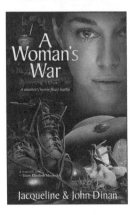

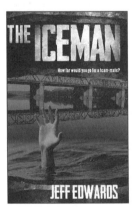

OTHER BEST SELLING SID HARTA TITLES CAN BE FOUND AT

http://sidharta.com.au   http://Anzac.sidharta.com

***

HAVE YOU WRITTEN A STORY?

http://publisher-guidelines.com